I0581420

ASH AND SNOW

ASH AND SNOW

USA TODAY BESTSELLING AUTHOR

SILVANA G. SÁNCHEZ

SECOND STAR PRESS

*To Dr. Essgard, and to all the health workers
fighting for humanity against the rise of darkness.*

VALATHÜRE PALACE
The Mighty Mountain
Hilgard Mountain
The Seven's Hideout
The Red Forest
Port Bree
Dark Sea
Iron River
The Devil's Throat
The Black Forest
WHITEHAVEN CASTLE
REALM OF MAN

REALM OF FAE
To The Netherworld
Mermaids' Cove
Silvermoon Ocean
Steelborn Castle
The Stone Keep

MALEATH SNOW

The king is dead… and I killed him.

I run in the darkness, through uneven planes where snow and rocks and twigs entwine like thorns slowing my pace. These woods I've known from a very young age; the playground of the young princess I used to be.

Tonight, my royal title has been shattered by the Evil Queen. I am no longer welcome in my own home, a pariah in the eyes of the court, a heartless killer… a monster who pushed her father off the castle's tower into an untimely death.

What do they know?

They are the monsters.

CHAPTER ONE

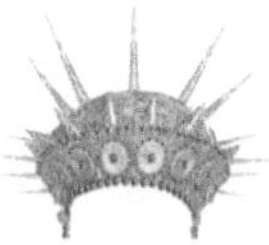

I moved through the buoyant crowds of drunken lords who shamelessly frolicked with kitchen maids, past the hordes of unspoiled maidens who secretly snubbed them. I dodged legendary minstrels brought from the north; their chants of knightly prowess echoed in the great hall, and tangled with the laughter and song of hundreds.

The warmth of a dozen blazing hearths set everyone's cheeks on fire. However, my skin flushed for another reason as I swept the room with a hastened glance, searching for a handsome face. Tall and well-built, with a regal air about him that inevitably drew all eyes. This was a man who stood out from the crowd.

I emptied my drink in one quick swig and tossed the glass into the fireplace. Tonight, I would have more than my fair share of spirits. This was an evening I longed to forget.

With a hand clasped fast on the mantel, I mounted a foot on the hearth's stone plinth. In one quick impulse, I bounced and loomed over the gathering, and kept my gaze sharp whilst biting my lower lip.

There he was, a most delightful sight, garbed in a royal blue coat and dark breeches. Gilded medals flashed on his chest as he gently moved sideways to attend the welcoming committee of maidens, old and young, their eyes sparkling with desire. Attractive to the bone, and next in the line of succession in his kingdom, Prince Phillip Steelborn was the most desirable bachelor in all the five realms.

I prowled towards him, stealthy as a lioness hunting its prey. "See me," I whispered, watching him intently from a cautious distance. "Turn away from your suitresses and notice me."

A joyous couple scurried out of the dance floor, the woman jostling close and pushing me toward the marble wall.

The icy stone against my bare back shot a bracing thrill that spread to my limbs. A slow breath escaped my mouth. I closed my eyes. And when I opened them, my focus locked on my fair prince.

At last, Phillip's gaze disengaged from the bevy

surrounding him. His stare found mine, feral with determination. A naughty smirk danced on his silken lips. I gave him a furtive smile in return.

The second he extended his farewells to the crowd, I took off to the stairway.

With my gown's tulle and silk crushed in my grip, I dashed upstairs, only to be stopped halfway by his firm hands wrapping around my waist. "Maleath," he whispered in my ear, his voice dark and lustful. "Going so soon?" His warm breath caressed my neck, sending endless ripples of desire through my body.

"Waiting for you," I said, swinging around to smooth a hand on his strong jawline.

Phillip seized my wrist. He drew my hand close to his lips and kissed it. When his fiery blue eyes cut to mine, my breathing hitched. "That's a good girl," he purred in his bedroom voice. My heart sprung into a gallop, foreseeing the delights ahead of us.

Our fingers interlaced as we climbed the remaining steps. "I thought you'd be congratulating King Edward," he casually said.

Downstairs, the ball continued. The cacophony of music and cheers seemed everlasting. "Oh, I spoke with him, yes…" I stared at him sidelong, full of boredom. "We quarreled, as usual."

We moved down the empty hallway. A sudden draft filtered through the embrasures, and despite the frosty air from the snow falling outside, I welcomed it with all my heart. Winter was all I'd ever known. It had ruled over Whitehaven for five hundred years… or so the stories said.

"I'm sorry to hear that," Phillip breathed, stopping at my bedroom. "You mustn't worry. Your father has married a wonderful woman." He pushed the door open and held it, waiting for me to step inside. Phillip Steelborn's chivalry met no equal. But I knew well once we crossed this threshold, his good breeding and manners would fade.

"Is she?" I told him, unconvinced.

His lips eased into a charming grin. "Can't you be happy for him?" he added, earning from me the harshest glare. "Or at least pretend to be?" His eyebrows arched softly, hopeful to persuade me.

I heaved a heavy sigh. I'd grown tired of pretending. Everyone wore masks in this kingdom.

I sauntered into the room and headed to the night table, where glasses and a jug of wine rested on a golden tray. I poured the drinks at once and gave mine a swig just as fast. "Have we come here to talk?" I asked, a malicious smirk blooming on my crimson lips.

Phillip's eyes grew alight with passion. He closed the door behind him, steady fingers unbuttoning his royal coat. And as he stripped from his clothes, I shed mine. Devastatingly appealing, he ambled towards me with a lover's confidence. Because that's what we were.

He pulled me to him roughly, his clean-shaven face inching closer, hunting for the sweetness of my kiss. His lips touched mine, and their velvet warmth set me aflame. I stood on tiptoe, clasping my hands around his neck, leading him back until my calves bounced against the bedframe.

Painted fire exploded in the evening sky. Vivid colors spread inside the chamber, brightening the old stone walls with flashes of red, green, and blue. It was a gift befitting a king. Such magic was all too rare and precious, and could only be found miles away in the eastern lands. One of many wonders brought to Whitehaven on the king's wedding day.

"Gods, I want you," he purred, eyeing me with a salacious stare. He then swept me off the ground, weightless, in his arms corded in muscle.

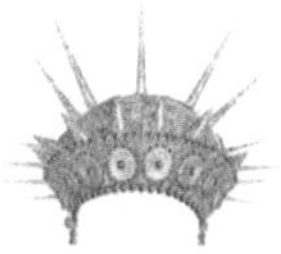

CHAPTER TWO

I straddled his waist with my thighs. And when he sat on the bed, my body molded to the hard planes of his. Phillip's panting breaths skimmed my ear, the sound as lulling as the beat of drums coming from the tents outside.

His thunderous heartbeat echoed in my chest. My breaths quickened, desperate to be full of him, eager for that blessed ecstasy that hushed my whirling mind and gave me peace.

Cries of the sweetest agony dripped from my lips when he sheathed himself inside me. And as our bare bodies rocked together in fluttering darkness, I became the goddess that served no other purpose than to push him to the edge of fathomless bliss.

"Maleath," Phillip moaned, shattered by unmitigated lust. "Maleath, slow down. If you don't stop..."

The words drifted into silence. His chiseled chest glistened in the twilight, heaving with excitement.

A quiver surged in my veins. In a flash, the tide of passion swept me whole, waves of pleasure throbbing through my core. Breathless, I reached the peak of delight, and as I did, I brought him with me.

When it was over, I tumbled to his arms, taken by pleasant exhaustion. Phillip tugged me close to his chest and pressed his soft lips against my brow.

Lights no longer painted the sky or flashed inside the room. But the music lingered. A low croon of zithers and flutes, soothing to my spirit. The three bronze bells tolled the midnight hour in the distance.

"Steel and blood roses," he uttered in a husky voice. The sigils of our houses. He loosened a sigh. "What a pair we make."

A pair. We were far from being a couple. I couldn't help but smirk. He was handsome, to be sure. With eyes green as the moss of the Forbidden Meadows, blonde hair that reminded me of sun-kissed wheat fields, and smooth, full lips that delivered me to heaven in more than one way. Every woman in court dreamed of having him. Many longed to prove the rumors of his proficient bed skills. In his arms, my restless evenings had subsided.

But not tonight. Tonight, I'd have to resort to other measures.

Pulling the red satin sheet over my back, I rolled aside, wrapping my narrow frame. I began gliding off the bed when Phillip caught my arm.

"Where do you think you're going?" he asked, gathering me to him in a single pull. "I'm not done with you yet." Undiluted lust hung from each word.

He took a hand to my chin and raised my gaze. A stray beam of silver moonlight slanted across my blue eyes. "But *I* am," I told him, slipping away, red lips stretched into a crooked grin.

Phillip started, confused. He wouldn't understand. He'd never come across rejection—not without inflicting severe penalties for it. The world and all its pleasures lay at his feet.

I swept a bronze candelabra from the nightstand. The sphere of amber light chased me across the chamber until I set the piece on the dressing table. It was carved in the finest wood from the Black Forest. Its value exceeded any estimation. Men had *died* on a mission to refurbish my rooms. The sole thought made me shudder in dismay. But on my stepmother's whim, treasures such as these now filled the castle.

"What are you saying?" he managed in a righteous tone without moving an inch.

My brow knitted as I leaned forward, studying the table carefully, searching for the latch that unhinged the secret drawer.

"Maleath?" he insisted, this time with a hint of vexation.

I looked over my shoulder to say, "It's over, Phillip." My focus returned to the table. I smoothed a hand over the surface, looking for a bump on its intricate carvings.

"Don't be like that," he barely whispered, taming his quick temper. My gaze angled up, catching his reflection in the mirror. He kept a flat expression, hard as iron. "Is this because of what I said about your father?"

"No," I managed. "It's not that."

My finger finally caught the pin. I pinched it fast and tugged until it clicked. The secret drawer popped open atop the dresser. At once, I glimpsed the small golden case waiting inside. I smiled as I brought it to the candlelight. The box itself was a precious oddity, forged in rose gold, engraved with ancient fae symbols; but what it concealed was a thousand times more valuable.

"Come to bed," he said. Not a question. A demand. Phillip's sultry voice, though harsh, offered the promise of reckless abandon. Indeed, the rumors were true. He was the finest lover in the realm, or at least, that I suspected. Making love to him again tempted me beyond any measure... But it would have to wait.

I turned the box in my hand, looking for the lock buried in its engravings. "Go back to Aurora," I taunted with a smirk, entranced by the shimmering case. Legends warned that any fae-made object brought forth evil in human hands. But that did not dissuade me from collecting them.

"Back to a bed of stone?" He growled, dragging his fingers through his mane of blonde hair. "You know very well she's cursed in that tower."

The words snapped me from the daze. I turned towards Phillip. "Waiting to be rescued by her one true love," I added knowingly, seriously. "That's you."

Phillip's eyes danced with uncertainty. He sat on the bed. Folding his arms across his chest, he said, "Is that really what you want?" His voice was stern and dauntless. "Maleath?" He frowned. "If I go to her now..."

A threat of loneliness. The lengths to which he'd go to get his way. And thus, Phillip had kept me in his thrall for months.

"If you go to her now," I said, "you will break the spell. You will claim your love and live a happy life." I clicked the lock, and the lid finally opened.

I dragged my bare feet to the nightstand and moved my wine glass closer to the edge. Unexperienced eyes would have seen no more than gold dust inside the box I carried. But appearances could often be deceiving.

"How can you say that?" He gasped in sheer shock. "How," he continued, narrowing his eyes, "when none of this would have happened without you?" Phillip paused, catching his breath. "It was *you* who summoned the monster that keeps her asleep."

"I do not deny it," I said in a cool voice, and dipping my fingers in the container, I took a pinch of dust. "But we cannot forget your part in this."

Phillip's mouth slackened. "Is that…?"

"Pixie dust from the Lost Realm," I said, smearing it on my fingers. "You won't find this anywhere else."

Fascination gave way to disapproval in Phillip's countenance. "Where did you get that poison?" he asked with a righteous frown.

"It came with the furniture." I shrugged.

"It's dangerous," he warned me.

"It might be perfect for my restless nerves," I uttered, dragging my wine glass closer. "A pinch of this, and I could sleep through the night like a babe."

"I wish you wouldn't," he mumbled, shaking his head.

I set the container on the nightstand and sat on the bed. My hand cupped the side of his face. "My sweet Phillip," I breathed, leaning closer. "You should know by now, wishes never come true in Whitehaven." Tears loomed in my eyes. How I'd wished my father would not marry.

His rough hand scurried up the slope my neck, firm fingers gently pressing down. "You're just using me," he whispered with no inclination, "too frightened to be left alone with your grieving heart."

"And you're stalling," I replied, my lips brushing his. "Too scared to be a hero and claim your true love." I swallowed hard. "We are wounded, you and I. And we've licked each other's wounds to find solace from our crumbling worlds long enough."

"Maleath..." he managed, taking his grip to my waist. "You've had your fun. Now, I'll have mine."

A stuttered breath left my mouth. "This will be the last time," I said, striving to convince myself.

Phillip's eyes hooded with desire. Lazily, his thumb stroked my lower lip. "Then make me remember it for years to come," he said, his voice darkened while his thumb entered the slit of my mouth and smoothed over my tongue; seductive, as he dragged me to his arms.

Rising before him, I pinched the satin sheet and unveiled myself to him like a royal rose. Phillip's head leaned back against the headboard, his lustful stare roving my bare body.

"I will be yours again, my prince," I murmured.

A quick breath rushed through his mouth. On a

whim of passion, he hauled me to the bed. His taut body rolled over mine, spreading me beneath him. "You will be," he purred, pinning my wrists above my head, "whatever I tell you to be."

"Your Highness," a voice said.

Startled, we both turned to the door. Barely fitting in the doorframe, there stood a man clad in golden armor, with a blood rose chiseled on the burnished breastplate. His scintillating helmet rested trapped beneath his arm. He was a burly man, whose sole presence gnawed away at my confidence.

Although unwelcome, the guard stepped inside. A pool of candlelight spilled on his face, revealing the deep scar that crossed it from left ear to cheek, barely touching the corner of his lips. The mark was hideous enough to make it memorable and his identity clear.

Daron Blackstone. The fiercest warrior in the kingdom. A heartless killer, and captain of the King's Guard.

"The king requests your presence in the North Tower," Daron said, his tone crude and hoarse. Not once did he look away from our lovers' scene. He knew better than to lower his guard in times as treacherous as these.

"The North Tower?" Phillip groaned, annoyed, as he swept back the hair from his face. However, I glimpsed alertness in his blue eyes.

Flustered, I gathered the sheet and covered myself. "I'm otherwise engaged at the moment," I told him. "As you can well see." The sole mention of the tower had rattled me to the core. I tried my best not to show it. I feared Daron could see through me like a pane of glass. He would not hesitate to use any weakness to his advantage. Daron Blackstone was as rotten as they came.

Phillip slipped on his clothes. He picked up my gown from the floor and laid it on the bed.

"Tell the king I'll see him tomorrow," I said as I got dressed. The minute I slipped on my shoes, I grabbed my glass of wine and took a swig. I'd have to drink the entire jar if the night didn't improve.

"You can tell him yourself, Your Highness," Daron said. "Right now." With the helmet still locked under his arm, he swiveled on his feet and marched to the doorway.

Insufferable man. How dared he speak to me like that? My jaw clenched tight.

Phillip filled his glass offhandedly. "Mind your manners, Daron," he said, calm and detached, and then sipped on wine.

The fearsome guard stood impassible, inches apart from the jamb, with dark angry eyes fixed on the hallway. Daron harrumphed. "King's orders, Your Highness," he amended begrudgingly, without looking back.

"I think you should go," Phillip whispered, stroking my cheek. "This might be good for you. *Both* of you."

I blushed. "Maybe you're right," I said, nodding.

"Your Highness?" Daron pressed, slipping his horned helmet on.

Daron thought himself untouchable. An appalling truth. He could get away with anything as long as he served under my father's shadow.

Phillip finished buttoning his blue coat before kissing me on the cheek. "See you soon, my darling," he breathed impishly.

"Farewell, my prince," I mumbled in a daze as Phillip left the room. But what I really meant was *goodbye*.

On my way to the doorway, I grabbed my white furred cape. The North Tower. No place was chilliest in the castle. Why would my father summon me there?

"Are you ready *now*?" Daron asked, mocking me with undiluted contempt.

I stood before him and swung my face up to catch a glimpse of his. "You're a lapdog," I told him through clenched teeth. "Lapdogs don't last around here."

The captain remained unmoved despite my

unkind words, the same hideous statue standing by the door. It soon became clear to me he would remain in his post until I followed his instructions.

I looked away and sucked in one deep breath. And as I exhaled, I hoped myself ready to face my father.

"Take me to him."

CHAPTER THREE

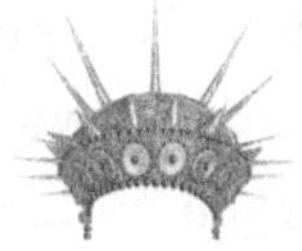

The sharpest apprehension tightened my chest as we climbed the North Tower's spiral staircase. Daron went ahead, guiding the way with torchlight. In his massive shadow, moving upwards proved a greater challenge than the narrow, slippery steps that made me stumble.

A decade had passed since I'd last ventured to this part of the castle, and I'd done it defying my father's explicit orders. Strange that I should be here now, at his behest.

Moments away from reaching the landing, my foot slipped. A desperate gasp clipped the silence as I lost my balance. My nails clung to the icy wall, barely sparing me from a lethal drop. Every muscle in my body went rigid in an instant. I took my free hand to my dry mouth and leaned against the freezing stone to catch my breath.

From the landing, Daron looked down at me with indolent brown eyes. He couldn't care less if I cracked my head open. Oh, why would my father summon me at such a late hour, and here, of all places? I picked up my gown and walked up the remaining steps with even more caution.

When I stood before the towering doors that led to the Throne Room, memories of that day flashed through my mind. I, as a girl of eight, standing in the place where it all happened. The place where my mother died. Where the black dragon killed her.

Ever since that harrowing day, the grieving king had sealed off the tower under penalty of death. He'd convinced himself the place was cursed, haunted by my mother's restless spirit. I disagreed. For I knew well my mother could never be a monster. Queen Laeessa's beauty had inspired several songs when she lived. However, hundreds followed her demise. Even today, the bards sang about her flawless grace, and the tragedy that befell the kingdom when death came for her with swift wings and scintillating scales. There hadn't been a dragon sighting in all the five realms in centuries. Not until that fated night.

My heart leapt like a wild stag in my throat. I

sucked in a long breath, watching the doors as though they truly were the gates to the Netherworld.

Daron harrumphed. He stood by the entrance, a gloved hand resting on the hilt of his golden long sword. The sole gesture filled me with unease. I strived to keep my frail control. But the truth was, I didn't like this. Any of it.

The captain squared his shoulders. He lifted his chin and focused his gaze on the pitch darkness of the stairs. This was as far as he'd go.

The doors' spiked iron nails, though worn with time, seemed sharp and threatening. I laid a leery hand on the handle and pushed hard until the door budged on its rusty hinges. A gust of freezing wind lashed through the crevice. My arms tingled in a sudden shiver. But I pushed further, widening the space enough for me to pass.

Once I stood inside, the room humbled me. Not because of the grandeur it once held, but with the sheer desolation it embraced.

Swathed in silver moonlight, the hall's white marble columns stood tall. Tattered banners, loose and crooked, still hung from their strings. As I glanced to my side, I faced the sooty walls, red velvet benches and chairs charred shapeless. A lineup of strangely unscathed long mirrors hung from the walls on both sides, antiques framed in gold with fae symbols, forever reflecting the desolation on their barely dusty surfaces. Legend had it they'd not only been forged by the fae, but possessed mysterious magic only the fae-born could unlock.

Undiluted sadness permeated the icy air. Grief clutched my heart as I meandered inside this forlorn space, frozen in time. I sensed no ghosts in here. Nothing, save absolute stillness. Utterly unbearable.

My thoughts went back to that painful day, to the many lives lost, as guards and members of the court assembled in one last act of bravery. I remembered the flames shooting furiously through the room. I remembered being swept away in Sir Trevan's arms, watching in dismay the devastation as smoke and cinders filled the chamber.

The wind tore me from the trance.

I moved down the central aisle. With each step, my leather boots crushed shards of glass. The carpeting that led to the throne, once shimmering gold, was now frayed, darkened with smoke and old ashes. At the far end, the dais stood, swallowed in shadows. And behind it, the tower's stone wall crumbled, along with the remains of colorful stained-glass windows.

The full moon appeared through the wall's opening. It called me closer, to where the dragon had stormed inside to steal half of my heart. The blood in my veins chilled. But the memory burned me to the bone, prickling like a thousand needles.

Lacy snowflakes drifted in the chamber. Low heaps of snow piled upon the dais. My steps turned sluggish as I got closer. Dread and cold tangled in my core and hindered my breathing. I hugged my arms and rubbed them, fighting the shivers that swept me in unstoppable waves... I wanted to leave this place, but what choice did I have when Father had summoned me?

When I stood scarce feet away from the enduring throne, my gaze sharpened, picking apart the shadows. I'd spent precious moments playing around that seat, running in circles, resting on my mother's lap... And it was because I knew this chair so well that I noticed the faint difference. Something had been added to the picture.

Someone was sitting on the White Throne.

As the moon shifted in the hazy sky, slanted light beams spilled upon the second throne's remains. A pile of molten marble, nothing more.

I took a step further, then another. The sharp echo of my footsteps made me restless. And then I saw. I chewed on my lower lip until the taste of sweet iron hit my tongue. And slowly, my expression slid into a frown.

"You," I all but hissed, stopping inches away.

I started as the crooked chandeliers came alight in a flash, flooding the throne room, spilling amber light on the carmine velvet train of the queen's gown.

Queen Roslyn's lips stretched in a bitter smile. "Yes," she said, her silken voice posing a challenge. "It's me." Lazily, she tapped the throne's marble arm with polished red fingernails.

I speared her with a furious glare. My hands dropped to the sides, curling into tightened fists of tension. Meanwhile, Lady Roslyn sank into the seat, spreading the long train of her gown across the dais. Her sleeves glinted with gold-embroidered trimmings, as did the brooch tailored to her bodice. A golden heart enclosed in filigree... The irony did not escape me. This woman had no heart.

"You shouldn't be here," I breathed, shaken by her presence.

The queen threaded her fingers through locks of light blonde hair that bounced on a deep red cloak edged in pristine white fur and rippled below her shoulders. Gleaming snowflakes lingered about her, suspended in the air. Prisoners of time. Much like this chamber.

"Where is my father?" I demanded, my tongue heavy with impatience. "He summoned me here."

The queen's lips twisted with derisive triumph.

"We missed you at the wedding," she sneered, turning the gold ring on her left hand.

"Did you?" I uttered through clenched teeth. My station as a princess prevented me from tearing her away from the throne, but if she sat there one more minute, I doubted I could master my restraint.

The onset of a laugh fluttered in her throat. At last, she rose from the seat, eyeing me sidelong while she turned. "It was quite the celebration," she continued. With light and graceful movements, she sauntered to the broken wall, where the snow stacked higher.

She stopped at the edge; her gaze lost in the night. "I want you to see this," she said. The sweetness of her tone belied the words of her choosing.

"Come." She called me near with a gentle hand wave.

A ripple of numbness washed through my being. Every instinct inside me screamed I should not move. However, I took a step towards her. Then another, driven by an invisible force. And when I least expected, I stood next to my father's bride.

"Look at them," she said, her gaze angling to the tents below. People gathered by the firepits, dancing and singing old songs of lore. "These peasants celebrate under the direst storm. The fools." The queen pursed her lips and shook her head.

The cool wind blew and picked up my hair, pitch black tendrils caressing my cheeks. "We people of Whitehaven love our winter." I lashed back at our new queen, an outsider of whom I knew very little.

"Mm..." she uttered with indolence, watching me out of the corner of her eye. Her delicate hand eased on the stone wall's rim.

Her empty stare became full of longing. "You speak like that because you've known nothing else," she decided. "But I promise you, this awful winter draws close to its end."

I frowned. The queen's intent escaped me. And yet, the cool determination of her voice heightened my disquiet. "Where is my father?" I hurried to say, unable to control my quickened breaths.

Queen Roslyn finally faced me, with widened eyes that claimed full innocence. "Oh. He's not here," she said, clasping her hands over her gown. "You should have been at the wedding, Maleath." She loosened a sigh.

I flinched, confused. "You've already said that..." I managed. And as I took a step back, the queen seized my shoulder. Her scarlet claws dug into my skin when she pulled hard, dragging me to the tower's unstable edge. Sheer black fright flew through me, faced with an imminent fall. Inches away from meeting my death, I whimpered.

"Don't you want to know why?" she asked with the same unnerving sweetness.

Shocked by paralyzing fear, I watched her in absolute silence. "Why...?" I said in a stuttered breath.

Gently, the queen leaned forward, stopping inches away from my face. "So that you might see your father one—last—time," she whispered, pulling me closer.

Out of her cloak appeared a silver dagger clutched firmly in her hand. What power had she over me? I tried to fight. I couldn't move. But I could scream. "Let me go!" I cried, clinging a hand to the wall, struggling to become free from the queen's hold.

"You're not going anywhere," she hissed in my ear, "but down." When her gaze swung up to meet mine, the queen's eyes burned with spectral fire. And then I knew.

"You have magic..." I mumbled foolishly, shuddering in undiluted dread. The weakness extended to my arms and legs. This must have been a spell. She was a sorceress!

"I do. And before your fall, *princess*," she whispered, holding the dagger close to my cheek. "I'll need your heart."

I gasped in horror. My body jittered on its own, sending icy rubble drizzling to the bottom of the tower. And all the while, below, the people chanted drunken songs that lingered in the air, oblivious as I faced my life's end.

"Why are you doing this?" I stammered, desperate to escape.

A flicker of wonder surfaced on the queen's countenance. And I could have sworn sadness had loomed in her eyes. "Darling girl," she said in the lowest of voices, "your heart will set me free." Queen Roslyn tilted her head, watching me with condescending pity.

"You're a vile and evil queen!" I roared.

All emotion vanished from Roslyn's expression. "Yes. I am an Evil Queen," she said. "And my curse roots deeper than anything you could imagine." Her voice came gravely. "Now, I will have that heart of yours." The knife's edge grazed the lacing of my bodice. A scream caught in my throat.

A harsh draft rushed between us and whisked the queen's cloak from the ground. The swaying velvet shrouded her face, her grip finally faltering. I took the chance and grappled to break free, and in the struggle, the wall crumbled behind us. The largest bolder dropped behind the queen and pinned her gown's train to the floor.

A spurt of strength shot through me then. I all but dragged myself away from the edge, my chest heaving with panting breaths.

"Come back here!" she roared once the cloak settled. As the queen attempted to move, she realized her disadvantage. Her jaw clenched tight in restless fury.

"Look at me!" Roslyn commanded.

I remembered her eyes—fierce, not human—and refused to look at them. Hugging my arms tight, I turned away. Gradually, the numbness of my limbs dissolved. Strength came back to me in slow, pulsing waves. My gaze locked on the door, which seemed a world away. "Help..." I managed, my legs lumbering as I moved across the dais.

"Daron!" the queen shrieked, jerking off the cloak in unmitigated anguish. Caught in the cruel winds, the red piece flew away, scurrying into the snowy night. "Daron! She's running away!"

Daron. I'd forgotten about him.

Panic as I'd never known before welled in my throat.

Instantly, the thrash of metal armor echoed in the hall. When Daron Blackstone's footsteps stormed into the room, all hope in me withered. I'd been a fool. There was no escape.

The captain reached the steps. And within seconds, his gloomy shadow fell upon me. "I never liked you, girly," he said in a gruff voice. "This should be fun." His gauntlet plunged into my hair. In one heartless move, Daron Blackstone tugged hard and hauled me back to the broken wall.

"I need her heart!" the Evil Queen cried, flustered and still trapped in the tower's debris.

Daron scoffed, shooting her a glare of annoyance. "I'll get it when she's dead," he grumbled, recapturing his grip on me, driving me one inch closer to the edge. "Time to fly, little bird." The captain grinned, revealing black and yellowed teeth.

My vision blurred with forthcoming tears. This was where I'd die. The same place as my mother. Now our ghosts might haunt together Whitehaven Castle's halls.

A tear spilled down my cheek as I closed my eyes and prepared to meet my gods.

"Daron?" The familiar voice echoed in the hall. "What is the meaning of this?" Spite drenched every word.

My eyes flew open. Relief washed through me when I glimpsed the man standing at the bottom of the dais.

"Edward..." the Evil Queen managed with a nervous tone.

My lips parted to speak, but no words came. The king had arrived. All would be well.

CHAPTER FOUR

"This is the highest of treasons," he said, spearing Daron with a glare. "Release my daughter at once!" Father climbed the steps and finally stood on the dais.

Daron's grip relaxed, his rough metal fingers drifting from my neck. The muscles in his jaw tensed as he turned to face the king. "I've had enough of you too..." he muttered. And in a flash, his blade swung free from its sheath.

At my frailest moment, I found courage. "No!" I growled, wrapping my arms around the captain's waist. And just as fast, Daron's hand came flying back and slammed against my chest. The blow shot me to the wall, where my back slipped until I dropped to the icy floor.

The clean-cut sweep of metal followed as my

father's sword tore free from its scabbard, ready to engage the guard in combat. Yes, the king's skill with the blade preceded his fame, but compared to Daron —a ruthless monster—his chances of prevailing were quite dim.

I turned to Roslyn. "Stop this," I begged. And still, she remained untouched by what transpired amid us. "Do something!" I spoke through gritted teeth. But it was useless.

The swords clashed in a mighty clang that shook the castle walls. The first strike came from Daron, a heavy blow that almost cost the king's right arm. But he'd been fast and dodged the vicious arc. Rabid as a dog, Daron lunged at the king. His fearsome fist clenched in the air and swung down, striking my father's face.

The king wiped the blood off his burst lip with the back of his hand. He shook his head, and sharpening his vision, he renewed his guard, gripping the sword tight with both hands. King Edward was a taut and agile man of forty-seven. And his swiftness played to his advantage as, in one quick move, he disarmed Daron Blackstone.

A faint gasp sailed through the queen's lips. Her countenance suddenly slackened.

The king's sword thirsted for death, his blade nipping at Daron's neck. With a hand on the pommel, and the other on the grip, my father braced to deliver the final blow.

"Don't kill him!" Queen Roslyn said in a ragged voice. "I need him."

My father looked back, confused. When he locked stares with his new bride, heartbreak glistened in his eyes. "You did this," he breathed, his grip on the blade suddenly weakening.

"Edward..." she managed, holding up a wary hand.

Out of the shadows, Daron's arms sneaked behind my father and grasped his chest tight. The king paled. And as he startled, the sword dropped from his grip. Quick as lightning, Daron hauled my father towards him. He raised his arm and flashed the dagger in his hold, hinting death. A wry smile curled the captain's lips. The sharp blade slipped beneath his chin, grazing the king's neck.

I dove for my father's sword on a reckless impulse. My shaking hands smeared in his blood as they fastened on the grip. I swung the weapon upwards and leveled it at the fiend. But the captain blocked my aim, dragging my father between us.

I steadied my grip. The world froze around me. What more could I do?

"Maleath," my father said in a soothing voice, pale blue eyes resting on mine. "Finish this."

My expression slackened in sheer fright. "No," I breathed, white mist fleeing from my lips.

Unwavering conviction hardened my father's countenance. "Now!" he demanded, aware of the odds if I took no action.

Behind him, Daron sneered. In an instant, cold steel plunged into my father's neck. And at its touch, blood bloomed in crimson flowers.

A scream sliced through my heart.

With tears brimming my eyes, I thrust the sword forward. Steel pierced flesh, muscle, and bone. And I pushed through, with every ounce of fury rushing through my veins, and did not stop until the blade cut deep into Blackstone's chest.

A dark gurgle burst from Daron's mouth. His eyes lit with rage, untamed.

In his arms, my father slowly faded. When he stumbled, Daron's foot scurried near the edge. And once I felt the pull, my hands released the sword's grip. Stunned beyond any measure, I watched it tear away from me. Daron staggered, to no avail. His armor's weight and my father's struck the final blow.

The captain's body swung, whisked away from the tower into the winter night. And as Blackstone fell, he took my father with him, down into an eerie end written by my hand.

A wild roar of grief echoed in the hall. Soon, I

realized the sound emerged from me. My strength finally broke, and my knees dropped to the ground.

"Foolish girl!" the queen cried, heavily afflicted. My head swung up. I found her hunched, her face buried in her pale hands.

This couldn't be real. It felt like walking in the bleakest nightmare.

When the queen straightened, her cheeks were blushing. Her green eyes gleamed with forthcoming tears, but undiluted hatred twisted her expression. "You have spoiled *everything* for me, Maleath." She sniffed.

Caught in the daze, I shook my head. "What are you saying?" I mumbled, unable to make sense of a single word. And then it came to me, how she'd begged to spare Daron's life. Did she ever love my father at all?

Howls of dismay rose from the crowd below. They twined in the wind until I no longer could tell either apart.

"This was *not* how it was meant to be!" Queen Roslyn clenched her jaw. And in that moment, any shred of pain in her vanished. "You will pay for what you've done." Her eyes grew aflame, mirroring the darkness she carried.

The room shook with the violence of a powerful earthquake. Snow and rubble rattled in our midst. In a flash, a dozen torches burst alight, lining the hall with an incandescent gleam. And then I saw. Something terrible and extraordinary was happening to the White Throne. Rivulets of blood streamed out of nowhere, scurrying down the seat, coating pristine marble with a crimson swathe.

This was magic if I ever saw it. The darkest, vilest kind.

As the floor settled, I got to my feet. My gaze narrowed on the Evil Queen, unable to make peace with what had just transpired. "Why are you doing this?" I asked in the lowest whisper.

The queen raised her chin. "Murderer," she proclaimed, pointing at me with a denouncing finger.

"No..." I said, stepping back.

"Guards!" she howled in rampant fury.

"No," I managed, taking one more step back, shaking my head.

"Seize Maleath Snow!" the queen commanded. This time, her voice unnaturally loud. The roar resounded in the vaulted hall and poured outside, reaching the restless horde gathered by the gates.

The queen summoned one deep breath. She met my unrelenting stare, then looked away into the broken wall. "Maleath Snow killed the king!" she wailed, casting echoes in the darkness.

Her head swung back towards me. "I would have

given you a merciful death," she added in a subdued tone. Then, slowly, the Evil Queen's quiet demeanor thawed back into hate.

One more step back.

"But now you'll have to run." She paused. "I want you to beg before I take your life."

At the sound of those words, my heart shuddered. The thought fleeted across my hazy brain—to jump into the end, into the Netherworld, to join my father. But then another voice spoke in my head. *It does no good,* it told me. *Clear your name and avenge him. Destroy the Evil Queen.*

Anger spiraled from the pit of my stomach. My fists clenched tight. "Not if I take yours first," I muttered. I then turned on the ball of my feet and started running.

CHAPTER FIVE

 stormed out of the castle into the bailey, a white speck drifting in the snowy fields. Never had I appreciated the secluded life that came along being the single daughter of the ruling king. Not until this day, for no secret passage in Whitehaven Castle escaped me. I knew the fortress better than any of its keepers.

With my heart throbbing hard against my chest and in my ears, I speared through the dark. I trudged on slush and mud, finding my way to the stables. Luckily, Sir Trevan had once told me of this place.

Stealthily, I peered into the stalls. Not a soul dwelled inside. Every man and woman in the castle surely jostled at the Keep's gates, drawn to the harrowing scene lying at its base.

A shiver skittered down my back. I clenched my eyes and pushed away the horrid images taking shape in my mind. There would be a time to grieve, but this was not it. I hurried to the farthest stall. A gorgeous black Friesian paced inside. "Easy, Thera..." I told her in a quiet voice as I entered. My hand smoothed on her neck. "It's me, girl."

The mare's sweet temper did not change as I began to drag the haystacks near the wall. I piled a couple, winded from the sprint. I scurried behind and dropped to my knees. My shaking hands cleared the ground at a frantic speed, soon revealing the hidden iron latch.

I pulled until the secret door swung open.

A horn blared in the distance. The somber noise, a grievous call I recognized too well. It was the call that summoned the King's Guard, the one that announced war and ruthless devastation. Would the Evil Queen send an entire battalion after me? As things stood, the kingdom's resources lay at her disposal.

Meeting no hesitation, I leapt into the darkened pit. A cloud of dust lifted as my feet touched down on the hard ground. It prickled my nose and stung my eyes. I coughed a few times as my hand blindly searched the wall. Finally, it caused a clatter. I found an oil lamp hanging from the crude stone wall, carefully stowed for such an occasion. I grabbed it and turned the dial, ready to move forward.

The flame grew steady, by and by. I held up the lamp, revealing the long tunnel that would grant me an escape. I did not know where it might lead, but for now, that mattered little. As I hurried, covering the distance as fast as I could manage, Roslyn's words came back to haunt me. She would see me dead. She would have my heart, she'd said. Why? Who was this woman? She claimed to be a noble from a distant kingdom, but tonight she'd proven to be more than that. The woman was a sorceress. An evil one.

I ran until my legs scarcely endured. And just as my conviction wavered, I glimpsed the exit ahead. A simple rusty door, so ordinary, yet full of promise.

A stuttered breath crossed my lips when my hand folded on the icy lever. I pulled it down, to no avail. "Oh, gods..." I mumbled. Sheaths of ice must have covered the other side. Determined to be free, I wrapped my cape around my hands and tried the lever again. After giving it one vigorous tug, something cracked inside. Still, it would not budge. I leaned against the door and used my shoulder to push it open. Sheer relief washed through me as the metal slab finally gave way.

I slipped my fingers through the narrow crevice and gave it one more push. The door opened wide enough for me to pass. And at last, I met my freedom; the land carpeted in snow.

The fiercest winds lashed when I stepped outside. I pulled my cloak's hood over my head, sharpening my gaze. At a first glance, I recognized the dark maple trees. It was then that my spirit waned. "The Black Forest," I breathed, my voice lost in the night's chilling air.

It took no more than a second to admit it. I had but two choices. It was death at the hands of the Evil Queen, or death at the whims of the cursed woods before me. My grieving heart thudded beyond control.

The choice was made long before I knew.

I dashed into the woods, through uneven planes of rocks and muddied slush. A mesh of tangled branches grazed my skin like sharpened thorns. I knew this land, if only barely. I'd secretly ventured into the Black Forest's outskirts many times as a girl. A few miles away lied the threshold into the Realm of Fae. Trespassers paid dearly on either side. Perhaps the King's Guard would not dare travel so far north. The thought hardly gave me peace.

Weary with grief and struggle, I slowed my pace into a walk. I didn't know how many hours had passed. The storm showed no signs of waning. I'd have to take shelter somewhere soon. And there was but one place I could think of. A place not a soul would dare disturb. The Devil's Throat.

I exhaled one long breath. Although my skin was numb with cold, my cheeks prickled and burned.

Branches cracked nearby. I swung my head towards the noise. The undergrowth suddenly juddered, breaking the thick layer of ice and snow coating the bushes.

I realized I was not alone. And then, I caught strong snarls carried in the wind.

Panic washed over me.

Hounds.

My body went taut in an instant, widened eyes lodged in the silvery bushes. I tried to scream, but my throat seized up.

Distant howls came in reply to the hideous call. The snarl drew closer, grumbling louder.

"Dear gods, no..." I managed, taking a step back when I knew it would do no good.

Silver eyes sparkled in the undergrowth. A grey muzzle emerged, flashing lethal fangs in a menacing grin. This was no hound, but something infinitely worse. A barghest. A daemon beast descended from the Hamman Mountains. The most gruesome death lay ahead of anyone unfortunate to fall at the mercy of their maw.

Larger than a wolf, the black-furred monster scurried into the clearing, stealthy, with feral eyes locked on its prey. The seven-foot-long beast stopped a few feet away from me. Watching. Waiting for its pack to arrive.

I gasped, panting in terror. I took one more step back, dreading the movement might stir its fury. And as I took another, I stumbled on a tree stump. The beast's snarls renewed as it crouched on its front legs, ready to pounce and seize me.

To die in the Black Forest's entrails hadn't been the end I'd imagined for myself. Moments ago, I'd considered jumping off the tower. I wondered now if not taking that chance had been a mistake. At least I'd have a grave. Here, there'd be nothing left to mourn.

"I'm sorry, Father," I mumbled as my vision blurred with streaming tears. I shut my eyes and prayed for a quick end.

The wind lashed once more. Silken feathers kissed my cheek. I started into alertness. My eyes widened in wonder as they traced the white bird spearing down over my shoulder with sharp claws aimed at the fearsome barghest. The dauntless owl rushed onto the monster's head and stabbed its eyes, making the beast wail in profound suffering.

The barghest fell back on its hind legs for an instant, only to charge against the winged creature with inflamed fury. But the owl escaped. It soared above the barghest, encircling the clearing before spearing through the air again and meeting its target. Clawing and pecking, it wounded the beast until it bled.

As my savior flapped to fly away, the barghest snatched the bird's right coverts, sinking fangs deep into flesh and bone. Crimson ribbons spurted from the owl's wing. Relentless, the beast yanked the bird and dragged it to the ground.

"No..." I breathed, creasing my brow into a frown. My heart shriveled in despair for my winged savior.

Suddenly, a voice whispered in my ear. *This is your chance to flee, Maleath. Let the beasts fight as they will and run to the Devil's Throat.*

Leaving behind the white owl would have meant sentencing it to death. Fighting for it would mean sealing mine.

"I won't let you die," I managed.

With revived conviction, I stepped forward. I swallowed hard, and swept the grisly scene with a glance. This was a forest. There were no swords or spears in here. Nothing but piles of snow, branches, and rocks surrounded me.

Branches and rocks it would be, then.

I sucked in a deep breath. In a flash, I grabbed the largest boulder I could lift. Fear, stark and vivid, streamed through my veins. But that would not stop me now.

I staggered over heaps of snow to reach the barghest as it toyed with its poor prey. The owl's wings batted, fighting strenuously to flee from the beast's grip. Slowly, I crept behind the monster, bolder in hands, summoning the courage to strike, when a loud crackle echoed in the woods.

The beast's ears stiffened, its silver eyes widening with alertness. Not a second passed when beneath the barghest, rocks, snow, and mud rumbled and plunged into an unseen abyss. Both monster and owl disappeared from my sight, swallowed by the precipice.

Carefully, I set the rock down, unable to move any further on the unsteady terrain. The harshness of reality came crashing over me. There was no justice in an unfair world. I'd lost everything I'd ever held dear, and I couldn't even save the ill-fated bird. The air froze in my throat. I couldn't handle one more loss. Tears brimmed in my eyes, and I wept miserably.

I heard flapping nearby. Taken by despair, I stared into the cliff. Suddenly, the white owl flitted from the abyss. It soared to the sky, its right wing smeared with crimson blood. The bird's frail wings flapped until it no longer sustained the effort. My winged savior plummeted to the ground, crashing inches away from my feet.

My knees buckled and dropped next to my wounded rescuer. "You're alive," I whispered, gently gliding my hands beneath the precious bird. "You've defeated the barghest, my friend." A bitter smile curled my lips. "I've never seen such bravery."

I stroked the owl's head with a delicate finger. The creature uttered a low hoot, gleaming amber eyes fixed on mine.

"You *will* survive this," I told the owl as I gathered it close to my chest. Quietly, I rose to my feet. "*We both will.*"

CHAPTER SIX

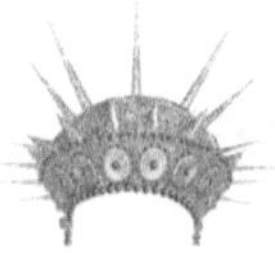

The night was drawing close to its end when I finally glimpsed the formidable cave. I stopped and checked under my fur cloak, as I'd done regularly for the past hour. The white owl was resting, nestled against my chest. "We're almost there, my friend," I whispered to the injured creature. And as if aware of my words' meaning, it chirped back the faintest sound.

The corner of my lips curled in a gentle smile. The owl shut its amber eyes, weary and subdued. I tugged on my cloak and covered the bird once more, pressing onward until we reached the cave's entrance.

The Devil's Throat. Only criminals and smugglers traveled this far in the kingdom. And by the looks of it, it hadn't been long since their last visit. While I meandered inside this raiders' sanctuary, I came across a stash of dry wood and some fire rocks piled next to a barren firepit.

Cold and exhaustion bit into my limbs. Sluggishly, I unlatched the straps of my cloak and spread it on the ground. A stuttered sigh escaped me when I got on my knees, and as I did, my winged friend lightly quivered. "Easy there," I breathed, and eased the bird on the furred surface. With a glance, I assessed the damage on its wing. The bleeding had stopped long ago. For now, that was enough to give me hope.

I shifted towards the firepit. I grabbed a handful of wood and tossed it in, then went for the stones and started a fire. My gaze lost itself in the rising flames when the flash of a memory sparked in my mind's eye. Camping in the woods with my father as we traveled to our neighboring kingdom.

I was a young girl of nine. Mother had died not six months back. I was sulking in the tent when my father walked in, carrying a stack of dry bark and twigs. He didn't have to, of course. Plenty of men could do that for him. But keeping himself busy was my father's means of escaping his pain. He dealt with grief as best he could. We both did.

His black leather boots halted in front of me, swathed with a sheath of crushed snow. *Care for a steaming bowl of mutton broth?*, he asked. His voice was smooth, but tired.

My head swung up to meet his blue eyes, weary from weeping silently at night. Despite himself, my father smiled.

I nodded. Mutton broth was Mother's favorite.

Then we must build a fire to make it, he added. All the goodness in the world reflected in his countenance. Father grabbed a piece of bark and offered it to me.

I wrinkled my nose, bemused. *It's snowing outside,* I told him with a hint of annoyance.

His eyebrows rose in amazement. *My darling girl,* Father said, *do you mean to tell me you've never built a fire in the snow?* A challenge lay buried in the words.

I pouted in frustration. *I don't know how,* I admitted, hardly matching his amusement.

Father returned the bark to the stack. He offered me his hand instead. *I'll show you,* he replied in a tender tone. *And once you've learned, you can start all the fires ahead of us, from here to Steelborn Castle.* His hand folded in mine, warm and caring. He tugged, and I rose to my feet.

As we walked side by side, I swung an arm around my father's back and looked up. *All the fires?*, I asked, an eyebrow shooting skywards.

Father cracked a smile. And this time, it was crisp

and natural. *Yes, my sweet,* he told me, his firm hand stroking the top of my head. *All of them.*

While my thoughts turned to the present, I found my lips had unconsciously thinned into a bitter smile. "A good man taught me how to build a fire when I was a child," I turned to say, but the owl had fallen asleep, beaten by extreme tiredness.

The warmth of forthcoming tears gathered in my eyes. "Dear gods," I breathed in a low, tormented voice. "I've lost my father." Grief and despair tore at my heart. My knees buckled, and I stumbled to the dirt floor. I rested my back against the knobby stone wall, curling my knees against my chest. And burying my face in my shuddering hands, I gave vent to the deepest agony.

Soon, the fire swelled, and warmth permeated the air, wrapping me in a pleasant embrace. I surrendered to the violent pull that begged to shut off all my senses. I closed my eyes, knowing myself damned into a lightless future, and I slept.

No dreams took over as I lay dormant. Nothing, but absolute darkness.

SLANTED BEAMS OF PALE SUNLIGHT SPILLED inside the cave when I woke up. The fire had died hours ago, leaving its comforting heat behind. My mind's blessed haziness swiftly dwindled. And it was then that the hurt began. In my limbs, strained and wounded by the harshest night. But also in my heart.

Reality rushed in. Unstoppable, merciless.

My hollow stare locked on the pit's charred remnants. "My father is dead," I managed, as grief slowly dulled the blood in my veins. Voices murmured in my ear, whispering that perhaps I could have saved him. Perhaps, had we not quarreled earlier... Perhaps, had I not stepped into that tower.

When I closed my eyes, tears glided down my cheeks. I hugged my arms tight. And I wept. And I mourned. I would have died myself, ripped to pieces by the barghest's fangs, had the white owl not come to my aid.

I raised my chin slightly at the thought. "The white owl," I said, remembering all.

Looking down at my cloak, I found no trace of my bird friend and frowned. "Where is it?" I sniffed, clearing the tears with the back of my hand. It took all the strength in me to rise to my feet. Pain and weakness had taken a great toll on my body this morning.

"Argh," I groaned when I noticed my bruised arms, though I couldn't care less about my gown's tattered sleeves and muddied hem.

I wandered in the cave, searching for a sign of the

wounded owl, but to no avail. It pained me to think that, aware of its dire fate, the owl would have fled to die in peace. Maybe the Devil's Throat was not cursed, as people said. But *I* was. And my darkness had stretched to the white feathered bird.

Crushed, I stopped at the cave's entrance. Within hours, I'd lost everything. Not only my father, but my home as well. In an instant, the Evil Queen had snatched my life away from me, sowing loss and desolation in my heart. What would become of me now?

Last night, the world had shaken and shifted on its axis. I'd become an outlaw. A traitor to the crown. I was the monster who'd delivered King Edward to an early grave. A crime, not only heinous in its nature, but punishable by death.

The Guard's horn roared miles away. Their chase resumed, probably with the best trackers in the realm. My chances of escaping were truly nil. But I couldn't give up. I had to survive.

The Devil's Throat had served its purpose. It was time to move on.

I swept my cloak off the ground, resolved to keep moving north. The Royal Guard wouldn't dare to cross the Iron River. It lined the border with the Realm of Fae. No one in their right minds would ever touch those waters. Dark legends riddled the woods beyond them. Myths of terrible magic and wonder.

They wouldn't stop me, though. Because the more I learned of the world, the more I realized, beneath the shimmering surface, everything was bleak and ordinary.

Outside, the snow had thawed. The woods seemed friendlier beneath the soft winter sun. My past fears and apprehensions concerning the Black Forest paled compared to what I'd already been through. My alertness, however, did not wane as I continued my journey.

Hunger rattled in my stomach. I'd have to figure out a way to hunt my meal fast. But in the middle of the harshest winter Whitehaven had ever seen, my odds were not looking that great.

CHAPTER SEVEN

$\mathcal{A}$ hazardous mountain pass and a rapid river edged the border between the realms of fae and man, the Black Forest being the sole point of entry. Sailing across the Black Sea or the Iron Pass was strictly forbidden. Our realms had been divided so for centuries. I'd heard stories of what lay beyond the Iron River, but not a soul who'd dared to sneak into the land of fae had come back to tell the tale.

As I moved through the forest, it seemed as though the sun shone brighter, its rays felt warmer. Even my thoughts turned back to happier days. To Sir Trevan Hillborn, and the many lessons in sword fight he'd taught me. My father had disapproved. A princess needn't associate herself with weaponry, he used to say. Still, he would not stop me or force me to give up practice. Training became my sole outlet of amusement in the first years of mourning after Mother had died. Then, I grew up. And I traded swords for dances and handsome princes.

What would Phillip think of me now? Honestly, I didn't care… I halted, distracted by a rumble ahead. The frothing and crushing of rough waters. Had I truly made it this far? There was only one way to find out.

I hurried uphill, slipping on moss-covered dead trees, climbing on a carpet of rocks and dry branches until I reached the crest. Breathless, I stood there, watching in absolute awe. The Iron River. Its crystalline waters splashed and crashed against giant riverbed boulders that split the hastened current in half. A few feet ahead stood the fabled bridge. It was narrower than what I'd imagined. A walking overpass, raised in stone. Three arches curved along its foundation, the vigorous waters tumbling below.

I closed my eyes and took in one deep breath. The wondrous fragrance of clover and wildflowers filled my lungs. It was the strangest feeling. Far from wariness, hope blossomed in my heart, because I knew whatever lay beyond this river would be better than the fate awaiting me in Whitehaven. Suddenly, venturing into the Realm of Fae did not seem such a perilous deed.

The way across the bridge was long, but I'd traveled longer to get here. "It's just a walk," I mumbled. "A simple walk." I spread my hands over my gown's skirt and harnessed my resolve.

When I took the first steps to the edge, I noticed the most peculiar thing. Planks of iron paved the threshold where stone met ground. The bridge's parapet was covered in it as well, sporting iron forged railings and horses sculptured in a gallop heading my way.

My feet touched the metal slabs. I noticed the simple inscription engraved again and again. "The road ends here for all fae," I read. Narrowing my gaze, I realized these were no ordinary scrapes of metal, but shields worn with time, adorned with the stamp of a rampant unicorn standing on its hind legs. My kingdom's sigil. The emblem looked older and rougher. But there it was.

Would the fae keep a similar threat on their end of the footbridge? I wanted to find out. Decided, I picked up my gown and took the first step that would deliver me to our neighboring realm.

While I moved onward, I found it hard to look away from the rushing waters. A myriad minnow darted between the rocks. Pink and red rose petals drifted in the current. I shaded my gaze from the scorching sun with my forearm and swung my head towards the mountain miles away. And I watched the torrent thundering down. I'd never witnessed such a stunning view, such life and color trapped within a single space.

A grand arch loomed ahead at the end of the bridge. Crafted in gold, adorned with gleaming filigree vines tangled with roses and leaves twirling down the walls.

At last, I reached the edge. I found no scribbling on the floor or the arch. No words of caution. No threats against my kith and kin. The legends had lied. This place wasn't dreadful or bleak.

"Well," I said under my breath, taking my hands to my waist. "That was easy." A proud nod. Satisfied, I crossed the brink.

I'd made it. I had crossed the Iron River, encountering no danger. A smile thinned my lips. I wished the people could see me now. I'd managed all this, and no one had been here to witness my...

I heard voices nearby. A conversation between two men. My eyes flew open. It then dawned on me. I was alone in the woods. Alone in another realm. A trespasser. Unarmed. I did not know what I was facing or could face in these lands. I knew nothing at all. My heart jolted with fright. What a fool I'd been!

At once, I sprinted towards the forest, fleeing from the voices. Curiosity compelled me to turn back, to see who these people were, and what they looked like. But the fear for my safety was stronger, so I moved forward.

A light and merry birdsong moved with me as I meandered in the woods. The trees were vivid red and green, their leaves rustled with a warm, soothing breeze. The air itself was fragrant with moss and the sweetness of rotten fruit. My mind whirled at the thought. Fruit. Something to eat. I had precious hours before this hunger turned unbearable. I decided I'd track the scent and wandered even deeper, hoping to find what my stomach desired.

Soon, I came across a vast clearing, carpeted with thick green grass and fragrant rosebushes tucked in the undergrowth. A stone well stood in the center, perfectly kept. It had a wooden roof, and a bucket tied with a splitting rope. The promise of fresh water led me closer.

Out of nowhere, buttercup butterflies encircled me in whimsical flight. It was then that I realized. "There's no snow," I mumbled. My mouth instantly slackened in wonder. I twirled, standing in the center of the clearing, delighted in the beauty of my surroundings.

Not a trace of ice or slush touched the land. I marveled at the vivid green of the shallow grass and tree leaves, and flowers in bloom crowning the hedges. Spring blessed this realm as it never had touched Whitehaven... But the quiet glee locked in the grove suddenly faded.

All sound came to an end. The stillness broke in swiftly, violently. Not a bird sung, nor a leaf moved. I became restless. "Something's wrong," I said under my breath, my brow creased with worry.

At once, the earth shuddered. The movement, gentle at first, quickly increased in strength and gained momentum. Thuds echoed in the distance and drew expeditiously near. Whatever was heading my way sounded reckless, and would charge against me without flinching.

I rushed to seek cover in the trees a moment too late. The violent herd had already arrived, unstoppable.

My throat thickened. I took a step back. Useless, as the horde quickly surrounded me. Shimmering black coated horses galloped in a circle, pinning me in the center. Their powerful stride made the earth rumble and my heart jitter in sheer fright. Amid whinnying and neighing, their pace came to a strut, slowing further as the circle tightened.

The gorgeous beasts swayed their necks, untamed and fierce under the blinding light. Humbled by their mighty presence, I curled up on myself, praying to escape their innate fury. It was only as they halted that I saw the pointy horn stemming from their foreheads.

Sheer shock washed over me. "Unicorns?" I managed in utter disbelief.

The creatures strutted closer. Their warm and smooth muzzles took turns to inspect me, their horns all but poking through my gown.

A loud whine rose above their noises. The horde suddenly broke at the sound, opening the way to another unicorn. A white wonderful beast, with snowy long hair rippling down its neck.

Every inch of my body went taut. A beautiful sight, a horde of wild unicorns. A vision so powerful and daunting that I thought I would die. These weren't the subdued creatures that filled the songs of bards, but fierce and violent beings. A fearsome sight to behold at such a narrow distance.

The white unicorn walked closer. The creature bowed its head and stooped before me, leveling our gazes. In silence, our eyes met in one long, meaningful stare. It wouldn't have surprised me if the unicorn had started speaking.

Trapped in the beast's spell of beauty, I raised a hand, impelled to glide my fingers down its muzzle. And as my touch hovered mere inches away from its immaculate coat, the unicorn brayed and shook its head disapprovingly. It straightened fast and marched back. The snowy creature then whipped its head, leading the others. It turned. And as it strutted back into the forest, the horde followed.

At the rattle of their gallop, a cloud of dirt lifted from the ground. Gradually, the dust settled. All traces of the unicorns had gone.

"It's real," I said, dumbfounded. "The stories are true."

CHAPTER EIGHT

Why had the wrathful unicorns chosen to spare me, even as they recognized me as an outsider? I did not know. But the day progressed, and I was standing here alone, in the middle of the radiant woodlands. I staggered to the well with quivering legs, desperate for a drink to soothe my parched mouth.

I tossed the bucket down the waterhole. It came back brimming with clear water that I lapped directly from my cupped hands. The fresh liquid helped revive my drained endurance, albeit not fully. My limbs throbbed with pulsing pain, bruised, and strained to the limit. I steadied my balance, clasping my hands on the well's rim as a sharp breath escaped me.

The stones, worn with age and weather, were smooth against my soaked palms. They shimmered ever so slightly where the water had touched them. I inched closer to look. To my amazement, mysterious engravings turned up on the dark surface. These weren't common rocks. It seemed everything in this realm had its secrets.

"What is this?" I mused, sharpening my attention. The letters spelled out a name. Lightly tilting my head, I read, "Akron." Next to this inscription, I found another, fading as rapidly as the water on the stone dried.

In a flash, I plunged my hands into the pail and drenched the well's rim. And just like before, the stones glimmered. This time, more names surfaced. "Thuriad, Millindrel," I read, spreading the liquid on the rocks. "Essgard, Romni, Leander..." A seventh name continued. I passed a rapid finger across the stone. Useless, as I couldn't make out the letters. They had been scraped unreadable.

I roamed around the well, close to its rim. I brought the bucket with me, splashing water on the rocks, discovering new carvings as I moved. The patterns eluded my understanding, cryptic and old, unlike any of the realm of man. When I got back to where I'd started, a last message appeared. This one I could decipher.

"To the Lair of the Seven Mages," I mused. The Seven Mages. I'd heard those words before in a song in court. The Tale of the Seven. I'd danced to the merry melody, learned its lyrics by heart since infancy. Before I even realized, I was already humming. And as those pleasant times rekindled in my mind, I began to sing.

> *'Tis the song*
> *Of the Seven sworn to reign*
> *For centuries long*
> *Wielding magic for all men*

I slid down, easing my back against the well, and rubbed my sore neck. My legs appreciated the much needed rest while I looked back on the stories of the formidable mages. Legends said a thousand years ago, the most formidable wizards in the realm of fae had left their homes and gathered on a mission to defy the laws that divided our realms.

They would share magic with the Realm of Men, teach humans their sophisticated knowledge. But when this news came to the fae council's ears, they were far from pleased. The day came when the council demanded the Seven ceased their efforts. They called for an immediate retraction.

The retraction never came. Against the council's expectations, the Seven stood their ground. At that moment, the mages sealed their fates. The fae quickly stripped them from their lands and riches. They became exiles, undesirables to the fae. In a world broken by magic, the Seven's rebellion had been nothing short of an act of heroism.

Winter came
To the Black Forest, they've gone
Carved their names
Into everlasting stone

I swung my head to the well. Could this be the stone from the song? The symbols surely seemed magical. But what did they mean? Had this been a spell, a last resort, to save their lives?

I'd never once believed the stories to be true. Like all fairy tales, I thought they were lessons in disguise, meant to subdue women and children. And yet... here was a well with those names carved in stone. And unicorns were real.

My gaze cut to the trees, startled by movement in the thickets. Instantly, I lunged to my knees and sharpened my focus. My breath hitched. Had the unicorns realized their mistake and come back to cast me off their land?

Frantic, my focus stumbled through the bushes. Again, the branches shuddered. It was real. I hadn't imagined it. Panic flittered through my heart. I got on my feet, slowly. It couldn't be the unicorns. The earth had not shaken as before. There definitely was something lurking in the woods. I had to know what it was. I was done with running.

I meandered to the undergrowth, determined, careful not to make a sound. With all the stealth I could summon, I crouched before the bushes, waiting. The next time the shrubs stirred, I dipped a hand inside.

As it happened, I caught nothing. But my spies scurried out of their hiding place. Two snowy furred creatures, leaping past me at dazzling speed. My tight lips slid into a smile of relief. "Fooled by rabbits," I mumbled, dusting off my hands. Not mythical creatures, but the most ordinary and beautiful bunnies. Hunger and tiredness were unquestionably taking a toll on my nerves.

I straightened with a grunt, ready to move onward. Then, turning on the ball of my feet, I crashed hard into something. "Oof!" I stumbled back at the blow and fell to the ground unhindered.

"Arg!" someone growled.

I lifted my gaze at the sound and found a man before me, sitting on a heap of maple leaves.

"By all the gods!" he muttered, wincing as he took a hand to his right shoulder. "Will you watch where you're going, woman?"

My brow furrowed, and my jaw slackened in sheer annoyance. "How dare you call me *woman*?" I groaned, rising from the ground. I looked down at the man, as he chose to remain on the ground, then dusted my gown with a few quick pats.

The stranger lifted his chin, shooting an eyebrow skyward. As he leaned forward, his face caught a stray beam of sunlight. Gleaming hazel eyes sparkled with awe as they found mine. The corner of his lips curled with mischief. "Aren't you one?" he asked with a sweeter tone, sweeping me with an appraising stare. He bit his lower lip, giving some thought to his own question.

His face was bronzed by wind and sun. His lips were firm and sensual. The skin, pulled taught over the ridge of his cheekbones.

"Well?" he said.

"Huh?" I started, frazzled and confused.

"Are you not a human woman?" he added, narrowing his gaze. He scratched his chin with gloved brown-leather fingers. "I don't see fae in you. But I could be wrong."

My stare lingered at the chiseled chest etched beneath his white tunic. The rich outlines of his shoulders strained against the sheer fabric. He looked tough, lean, and sinewy.

Stop staring at the man. "No!" I scoffed, outraged. A woman? I was no ordinary woman, but a princess.

A smile danced on his lips. "Are you sure about

that, love?" He spoke in a husky voice that made me shiver in delight. My cheeks burned in an instant.

A swath of tawny-gold hair dropped to his brow. His features were too perfect, too pleasant to look at. A pity he lacked any sense of decency. Why, he hadn't even risen or offered an apology.

I scowled. "Contemptible man," I mumbled, fixing my hair into a quick braid.

My stomach churned painfully. I would have bitten off the stranger's head if that had eased this straining hunger. Perhaps he carried something to eat.

Out of the corner of my eye, I caught the glint of metal. A sword, lying on the grass. In one quick move, I swept the blade off the ground. Heavier than I expected, but still manageable. My hands folded around the hilt and I held the weapon firmly as I moved closer, pointing the tip at the man's handsome face.

The stranger's strong jawline stiffened. However, his stare remained gentle.

"Who are you?" I urged, hardening my expression. "You're either a spy or a thief. If the first, you're not a very good one. If the second, I'm afraid the roles have changed as *I* will be stealing from you today."

The stranger raised his arms midway and flashed his palms in surrender. Slowly, he rose to his knees. "You might want to be careful with that sword," he said in an appeasing tone. "It's pretty sharp, *my lady.*" He raised his brow, giving me a knowing look.

A brief gasp fled my lips. "My lady?" I repeated, stunned. "How did you…?"

"Your manners," he added with half a shrug. "And that dress." He pointed with a finger, never lowering his arms. "It's Lathiriua silk. Expensive material. Quite rare."

I swallowed hard. My confidence wavered. Perhaps there was more to this man than met the eye... No. He was a stranger. I shook my head, driving away any doubts. I shifted an angry glare at his face, readjusting my grip on the sword. "Pears?" I asked, lifting my chin.

His brow creased with bemusement. "Huh?" he uttered.

"Or grapes, perhaps?" I added with fluttering lashes.

He tisked. "My, my…" he mumbled, shaking his head slightly. "You *are* a strange woman."

I released a gruff breath of frustration. "Food," I explained, moments away from losing all patience. "Do you have anything to eat?" The question sailed more like a plea than a demand.

"Yeah," he said. "I do." And at those words, the man cocked his head, a finger pointing at the ground at a leather satchel lying inches away from where he'd fallen.

"Toss it here," I replied in a smoother tone.

He did as I asked, with no objection. I grabbed the satchel and peered inside. Undiluted relief washed over me when I saw it contained several pieces of fruit. I took one and held it in the light, still gripping the sword in my right hand. My mouth watered just by observing it, the rarest food I'd ever come across.

"You won't find pears or grapes around here, my lady," the man said.

"A black apple?" I asked with a frown, watching the curious fruit. "How very strange. Is it poisonous?"

The stranger did his best to choke a laugh. However, he failed. "Now, why would I carry poisonous apples?" he said, amused.

Warmth rose to my face. My gaze whipped to his. "I wouldn't know," I lashed back, annoyed. "There's one way to find out, I suppose. Catch!" I tossed him the piece of fruit.

The stranger caught the apple in the air. Quick to prove himself, he sank his teeth into it and swallowed. "See?" he said, showing me the fruit's fleshy red interior. "They're not apples. They're plums." He smirked. "They're quite sweet."

"Mm..." I pursed my lips, doubtful as I dug a hand into the bag. I grabbed another plum and took the first bite. Its juicy sweetness led me to a second, and a third, until I finished it.

"That was actually very good," I said, genuinely surprised. "Thank you. I think I'll have one more." My hand slipped into the satchel, happy as I could be.

The man harrumphed. "If you really want to

thank me," he said in a silken voice, "you could drop that sword." Rubbing his nape, he tipped his head and flashed me half a grin. Tempting, all in all.

"Nice try," I conceded, matching his cheerful mood. "You should leave." I waved the sword up, instigating him to stand. "I'm here to see the Seven. They don't take kindly on strangers as nosey as you."

The man got to his feet. He stood there, inches away, handsome and boldly intimidating. "Is that so?" he asked, taking his hands to his waist, expanding his shoulders. "Good thing I'm with the Seven, then." The pitch of his voice dropped at those last words.

Ice skittered down my spine. "*You?*" I managed as the blood drained from my countenance.

The stranger nodded. "Yes," he said, folding his arms over his chest. "Me."

I flinched. "You're lying," I hurried to say.

He gasped in disbelief. "Really?" he said, stepping closer. I readjusted my grip on the sword as it wavered with uncertainty. "I have proven myself to you twice already." He stopped, his chest inches away from the blade. "So, will you give me back my sword, or shall I curse you for it?"

This was real. He was one of them. One of the legendary Seven Mages, the only one who might help me, and I had threatened him more than once. Reluctantly, I loosened my grip and allowed the blade to drop at the mage's feet.

Magic glinted in his eyes, precious amber gems. "That wasn't so hard now, was it?" he purred with obnoxious self-assurance.

"A mage *and* a thug," I said through clenched teeth. This was such a disappointment. He was nothing like the wizards of legend. This man was proud and annoying. And I absolutely couldn't stand him.

Like a chivalrous knight—which he was not, and I was sure he could never be—the mage got on one knee. He picked up the blade with his left hand and sheathed it quick. "It could have been worse, my lady," he said, looking up. An egregious smirk curled his lips as he stood. "Such horrors fill these woods as your blue eyes have never seen."

I scowled, crossing my arms. "Oh, I see them," I said, twisting my mouth into a derisive grin.

Astonishment fleeted across his countenance. "My lady," he began with a righteous frown, "I assure you, my friends consider me perfectly charming."

"Charming?" I sneered, shooting up an eyebrow. "That's a bit of a stretch, isn't it?" I reached an arm out, offering him back his satchel.

The mysterious mage drew closer. He narrowed the distance, leaving us but a breath apart. The air charged with an energy so strong I could almost touch it.

"Stick with me and find out," he told me in a sultry tone.

I froze. A ripple of excitement spread through my limbs. Was this his magic's doing?

The mage winked and took the satchel off my hand. He stepped away slowly and turned. And all the while, I remained standing there, like a complete fool, unable to come up with a witty remark to silence him.

Suddenly, he looked back. "What do you want from the—from *us*, anyway?" he asked coolly. The mage strolled, moving around me, eyeing me like a lion studying its prey.

"I need a spell," I said simply.

He lashed his head back. "Well, that's obvious," he blurted. "Why else does one seek the mighty Seven?"

"Mighty?" I glowered, but my temper waned immediately. I could not afford to cross the man if I wanted his help. "I need to be invisible to someone," I added in a softer demeanor.

Charming halted. "Oh. I see how it is," he said, decided. "You're a posh runaway."

My lips parted to speak, but he went on.

"Stole from your mistress, did you?" he asked,

furrowing his brow. The mage licked his lips before going on. "What was it?" he added with an inquisitive glance. "Diamond earrings, a bracelet..." A crooked finger swept my sleeve. "That expensive gown, maybe?"

I blinked, aghast. Never had I been so insulted in my life. "How dare you?" I demanded, scrunching my nose.

"Well, I'd say it's obvious enough," he continued, smug and unbearable. "You were the handmaid of royalty. You must have done something truly terrible to wind up here." The mage nodded.

I narrowed my eyes. "Why would you think that?" I asked, honestly curious.

Silence sailed between us as he considered his following words. All amusement fled his countenance. "We're all outcasts on this side of the river," he said, and his stare darkened.

The words made me restless. But I shed from their powerful effect and asked, "Are all mages as insufferable as you?"

At once, the brooding glint vanished from his hazel eyes. He smiled, carefree and genuine, and it was like glimpsing summer for the first time all over again.

"Insufferable, you say." A terse laugh slid under his breath. "I believe that title is my own to bear."

Charming bowed his head graciously, without pretense or affectation. The frivolous mask was gradually coming down, and I found what hid underneath it quite enjoyable.

He leaned against the wide trunk of a maple tree, squinting as he tried to decipher me while I did the same.

So this was a mage of the Seven. A man who seemed no older than me. Then again, mages aged slowly, their lifespan stretching over a thousand years... or at least, those were the stories.

He was attractive and tolerably confident. Not the bespectacled white-bearded wizard I'd expected. He carried a sword instead of a wooden staff. He was witty and cynical, not wise and contained. Charming defied every preconception of his kind.

"I think we've started this all wrong," the mage said out of the blue before taking a bite of his plum.

"I am not a thief," I told him in a whisper. Oh, but what did it matter what he thought of me?

"I'm sorry I said that," Charming added, subdued. "But you *are* running," he pointed at me with his bitten plum, "from the King's Guard."

My eyes flew wide open. "How do you know that?" I pressed a hand on my chest, trying to ease my quickened heart. What powerful magic was this that he could go through my thoughts?

He curled his lips, pleased. "I know many things." He shrugged. Charming gave one last bite into his plum, then tossed it away. "So, you must be from Whitehaven," he concluded. "The king's dead, have you heard? Stabbed and pushed off the tower by his own daughter."

Horror and fury flashed in my gut. "Stabbed and pushed off the tower... by the princess," I repeated with a tight jaw. Rumors spread fast. The warmth of forthcoming tears rose to my eyes.

"What did you say your name was?" he asked, moving closer.

"I didn't," I mumbled, my mind whirling miles away. He'd heard the story. I couldn't reveal my identity to this man—mage or not. "It's Snow."

"Now listen, Snow..." He glanced away while rubbing his nape. When he faced me again, he did it with stern conviction. "You're deep in the Black Forest," he warned me. "This isn't the citadel. There are things here far more dangerous than any penalty waiting for you in Whitehaven."

"I can't go back," I said in a blurt, with faintly trembling lips. "They'll have my head if I do." My throat seized up.

Charming's expression slackened. "Your head?" He started, astonished. "Gods! What did you do to deserve such a punishment?"

"I…" I bit my lower lip. Stepping back, I swallowed my tears.

The sheer shock of discovery fleeted across Charming's h

azel eyes. "Wait a minute." A harsh exhalation. "It was you. *You're* the runaway who killed the king." He paused in dismay. "But if that's true then… Then, you're Prin—!"

"Stop. Right. There," a voice said.

CHAPTER TEN

"I said…" The man harrumphed. "Don't. Move."

A towering figure emerged from a pathway concealed between the trees. The man must have been six and a half feet tall. A black cloak covered his burly frame, the details of his face buried in the shadows of its hood.

My heart jolted into a wild gallop, taking my breath along for the ride. The very way he stood told me he was far from friendly. Was this the Evil Queen's emissary, a hunter sent to kill me? I swallowed hard, bracing myself to run if it came to it. On sheer instinct, I stepped back, but slipped on a stack of twigs and pebbles and almost lost my balance.

The cloaked man reached us in a few long strides. With a lazy brush of the hand, he tugged at the back of his hood, letting the fabric slowly slip down. Stray strands of pitch-black hair came loose and swathed half his face, accentuating the moon-like pallor of his skin.

His profile spoke of power and ageless strength, with chiseled lips and an aquiline nose. The one eye visible was blue and shone like cobalt, with an unnatural fire that gently burned. I'd yet to see this in any man.

Heaving a sigh, he swept a hand over his stubble. His gaze cut to the ground behind my foot. A muscle clenched along his jawline.

"Leander," Charming said, putting on his best smile. "It's only me."

My lips parted in awe. Leander. I'd read the name on the well. He was another mage. More imposing than Charming somehow, with an ethereal air about him, impossible to pin down. A subtle pulse of light beamed off him, like the moon's faint gleam. It had to be magic.

That left five other mages to meet. Were they hiding in the woods? My shuddering eyes swept our surroundings, fearing they might suddenly step out of the bushes, wrathful as the unicorns.

Leander scowled. "I wasn't speaking to you, laddie." He groaned as he trudged towards us. "*Don't move,* says I. And what does she do?" he mumbled.

"Steps back and smashes everything." He snapped off his cloak with haste and slipped it around his arm. It was then that I noticed the glyphs inked on his neck and around his forearms. They matched the ones I'd discovered etched in the well. Secret words of magic only a mage could understand.

He halted in front of me, spearing me with a powerful glare that rattled me to the core. I felt he could see through me and learn my darkest truths. Instantly, I lowered my gaze.

Leander marched past me and crouched carefully. He pulled back the strands of hair away from his face and locked his attention on the ground. On the rubble I'd stepped onto. His lips pursed tight, and he grumbled.

The mage's head suddenly swung up. He looked over his shoulder as though someone had called him before raising his hand and opening it with care.

I moved closer to catch a glimpse. The faintest flicker of a creature with fluttering white wings hovered above Leander's palm. Too small for a butterfly but bigger than a fly. What was it?

Leander brought his hand to eye level. *"Svestia drug on aerios, Marioth,"* he whispered to the critter. Even though I failed to understand the language, I caught the heaviness with which he'd said the words, the absolute dismay in the mage's voice.

"We will try again," Leander said to the creature. A bitter smile curled the corner of his lips. The being then batted its wings and drifted away like the faintest snowflake in the wind.

I took one more step and stood beside him. "What happened?" I asked Leander, holding back countless questions.

The mage smoothed a hand on his brow. He straightened before giving me an answer. "Your little roundabout destroyed Marioth's new home," he finally said, dusting off his knees.

My jaw slackened. "Faeries…" I whispered in wonder.

A wry grin twisted Leander's lips. "Pixies," he corrected, not particularly enthused. "They've lost their home and everything they ever held dear. I promised Marioth, their queen, I would not rest until we found them a new sanctuary." He paused, hesitant to say more. But then, he added in a burst of frustration, "I thought I'd found the perfect place for them. Until now." Leander straightened and sauntered towards Charming.

"I destroyed the pixies' home?" I asked, appalled. My voice's pitch went a tad higher.

"A colony," he added, as he eyed me sidelong. "An empty one. Don't you worry."

I exhaled in utter relief.

The mage smiled and shook his head. He turned to Charming. "Who's the girl?" he asked, amused.

My gaze angled straight to Charming, anxious he might reveal my secret. He hadn't said a thing so far, but that gave me no assurance. I hated to admit it, but my life hung from the frailest thread. And that thread was in Charming's hand. If the Seven learned the crown was after me, they'd surely turn me in. No one in their right mind would take on the kingdom of Whitehaven.

Seconds lasted an eternity until Charming's mouth opened. "A handmaid from Whitehaven," he said. "Got caught stealing from her mistress." He shrugged matter-of-factly.

Leander glowered. "You've brought a thief to our lair?" he said, each word drenched with glaring disapproval.

"A thief," Charming repeated under his breath, strolling to meet his friend. His hand landed on Leander's shoulder. "Aren't we all?" He flashed a smile.

Charming made justice to his nickname as Leander's sternness thawed, and he returned his smile. "All right, *Handmaid from Whitehaven,*" Leander told me, reaching into the satchel fastened to his hip. "You may stay with us for now." He drew out a silver dagger embedded with sapphires. The blade glinted with spectral blue light.

Leander shifted towards me. Wielding the blade in his grip with amazing prowess, he marched forward with sheer determination. My breathing hitched because in Leander I recognized the untamed quality of the unicorns. The same bold beauty, so terrible and imposing... What did he mean to do with that dagger?

When the mage strolled past me, a long sigh fled my lips. I looked back to see him walk further in the clearing, until he stopped inches away from the well.

Charming followed. I went after him.

The wind picked up, whirling strands of hair that stroked our faces. The leaves shuddered on rustling branches. Even the birds stirred.

Holding a hand in the air, Leander whispered a phrase in a language unknown to me. The words were melodious and sweet, the string of them as pleasant as a lullaby. Suddenly, the inscription in the stone came alight, gleaming the brightest blue. Leander lifted the dagger in his left hand and swung it firmly, making clean cuts into the afternoon air.

I watched in awe as the woods split before him. A rupture in a vividly painted canvas. Without saying a word, Leander walked through the rip. Charming moved behind him. Overwhelmed by the marvel before me, I hesitated. I didn't think my fears were unreasonable. As I saw the flawless portal opened, every certainty I'd ever had fumbled.

The portal's light flickered. The magic began to fade.

"Snow!" Charming called, looking back. "It's one side or the other. You must choose now!"

This was it. It was a choice more crucial than crossing any border, because once I stepped inside, I'd be leaving everything behind. Everything.

"Snow!" Charming insisted. He reached a hand towards me.

With no time to lose, I nodded and fastened my hand on his. The sole touch sent a ripple of lightning through my being. A magic so strong that it swept me in a daze. Could he feel it too? Charming pulled, and I rushed to him. And as I crossed the severed veil, the door closed behind me.

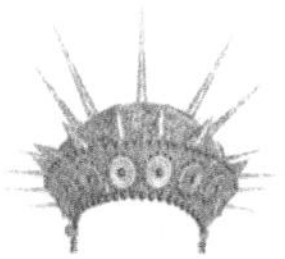

There was darkness. And in the darkness, a low bank of fog scurried. The mist's coolness climbed to my knees, higher, until it enveloped me fully. My heart rattled in my chest, doused with uncertainty.

"Don't stop now," Charming said. The soothing firmness in his voice eased my restlessness, even though I couldn't see him.

It didn't take long before I glimpsed the first sign of light. Faint, but enough to outline the mages' silhouettes as they moved ahead of me.

By and by, the darkness faded and the fog dispersed, revealing our surroundings. There was no forest. We stood at the top of a hill, in the center of a ring of vertical blue sarsen stones, at least fifteen feet high. When I looked back, the portal had vanished, leaving a mild mist behind, which quickly dissipated in the moors.

The wind lashed, cooler and harsher. It picked up my hair, whimsically tousling my long black locks. A shiver skittered down my spine. I hugged my arms and stroked them, losing my gaze in the wondrous green fields that stretched before me. Dusk washed the horizon with crimson streaks and amber hues.

"Look at you," Charming said. "You made it." He was standing in the ring. His taut muscular body leaned against a sarsen stone. That everlasting smirk of his stretched his tempting lips.

"Is that a surprise to you?" I asked, perplexed. But astonishment gave way to fury, and a glower promptly burdened my eyes. "Do you mean to say I could have died?" I skewered him with an unflinching stare.

"Well, I wouldn't call it *dying*," he hurried to amend in an offhanded manner. His head bobbed sideways, weighing his answer. "Not technically." He shrugged.

I marched towards him. "What would you call it?" I said, leaving a safe distance between us when I halted.

Too late did I realize, whether near or far, there was no being safe around him. His hazel eyes bored into mine. His wide pupils, fathomless ponds of darkness, lured me closer. "You could have lost your way in there," he conceded in a low, dispassionate tone. "But I would have found you." Charming paused, maintaining his resolve. There was something appealing in the sternness of his character, a quiet conviction lingering inside him.

It occurred to me then, I might have misjudged him.

I bit my lower lip, feeling an unstoppable wave of warmth rising to my cheeks. "What exactly did we cross?" I asked, arching my eyebrows softly. "Where are we?"

"The answer to your first question is," he began patiently, "a magic portal. Keeps us hidden from unwanted eyes." His gaze emptied and drifted to the fields. "As to your whereabouts," he added, facing me once more, "you, my lady, are standing in the secret lair of the Seven." He stepped back. With a hand wave, Charming showed me the way downhill.

I stepped outside the ring and saw the blooming valley, and beyond, a dense stretch of woods, vibrant with red maple trees. Hugged by the forest, I saw the house. Raised in red stone, two-story high, with slanted rooftops covered in green moss and morning glories twining on the walls. A tall column of smoke puffed out of the chimney top. Amber lights gently swelled thorough the windows, the finishing touch that gave the structure the coziness of home.

"It's beautiful," I said. I couldn't help a faint smile. A secret lair. Exactly what I needed. At last, I would be safe.

"I'm glad you think so," he said. "We should get going." Charming pointed at the burly figure strolling miles away downhill. Leander sure was in a hurry to get home.

I nodded, then picked up my gown and prepared to make the descent.

The way down was sheer misery. My boots were fit for court and dancing. They'd already exceeded my expectations as I'd made the journey through the Black Forest into the Realm of Fae. These leather pieces were all but spent and could hardly manage the muddy terrain.

Charming had the lead by at least twenty feet.

On my way down, I staggered, and grunted, and cursed the blasted shoes again and again. My feet hurt, and I couldn't wait to be rid of these boots.

"Everything all right, my lady?" Charming looked back, a flicker of concern marring his expression.

"Yes," I said, collected as I wielded the best skills I'd learned in court. "Everything's just fine."

He frowned. "Are you sure?" he asked intently.

I hesitated. Meanwhile, I measured with a glance the uncovered distance to the house. I'd made it this far on my own. I could surely walk a few more steps.

My lips parted to speak, but Charming already stood before me. "The slope is steep," he stated. "Do you want me to carry you down?"

"What?" I breathed, absolutely stunned.

He leaned closer. "Do you want me to carry you?" He repeated the words with no inclination.

I blushed and blushed again. "No..." I managed. Then smoothed my harshness with, "Thank you."

"Very well." He bowed his head.

As he was about to turn, I added, "Just... hold my hand?"

Charming did not show any delight or amusement. "Of course, my lady," he said, offering me his hand.

I swallowed hard, painfully aware of my feelings the last time we'd touched. Slowly, I lowered my hand until our palms barely grazed. When my hand folded on his, my skin tingled. A tide of warmth swept through my limbs. A sensation so powerful, my breath ceased for an instant.

His eyes grew alight as they found mine. And then I knew. He felt it too.

Stunned, we held each other's stare in silence.

"Hurry, lads!" Leander called in the distance. "The evening's upon us!"

Flustered, Charming turned away. "Right," he mumbled, clearly shaken. "We should make haste."

His grip tightened, firm fingers burning into my skin, sending thrill upon thrill through my body.

"What's so scary about the evening?" I turned to ask Charming as we covered the last stretch downhill.

He forced a smile, but it came bitterly. "You don't want to know," he said, closing the door to that conversation, or to any other.

When we reached the valley, and his fingers glided away, my hand ached with cold. The walk down the treelined lane that led to the house felt like a breeze in light of all my misfortunes.

Charming opened the door and stepped aside on the front porch, allowing me to pass. My belly ached again; this time twisting in knots. I took a trembling hand to the door and winced.

"Is something wrong?" he asked, stooping closer, so close that his warm breath caressed my ear. In this nearness, I caught the scent of musk and woods on him. He was all man and incredibly intoxicating. There was no doubt Charming tested all my self-restraint... I shut my eyes and quietly thanked this gruesome hunger for taking those thoughts away.

"Snow?" Charming's brow creased. Unquestionable wariness gleamed in his eyes. Oh, gods. He was so close. I noticed then his lips, smooth and full. They must have been glorious to kiss... *Go away, Charming. Go away or I might devour more than your mouth.*

"What is it?" he asked in a husky voice that shot a thrill to my core. I blushed without remedy.

"She's starving, lad!" Leander said, standing in the back of the room. "Let her in, why don't you?"

Flustered, Charming looked away. A heavy sigh fled from his lips. "Come on," he mumbled, holding my arm. "It's this way."

He led me to the dining hall, where we found Leander, standing by a roaring grand fireplace. The mage was at his leisure, turning an iron rod, roasting three chickens. My gaze angled to the long oak table on the side, laid out with a feast that rivalled any royal banquet. Pots of steaming broth, countless loafs of freshly baked bread, at least eight meat pies, a plate crammed with butter and cheese, and in the center, two baskets full of plums.

My mouth watered at the blissful scene. It took everything in me not to throw myself at such a wonderful layout.

Charming pulled a chair back and waited in silence until I glided on the seat.

"Go on then," Leander said, taking a seat himself. "Dig in, lass."

I stared at the colorful dishes. This would be my first full meal since I'd fled Whitehaven. It felt like an eternity had passed since. Charming set a dish before me, topped with roasted chicken and boiled potatoes.

Leander laid out a fork and knife next to the plate, but I'd already grabbed the chicken leg and sunk my teeth into its tender meat. I moaned as the juicy chicken melt in my mouth, caring little to nothing of what either of them thought of me.

My royal manners had flown away, and I couldn't care less. Out of the corner of my eye, I saw Charming saunter to the window. He stood there, looking outside. Even better. I took a loaf of bread and jabbed it into my mouth.

"Whitehaven, you said?" Leander poured a glass of red wine. He set it on the table and nudged it towards me with the tip of his fingers.

I took a swig and silently agreed. My mouth served a better purpose eating than talking at the moment. I took the fork and stabbed a slice of boiled potatoes, then shoved it into my mouth.

Leander glided a piece of linen over the table. It was a handkerchief embroidered with the finest silk.

"Your land is cursed," he continued. The calmness of his tone belied the grimness of the words. "They say your queen is the queen of death. That everything she touches invariably meets devastation."

I dropped the fork as an image flashed in my mind's eye. My father's face, seconds away from falling off the crumbling tower. And I understood it then. His empty stare would haunt me forever.

I grabbed the glass and had another drink. "The queen is an evil monster," I said through clenched teeth.

"Aye, but she *is* queen," Leander said all too knowingly. "Your *Evil Queen* is the only sovereign now that the king is dead, and the princess is missing."

"As was surely her plan," I mumbled. The hunger in me had met satisfaction. But my heart's thirst for vengeance endured, dulled only by my body's strain.

"Are you certain about that?" Charming said, looking back into the dining hall from his post by the window.

The question disarmed me. He knew nothing of my story, of course. I had no reason to doubt the queen's wickedness. She'd made it abundantly clear that she would see me dead. My father's death had seemed to grieve her, however. Perhaps the queen's selfish heart had found no place for me in their lives... I didn't know. I didn't care to know.

"Where do you suppose the princess is now?" Leander asked as he sluggishly carved a slice of cheese. When the creamy square fell on the wood board, he poked the slice with the knife and dipped it into his mouth.

"Miles away," I said absentmindedly. "Untraceable. A woman like her has all the means to disappear and become no one." If only that were true.

"It doesn't matter where she goes," Charming said in a gloomy tone. "The burden of her sin goes with her." His harsh words pierced my heart as strongly as Leander's knife when it stabbed that slice of cheese. What could have prompted them, I wondered. Only a moment ago he'd been so helpful and... we'd connected, hadn't we? And now this?

"So what if she killed her father?" Leander shrugged dismissively. "A princess would not kill indiscriminately." He slouched in the chair. "I'm sure she had her reasons."

Charming's fist slammed against the sill. "What reasons can a child have to destroy a most beloved father and king?" he said through clenched teeth. "Either by sword or neglect... It's an unforgivable crime to slay one's father." His expression darkened. Defeated, Charming looked away.

At once, Leander straightened. He pushed back the chair and got on his feet. "Ashton," he pleaded in the lowest voice, concern creasing his brow.

I should have thought a million things, and in the back of my mind, I surely did. I questioned Charming's reaction, the harshness of his words, when he knew who I was... or he thought he knew. Still, in that moment, a single thought outshone the rest.

Charming has a name.

"Forgive me. I cannot stay here," Ash breathed, stepping away from the window. He marched to the door and left the house without saying another word.

He never once looked at me.

CHAPTER TWELVE

My gaze lingered on the door. "What's *his* problem?" I mumbled, dreading the answer. *You're the problem,* a voice whispered in my head. *Ashton knows you're the princess who killed her father.* But he was wrong. Daron's unforgiving blade had kissed my father's throat long before I'd stabbed them both. And I'd done it because, in my father's darkest hour, he deserved at least the certainty of my survival. And the only way to ensure that was by pushing Daron Blackstone off the crumbling tower.

In silence, I told myself the story again and again. Even so, guilt and grief consumed me. Ashton's sudden disdain only deepened my misery. I could not bear him thinking so ill about me.

Leander rubbed his hand across his mouth. He

stood by the door, watching, perhaps hoping Ashton might return. His shoulders heaved with a deep breath that he immediately released. Slowly, he turned. "Sometimes, lass..." He hesitated. His piercing blue eyes glistened with sadness. Finally, Leander cleared his throat. "There are certain things..."

The door burst open violently, letting a boisterous group of men pour into the hall, spreading laughter and cheer.

"Leander! We lost you in Port Bree!" a red-haired man said. He slammed a black leather satchel onto the table. The bag opened at once, scattering gold coins, emeralds, and rubies. "Your share, man."

Leander darted towards him, and stopping between us, he glided a smooth hand on the table. "Thuriad, we have a guest," he said with a gentle voice, the kind that subtly urged someone's best behavior.

Thuriad. Another name from the well.

His head peeped over Leander's arm. The same unnatural fire burned in Thuriad's green eyes, startling against his beard and long wavy hair tangled with narrow braids. His freckled skin was weathered from many sunny days. His profile was strong and rigid, which he compensated with a grinning, kind mouth.

"Well, what do you know?" Thuriad said in a low, raspy voice. "We *do* have a guest." His expression slipped into a frown, and his lips twisted in a faint smile. "What's your name, puppet?"

"It's Snow," Leander said, notably annoyed. He sighed, reluctantly parting from the table.

Save for their condition of mages, Leander and Thuriad could not be more different. Two sides of the same coin. Leander, the moon, quiet and graceful. And Thuriad, the sun—tempestuous, bleeding light off the edges.

Thuriad reached an arm in front of me, across the table. When his shirt's sleeve rode up his arm, I glimpsed the tattoos that inked his forearm, down to his wrists and knuckles. The symbols, ancient runes of magic. He grabbed a jug of ale and a cup and dragged them to him.

The mage poured his drink, then snatched a chair and pulled it next to mine. In a single move, he flipped it backwards and sat. "Now then," he began, holding his cup while he swept me with an assessing stare. "Are you a witch, Snow?" He leaned closer to me with narrowed eyes, seeking to speak in confidence. "I don't like witches, you see."

His untamed braided hair reminded me of paintings of the Masters of the Nine Seas, heroes who'd conquered the five realms centuries ago.

"Nah... She's not a witch," someone spoke behind me. The voice was harsh and unfriendly.

Heavy footsteps approached the dining table. The man hauled back the chair to my left and set his muddied foot on the seat. Long, delicate fingers moved swiftly along the side of his boot, pulling out three hidden daggers. He carefully laid each one over the table in a perfect line next to my empty dish.

Out of the corner of my eye, I glimpsed his elbow as it glided on his knee. My head swung up to meet him, but a black mane of wavy hair veiled his face. Aware of my interest, he slipped a hand underneath and carelessly tossed his hair back. Only then did I realize he'd been smiling all along. A thin scar sliced his left cheek, etching a white line across his short beard. The same glyphs as the two others marked his neck and hands up to his forearms. Despite the brashness of his manors, his chestnut eyes were gentle as they met mine. His lips then eased into a pleasant smile.

"What makes you so sure she's not a witch?" Thuriad asked, clearly vexed.

The mage arched up his eyebrows. "Witches are awful," he assured him while peeking at me. His gaze cut back to Thuriad. "This one, not so much." He gave me a teasing wink, then snatched a plum out of the fruit plate.

"They're not ugly at all," Thuriad argued as his frown carved deeper into his brow. "Brindel's a gorgeous woman. Voluptuous, sensual… an absolute weakness to any man who's not blind!"

The mage chuckled. "Brindel's a faerie!" he blurted, meandering to the hearth.

This didn't sit well with Thuriad. His lips pouted. His shoulders slouched in defeat. "Same difference," he mumbled. "She's bewitched me."

"Pay no attention to Thuriad," Leander said with a dismissive hand wave. "*Or* to Essgard." He pointed at the dark-haired mage standing by the fire.

"I am drained out of my wits!" someone groaned. The voice came from the dining hall's entrance. The mage's head grazed the lintel. He was a mountain of a man—tall, with a taut, muscular build. He dragged a massive chest into the room as if it were completely weightless. Long silver hair rippled below his broad shoulders when he popped open the lid. And he did it with such strength that the chest tumbled and fell back, spilling on the ground a treasure worth a king's ransom.

"Must we keep striking these raids in the wee hours?" he grumbled, raking back his silken hair with tattoo-covered fingers. A harsh exhalation sailed through his lips. "The journey back home takes so long…" He yawned. "Leander, I can't go on like this. I need my sleep, you know?"

Leander pursed his lips. "I will remind you not to call them that, Akron," he managed. "These aren't raids, brother. We're simply…" he shrugged, "*evening out* the playing field."

"Stealing riches from the Fae Council?" Akron said curtly. "Sounds like a raid to me." A dimple pierced his left cheek as he gave Leander a lopsided grin. The smile soon faded when Akron noticed me.

"And who might you be?" he said, stooping before me with such kindness that it felt as if he were speaking to a child.

"This is Snow," Leander said, referring to me with a hand.

"She's a witch," Thuriad added with such conviction it made my jaw slacken in disbelief.

I faced him in immediate protest. "No! I'm…" I uttered.

"I've already told you, she's not!" Essgard interrupted, each word drenched with frustration. "Thuriad, honestly. You think everyone's a witch."

Thuriad cocked a red eyebrow sky-high. "Aye, but can we trust her?" he pushed back, wiggling a lecturing finger in the air.

"Silence," Akron said, his voice so loud and resonant it brought all noise to a stop.

"She's here, isn't she?" he continued in a warmer manner. "If Leander approves, then that's good enough for me." He stopped to give me a tender smile. Akron then turned to his brothers once more. "It should be good enough for you, too."

He yawned again. "Please excuse my brothers," he told me with droopy eyes. "I'm sure you have an interesting story, Snow. And I cannot wait to hear it, but for now I'm going to bed." He nodded. "Welcome to our lair, child."

I started. *Child?* Akron looked no older than me. But if the legends were true, then these men must have been at least a thousand years old. The thought was enough to stun my whirling mind.

Akron yawned yet again, stretched his arms, and turned to the doorway. "Good night, everyone…" he said, trudging all the way to the staircase.

"Romni and Millindrel," a pair spoke in unison. The men stood across the table, pointing at each other, so I could tell them apart. However, it was still confusing.

They both seemed callow men with firm, athletic bodies. Their light blue eyes glinted with magic. Braids tangled in their long blonde hair.

"We're twins," they added, leaning their elbows on the table. Brands like the ones on the other mages inked their wrists and hands with subtly different glyphs.

"I'm the handsome one." Romni winked. His nose was a tad rounder, I noted.

Millindrel shoved his brother away from the table and took his place. "The nasty one, he means!" He snorted.

I stared at the gathering, marveled. These were the Seven. I'd expected to be humbled by their wisdom, but they looked like ordinary men. A paradox of magic, truly.

"Everyone, please listen…" Leander called, standing in the middle of the room. "Snow will stay with us for a few days." He paused to look at each of his brothers' faces. "We shall all do our best to make her feel welcomed and comfortable for as long as she's here."

"A house guest. Such wonderful news calls for a celebration!" Romni cheered. Aware of his intentions, Millindrel grabbed a jug of ale and served two drinks, one of which he glided to me across the table.

"Drink up, Snow!" Millindrel cheered.

"Good gods!" Thuriad groaned in wonder. His eyes flew wide open. His thin lips curled into a smile. "Is that the good ale?" He inched close to look. "I want some of that!"

"The finest in the five realms," Leander added,

enticing me to taste it with a subtle nod. "Go on, lass. Try it."

"Essgard, how about some music?" Romni said, stepping back towards the fireplace. He turned to the wall and removed the blue zither that hung from it. A beautiful work of craftsmanship, enameled in gold leaf.

The mage took the zither as Romni offered it. He dragged his seat close to the hearth, setting it against the wall. "Mm... Why not?" Essgard mumbled, lifting his drink. With the instrument in one hand, the ale in the other, he gave the drink one long swig. He then ambled to the chair and sat with the zither in his lap, tuning it.

Thuriad sprung off his seat. "I'll drink *that* if you won't, lass." He reached for my cup of ale. "No one matches my skills when it comes to holding liquor."

His certainty stung my pride. In a flash, I cut off his hand's target by slipping my own in between. "Oh, really?" I dared him, quirking up an eyebrow.

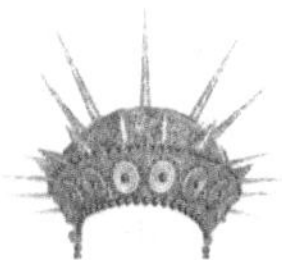

A thrill prickled every nervous fiber in my being. Wave upon wave of warmth rose to my face. The rhythmic pounding of the mages' fists on the table had more than encouraged me. I was gulping down my seventh cup of ale, frothy and fresh as it glided down my throat, and sweetened with a hint of honey. At least, I thought it was. I had no mind to ask. Not after I'd beaten Thuriad.

When I finished the drink, I slammed the cup on the table. I was so proud of my accomplishment, elated as the mages chanted my name amid roars of cheer.

With a flick of a finger, I dropped the empty jar on the table. "That was the last drink in the jug." I lowered my chin, flaying Thuriad with a teasing glaze.

"I believe that makes me the winner," I said, curling the corner of my lips ever so slightly.

Sir Trevan had once told me winning minor battles always mattered, because it was the smallest victories that paved the way to triumph... What would he think of me now? I'd surely be a disappointment. But I'd lost so much in the last few hours that gaining anything meant the world to me.

Thuriad's fiery brows knitted tight. He pursed his lips, stern as he locked stares with me.

"The last in the jug, aye," Romni uttered, leaning against the cupboard behind me. "But not the last of the ale!" He flung the door open, revealing a dozen more jugs stored inside the cabinet.

Oohs and aaahs stirred amid the mages.

I couldn't help but laugh at such a view. When I looked over to see my rival's reaction, his pleasant green eyes rested on me. Thuriad smiled, satisfied. And also, absolutely drunk. That sole thought pulled another burst of laughter from me, as Romni topped our cups with ale.

"It's your turn, Thuriad," I managed, blushing again and again.

With unshakable sternness etched on his face, Thuriad grabbed his cup. His grip faintly wavered as he drew it close to his lips. At that moment, he became the cynosure of all eyes.

Thuriad swallowed hard. He lowered his drink. "I don't want to humiliate you, lass…" he mumbled, and his face went notably pale.

My eyes narrowed. I leaned closer. "Are you unwell?" I asked, reaching a hand towards him.

Thuriad dragged back the chair and sprung off the seat fast as lightning. With eyes wild with intoxication, he turned to say, "Excuse me," covering his mouth with the back of his hand. And fighting the urge to retch right then and there, he dashed out of the room.

Bursts of laughter and shouts of disappointment rumbled in the dining hall. The mages gathered by the table, tossing gold coins and precious gems that traded hands.

"Come on!" Millindrel said, holding a hand out in front of Essgard. "Pay up!"

Wearing a lopsided grin, Essgard shook his lowered head. He dragged his fingers through his dark hair, uttering the quietest laugh. He then dipped his hand into his pocket and drew out a fistful of gold coins, which found their way into Millindrel's pocket.

"I wasn't expecting that, Snow," Essgard told me in a low voice. He poured himself a drink and went back to his seat, where the zither waited.

My eyebrows shot sky-high. "I'm sure I wasn't either," I mumbled, astonished. I'd witnessed these contests before, often taking place between the guards. This was my first, and hopefully, my last. "I guess I was lucky." I shrugged.

"Sheer luck, I say!" Thuriad belted out, stopping in the doorway. He looked mighty, standing tall with both hands on his hips and a steely expression.

Recovered from his drowsiness, the mage marched towards me. I watched him come closer, silently subdued. And as he stood inches away, Thuriad's stoic demeanor thawed. A warm smile stretched his lips. He offered me his hand. "Well done, lass."

When I grinned and shook his hand, the mage nodded in approval.

As the evening deepened, the gathering broke up and scattered in the house. Leander had snuck into an armchair by the hearth, where he now slept. Essgard remained in his post, next to him, playing a gentle melody on the zither. Romni and Millindrel argued in the hall about which one of them had made the best impression on me.

I lingered by the window, watching the woods, grateful to have found a roof... and friends. For the mages had embraced me as one of their own. I promised myself then, for as long as I lived, I would never forget their generosity.

The moon was long gone, and the starry sky faded fast before my eyes. The first streaks of dawn painted the horizon... And still, no sign of him. No sign of Ash.

"He's not coming back, lass." Thuriad stood beside me. He leaned a hand on the sill and stooped a little to peep through the window.

I blinked and turned to face him without saying a word.

"Not for a while," he added in staid calmness. The mage loosened a sigh. He then tightened his lips, wavering to say more. "We can't change what he is, Snow." He paused. "D'you understand?" Thuriad gave me a long, meaningful look.

No. I didn't understand. I didn't know what Ash was, the kind of man he was. I only wished I did. But now that I'd learned of his hatred, any hopes of being his friend had been reduced almost to nil.

Thuriad took a swig of ale, then leaned against the wall. "The lad's cursed, he is..." he continued with empty green eyes. "We all are, one way or another."

The words resounded deeply in my soul. "I am too," I said, unable to stop the words as they rolled off my tongue.

"The witch who cursed Ash stole everything he'd ever held dear," he carried on, oblivious to my confession.

I flinched, puzzled by the story. "Cursed by a

witch, you say?" I asked, leaning closer. "But how can that be? He's a mage, like you. A powerful one."

Thuriad whipped his head back. His expression twisted with a creased brow and a smirk of amusement. "A mage?" He snickered. "Ashton's not a mage!"

I sat back, momentarily rebuffed. Then I snapped. "What?" I uttered with a scowl, my voice's pitch higher than I had expected. "But if Ash isn't a mage, then that makes six of you." I paused to wrap my mind around this business. "Where's the seventh?" I had to ask.

Thuriad's face suddenly sagged. "We lost Galhöe years ago…" he said under his breath. The sole name invoked darkness in his countenance.

He sucked a deep breath and exhaled sharply, then rubbed a hand across his brow. I fancied that gesture alone might cast away his bad memories. "It was Leander who found Ash," he continued in a sullen tone. "An orphan in the night. A victim of magic, most vile... Lost in the world."

My lips parted to speak, but no words came through. Ashton's charm and good nature had led me to believe he'd never come across a dire day in his life. He seemed anything but cursed. Perhaps out of shame, he'd not spoken of the fact. I certainly could not hold it against him, especially when I carried secrets of my own.

"Ash came to us broken," Thuriad said, looking down at the empty cup in his hand. "Leander saved him. But some wounds, not even the finest spell can fix." He bowed his head. "It took time to heal Ash." His gaze cut to mine. "Longer than it took any of us to make you smile."

Thuriad's eyes glinted as he threw me a knowing look.

Sheer panic flew through me. "I don't understand," I mumbled, restless.

The mage crouched before me. "Now, look here, lass," he said, anchoring his full attention on me. "I've lived long enough to recognize grief when I see it." He tilted his head. "And *you* are mourning, child. Someone close to you died?"

The blood in my veins chilled. "People die all the time," I blurted, pinned to the chair as every inch of my body went taut.

"Aye, but this one was special." His gaze hunted my evasive stare. "Why are you here?" The question sailed through his lips with no inclination.

I pivoted away from him in the chair. "I'm a runaway," I said, clasping my hands on my lap. My fingers interlaced so tight that my knuckles whitened. "Just like you."

Thuriad nodded. "Who are you running away from?" he said in a smoother, warmer tone.

"The Evil Queen," I partly admitted.

"A queen…" the mage said, stroking his beard. "What did you do to cross a queen?" He frowned, intrigued.

Don't say it, Maleath. Don't speak another word.

His green eyes stabbed me with sincere concern. Patiently, he waited for an answer.

"I…" I breathed, taking a hand to my chest. "I killed her king." The words rolled off my tongue, meeting no resistance. It surprised me how good it felt to say them aloud, even if they meant sealing my end.

Thuriad said nothing. He just stared at me blankly while gnawing the inside of his mouth. Finally, he bobbed his head. "You killed a king?" he said, and his lips tensed in a confident smile. "You're drunk, lass!" He chuckled. And sweeping a hand across his knee, he straightened. "And I am too!" More laughs streamed from his throat.

I began to relax as I realized Thuriad thought my revelation was a joke.

"Shh…" Thuriad took a finger to his lips and stooped a little. "Let's not tell anyone," he whispered in confidence, his cheeks blushing from the drink.

I agreed to his proposal in silence. He was right.

We were drunk. And thank heavens for that. It gave me carte blanche to ask Thuriad anything I wanted.

"So, about Ashton," I began. "His curse. How did *that* happen?"

Thuriad turned to the window. He stared outside longer than I would have wanted, holding back on his answer. "You can ask him yourself, lass…" he then said. "He's coming."

I sprung off the seat and joined him by the window. My brow eased into a frown as I slowly narrowed my eyes.

"He's not alone," I said.

CHAPTER FOURTEEN

Thuriad's countenance slackened when he saw the woman lying in Ashton's arms. Any dregs of alcohol in his blood vaporized in an instant. He pushed away from the window without saying a word and rushed to the hearth in lumbering strides, overwhelmed with restlessness.

"Leander!" he cried, despair straining his voice. "Wake up, man! Come quickly!" Thuriad frantically shook his friend's shoulder, wasting no time before he ran outside.

"What is it?" Leander groaned, rubbing his eyes with the heel of his hands. He got on his feet and followed the mage into the hallway, although not as promptly.

I kept my eyes on Ash as he drew closer to the house. The morning sun rose behind him, bleeding radiant beams that outlined his tall frame. He trudged down the treelined road, his expression marred with worry.

Who was the woman he carried? It dawned on me then. I knew nothing of his life. Was he married or promised to another? The sole thought made my stomach churn. I parted from the window, bitter and confused.

The door burst open.

I moved into the hall, but lingered back, standing next to a pillar. I dared not come closer. Ashton's harsh words had burned into my soul. I would not risk being slighted by him again.

He stood in the doorway, with blushing cheeks, his chest heaving with exhaustion. The woman in his arms lay unconscious.

"Ash," Leander said in the gravest tone.

Ashton walked inside. He stopped in the middle of the room, sullen and speechless. Then, getting on one knee, he carefully eased the woman onto the hardwood floor.

One by one, the mages gradually appeared, moving towards the pair with stealthy steps until they surrounded them.

Thuriad stood beside me, bewildered, as was I. "Oh, gods..." he whispered, putting a foot forward. Out of the corner of my eye, I watched him, hesitant to move. He pushed himself, though, and found his way into the circle.

I took his lead, meandering further. This time, I stopped by the staircase.

Thuriad took to the floor, kneeling next to the woman. "Brindel," he breathed, gliding his fingers through her smooth, wavy hair. His brows snapped together, glistening green eyes angling to meet Ash. "What happened, lad?" The voice came crushed, the gentlest plea.

Ashton's shoulders dropped with a heavy sigh. "I don't know," he told him, shaking his head. He ground his jaw. "I found her on the hill, by the stones." Ash took a hard swallow. "She was trying to reach us. She must have passed out, the poor thing."

My heart ached for the woman's condition, but it ached more when I glimpsed Ashton's suffering. Meanwhile, the mages stirred in dismay, murmuring into each other's ears. Their burly frames hindered my view.

Without making a sound, I climbed the first steps and peered at the woman lying on the floor. She was fair as few. Her face refined, symmetrical, and flawless. She had a delicate chiseled nose, high cheekbones, soft eyebrows, thick blonde eyelashes. Light freckles dusted her cheeks and nose. Her rosebud lips were plump and smooth as silk... No detail escaped me. The *blood* did not escape me either—streaming from her back, drenching the hardwood floor, pooling underneath her.

And then, I saw the wings. Light, as if made of the finest gossamer, weaved by spiders.

Brindel was fae.

"Her wing," I uttered, ambling towards them. I moved past the crowd. And in this nearness, I learned her wings gleamed, sheer and iridescent, when daylight spilled on them. Blue blood stained the left one while it gently poured.

"It's broken," Ash said, subdued, as his hazel eyes found mine.

I nodded.

"It's a clean cut." Ash pointed with a finger, careful not to touch. He exhaled, relieving the tension from his shoulders. "Whoever did this knew exactly what they were doing. The damage won't endure, but healing will be painful."

"Monsters," Thuriad growled, his eager stare sweeping Brindel's face in complete agony.

Brindel quietly moaned. Her eyelids tightened shut before they opened. Green eyes, sparkling with intensity. But even as magic glinted inside them, their light slowly dimmed.

The fairy drew in a sharp breath. Her body shuddered in full dread. She froze, eyes wide, surely struggling to understand how she'd gotten here.

"Brindel," Ash said in a quiet voice. He slipped a hand under her nape, comforting her as he spoke. "You're in our lair. I brought you here." A candid glance. "I found you on the hill." He moistened his lips. "Can you tell us what happened?"

Brindel's already pale countenance grew bleaker. Aware of her disquiet, Ash folded his hand over hers, then bowed his head. "Take your time," he told her.

She closed her eyes and summoned a deep breath, calling back the memories. "A harbinger of death," she said as she opened them. Her voice was soft and lightly grave, melodious though doused with horror. "With rotting flesh and empty eyes…" Brindel's lips quivered as she swallowed her tears. "He found me on the other side, in the Black Forest."

"Who was he?" Leander asked, gently leaning in. He crouched next to Thuriad, sweeping his hands over his knees. "What did he want?"

"A huntsman," Brindel managed, wincing in pain. "Clad in golden armor. And a rose… A blood rose sculpted on his chest plate." Her eyes shifted to Thuriad. "A hound traveled with him. A beast from hell with flaming eyes burning with dark magic!"

"That sounds like a barghest," Leander told

Thuriad in the lowest voice. Ice skittered down my spine at those words.

"Why would he do it?" the fairy added, confused, as crystalline beads rolled down her cheeks. "Why would he attack us?" She faced Ash, then swept her hand away from his and covered her mouth. "Dear gods, he killed her." Panic flashed in her wide eyes. "He killed Cindary!" Brindel broke into sobs of grief, crawling back into Ashton's arms.

"I'm so sorry. I know this is hard, Brindel…" Ash whispered, welcoming her with a tender hold. "You're safe now." Fury glinted in his eyes as, silently, he exchanged stares with the mages.

"I should have saved her, and I tried. But he came after me so fast," she said between quick, stuttered breaths. "When I took off in flight, the monster pinned me down. His fist crushed my wing useless." Her vacant gaze strayed to the doorway. "I escaped his grip and fled to the well. I opened the portal. But before I could cross, the huntsman gave me this." Brindel hugged her shoulder, displaying her wounded wing. Fortunately, the bleeding had stopped.

"You should rest," Ash told her. "Let's get you to bed." He gathered her to him, and as he picked her up, a moan escaped his lips. "Gods!" He paled, stricken by the rawest pain.

Leander stepped in. "I'll do it." He swept Brindel

off the floor, weightless, in his strong arms. "Ash, you've not healed yet. Rest, my boy," he said with a devoted father's care.

Ash took a hand to his shoulder. He nodded in silence.

Leander carried Brindel to the stairway. "We'll get that wing fixed," he assured her, staring at her warmly. "Don't you worry."

Locks of fawn hair rippled off her shoulders as her head swung to him. "Leander," the fairy breathed.

"Yes, Brindel?" he said, stopping at the foot of the stairs.

"I'm frightened," she confessed in a whisper.

"Of what, m'darling?" Leander's voice sailed like the gentlest croon, appeasing Brindel's hurt like the most powerful spell.

"The huntsman," she barely managed, sheer dread tightening her throat. "What if the monster got through? What if he's already here?"

Leander's expression hardened. "If indeed that monster has crossed over," he said severely, "then he's already done half the job for us." A quick glance over his shoulder met his brothers. "Rest assured, Brindel, his crime will not go unpunished."

Taken by exhaustion, Brindel nestled her head against the mage's chest. And as he climbed the stairs, Romni and Millindrel followed.

"We should all get some sleep," Essgard said in a darkened voice. "Come on, man." He nudged Thuriad's shoulder with his. "Leander will take care of her. You can talk to Brindel when she's good and ready."

Thuriad blinked out of the daze. "Aye..." He nodded gravely. "You're right." He slipped a hand over the mage's shoulder and patted it lightly.

Both men headed upstairs in silence.

An unsettling calm lingered in the air as morning light slowly crept in. I watched Ash rise from the floor, caught in the dullness of pain and grief. He trudged towards me—towards the staircase—with a hand locked on his bruised shoulder.

"Ash," I breathed like a fool. When his gaze stumbled on mine, its undiluted gloom made my heart shrivel.

"I'll be fine," he said under his breath. His hard stare followed me while he passed me by. He then mounted the first step and followed the way to his bedroom.

It stung. It became clear to me, Ash would not be persuaded. He'd already decided I was the foulest villain. And maybe I was.

"You must be exhausted." A warm voice spoke. When the mage stopped next to me, I turned to him. My face swung high to meet his. Akron tied his silvery hair into a low coil, looking down at me with infinite kindness.

"Let me show you to your room, child." A faint smile tugged the corner of his lips. "I hope you don't mind climbing a second staircase. It's the highest room in the house. Well worth the pretty view."

I smiled back, or at least I tried to.

Akron and I walked upstairs. The house was bigger than any cottage in the woods, with spacious halls and furnishings that, though far from splendid, added to a warm environment.

We moved down the hallway, passing door after door. I couldn't help but wonder which one was Ashton's, and what it looked like inside, the type of items he treasured... I scrunched my nose and scolded myself for thinking about him. Ash had clearly no intention to befriend me. I should vow the same.

"This part of the house is often chilly," Akron told me, signaling the way up the second set of stairs. I moved ahead and now he followed. "I've started a fire for you. It should be warm by now."

We reached the narrow landing. It led to a single door.

I raised my gaze to meet his eyes. "You've been so kind to me," I said in wonder. "You all have." If only they knew who I was. What I'd done. Darkness swelled in my heart.

Akron frowned. "Most people are leery of those on the run," he said in a quiet voice. "But here's something they don't know." He inched closer, seeking confidence. "There's always two sides to the story. If you stole from your mistress, I suspect you had good reason for it." His eyebrows arched softly. "Aye, we steal. But life has robbed us, Snow. Life has failed *us*. It came in the dead of night and sank its fangs deep in our throats..." The corner of his mouth lightly curled as he added, "We're just biting back."

I nodded. It was true. No matter what I'd done. Either a thief or a killer. Life had failed me.

"Now," Akron added with a gentle smile, turning the doorknob. "Welcome to your room, Snow." The door swung inwards without making a noise. With a slight bow, he stepped back.

I stood in the doorway, watching him descend the stairs until he disappeared.

The room was modest, with no more furnishings than a bed, a small dresser and a washbasin with a water pitcher set by the window... It was perfect.

It was home.

CHAPTER FIFTEEN

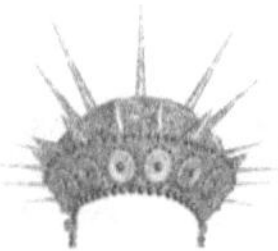

My eyes cracked opened to pitch darkness. The fire in the hearth had died long ago, but its warmth lingered in the room, delightful as I curled up underneath the blankets. To say I'd taken for granted the comfort of a plush bed would have been an understatement. More than ever, I was grateful to have found this wonderful haven.

I yawned. I'd slept through the entire day, but even then, my body claimed for more hours of rest.

Muffled thunder rumbled nearby. A howling wind lashed outside and shook the shutters. I yanked the covers higher, covering my face up to my nose. My mind started to drift into a pleasant dream, when a harsher gust of wind burst open the blinds. The cool draft that swirled inside smelled of woods and damp earth, a bracing perfume I took in with one deep breath.

Through a lazy squint, I saw a basket, caught in the light that spilled through the window. It was full of plums and berries. I glimpsed a wine pitcher too, set beside it. The fruit might have tempted me to rise from bed—closing the window certainly did not. But drowsiness took over me, overpowering all else. My dwindling thoughts invariably turned to Aurora, to the many delights that bound her to the realm of slumber... No wonder she refused to wake.

I dragged a pillow near and cuddled it to my chest. I felt myself letting go again.

A hoot snapped me awake.

My head swung to the window. Sheer shock hit me at the sight of the creature perched up on the sill. At once, I sat bolt upright and gained my feet, gawking.

The white owl remained stalk still, watching me with wide amber eyes that sparkled like precious gems. Its silken white feathers ruffled in the breeze, gleaming in the silver moonlight.

I blinked twice, absolutely tongue-tied. And when I realized this was no dream, my jaw went slack. "Can this be true?" I whispered in sheer awe, drifting closer to my friend.

The white owl cocked its head, and without moving an inch further, it cooed.

"My winged savior," I managed through my bewildered mind. "Is it really you?"

The owl opened his right wing ever so slightly. Yet not fully, as pain would not allow it.

"It *is* you." An involuntary twitch cracked the edges of my mouth. "You survived," I told him, awash with relief. I ambled towards the beautiful creature cautiously, fearing any sudden movements might drive him away. But the owl's stillness kept true while, patiently, he waited.

"You found me," I said, barely able to hold back a gasp of astonishment. Perhaps I should have expected it. Owls were hunters, after all.

One more step delivered me inches away from my winged friend. As I latched the shutters tight, my expression slipped into a frown. "You left me in that cave," I scolded him. "I was worried you might—" I pursed my lips. Was I really going to snap at the poor creature? Not after all we'd been through.

"Are you hungry?" I asked, dipping a hand in the basket. I snatched a blueberry between my fingers. "Do you want some?" I brought the berry close to his beak.

The white owl shrieked, flapping his wings in blatant protest.

"No need for that. I hear you," I told him, holding an appeasing hand in the air. "Forgive me, *Your Highness*." Taking the hand to my chest, I curtsied. "I have no mice to offer." I tittered, and when I straightened, I tossed the berry into my mouth.

Lightning struck. The room shuddered with the loudest thunder. A downpour suddenly unleashed. Unlike the storms in Whitehaven, this one was not ominous or bleak, but fresh and soothing. "I think you should come in," I suggested.

The owl lurched back and nestled against the window frame.

I gave him a little whisk of a smile. "Oh. You like it there, then?" I breathed. A yawn escaped me. I whirled back to the bed and snuck under the covers.

"Well, at least you won't get wet," I told him in a low, groggy voice.

My friend cooed.

Keeping my eyes on him became a struggle. The owl nestled in his spot, his gleaming eyes fixed on me. "You're not going away this time?" I told him. What was I doing, speaking to an owl? It didn't matter. Nothing did. Sweet drowsiness numbed my senses.

"Will you at least watch over my sleep?" I heard myself mumbling the words, but exhaustion quickly pulled me down into the depths of slumber.

CHAPTER SIXTEEN

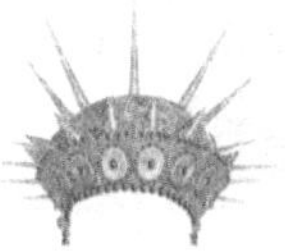

I woke up to the clang of cold steel coming from the garden beneath my window. The sound summoned back old memories of the soldier's practice square in Whitehaven Castle.

"Your grip is faulty," a voice said, stern yet dispassionate.

"Again," someone replied. Ash. I could recognize his velvety voice anywhere.

I sat on the bed and stretched my arms. At last, I felt truly rested. The soreness of my limbs had disappeared, though hunger rumbled in the pit of my stomach.

"You've not fully healed, lad," the other man added. This time, with a warmer tone. "I don't think you should—"

"Again, Essgard!" Ash all but growled.

Steel met steel once more while I sauntered to the window. On my way, I grabbed a fistful of berries, then leaned a shoulder against the wall and peeped outside, careful to remain unseen.

The fragrant vines that climbed the trellis glistened with the last drops of morning dew. The cool, crisp scent of night gave way to sun-warmed earth, as the sky became awash in pink and orange hues. I took it all in with one deep breath, and relished in the peaceful comfort of the Seven's lair.

From my peeping post, I watched the men below. Ash flashed his blade in a practiced arc, meeting Essgard's sword in silver fury. Both men locked blades and shoulders, sealed in a struggle. The mage pushed forward. Ash winced in sheer pain, and when his grip faltered, Essgard's sword glided free. The movement cost Ash his balance. He stumbled back and dropped on one knee, and just as swiftly, the mage's blade kissed Ashton's throat.

"That's enough for now, lad." Essgard's voice was calm, his sword steady. He whisked the blade away and slipped it into its scabbard, then offered Ash a hand to stand.

"You mustn't try so hard," the mage warned him, swinging an arm over Ashton's shoulders as they walked to the backdoor.

Ash kept his head low as he nodded.

A few feet away from the doorstep, both men halted. Essgard turned to Ash, his expression cold as the grave. "When evil strikes, we'll need each and every sword," he told him.

"I'll be ready, my friend," Ash replied. "I promise you."

A moment of silence sailed between them.

Suddenly, Ash looked over his shoulder. When his head swung up to the window, I moved away fast, praying to all the gods he hadn't seen me. I slammed my back against the wall, pressing a hand to my chest, trying to ease my racing heart.

When evil strikes. The words made me shudder. What evil lurked outside this haven, fiercer than the queen's? Her dark hand stretched beyond the Realm of Man. It already might have reached the Red Forest that concealed the Seven's lair. If indeed the guard who attacked Brindel was her emissary, it made no sense that he'd travel with a barghest. Those hellish hounds had no interest in humans unless they met the might of their fangs.

"Time for breakfast, lads!" Romni called into the garden. "It's moon sugar cakes today! I'm waiting for no one."

I'd never tried those before, but they sounded scrumptious. With that feast in mind, I dashed to the washbasin.

As I reached the pitcher, I noticed the dirt on my hands, and only then did I realize I hadn't really washed myself since I'd left Whitehaven. My gaze traveled down to my gown, past the dirt and mud that tarnished the hem, until sheer shock struck me when I saw the crimson spatter smudged on the tattered silk. Blood... Mine? No. My father's.

I gasped and raked my fingers through my hair in dismay, the dreadful image reviving the terror I hadn't felt since reaching the safety of the Seven's lair. When my hands came down, I spotted more flakes of dry blood my hair had retained as a keepsake from that tragedy. "No..." I mused, my misery so acute, it shot a blow of physical pain across my limbs. "Gods, no."

At once, I dipped my hands into the lukewarm water and scrubbed them clean with some soap. This would not do. I quickly disrobed and, with a piece of linen, I washed every inch of my body as thoroughly as I could, until my skin felt renewed. As if the act itself could rid me from the harrowing memory of my father's fall.

Pouring more water, I washed my hair. I watched as the red-stained liquid dripped into the basin until it finally rinsed clear. By the time I finished, it pained me to have to wear that dress again. I decided to be bold and ripped off the bottom of the dress, only to keep my underskirt and the disheveled bodice. I threw the tattered rags into the fireplace, promising myself I'd burn them as soon as breakfast was over.

I glanced at the mirror on my way to the door and came to a full stop. A shadow of chagrin fleeted across my countenance. I'd have to figure out a way to get new clothes *after* I'd tasted those delicious moon sugar cakes.

"Goodness." With a sweep of my fingers, I untangled the strands of my soaked mane of pitch-black hair as best I could. Once I managed that, I quickly tied it into a braid—the only trick I'd picked up from my lady-in-waiting when it came to hairstyling.

"There you go, Agnes," I said under my breath, somewhat satisfied and nostalgic, as I inspected my work in the reflection. "I hope you're proud."

I exhaled one long breath, shedding the gloom from my heart.

My stomach churned, so I hurried to the door and swung it open. I startled as I found Millindrel standing in the doorway, a frozen hand in the air, ready to knock.

"Snow." The mage's cheeks burned red scarlet. "We thought," he mumbled, taking the hand to the back of his head. "Since you slept all day yesterday..." He bit his lower lip.

"Yes?" I asked, smoothing my hand along the jamb.

Millindrel knitted his eyebrows. He picked at his nails for a second. And finally, he blurted, "Thuriad said to check if you'd been poisoned."

My eyes flew open. "Poisoned?" I took a hand to my lips, stifling a laugh. Of all the things, I never expected *that* to come out of his mouth.

Millindrel pursed his lips. "That ale, you know..." he mumbled, scratching his trimmed beard. He nervously raked back his blonde mane with his fingers. "It's powerful stuff." When his piercing blue eyes met mine, a mischievous grin appeared.

"It really is. Thankfully, I survived," I conceded with contained amusement. "I'll be happy to tell Thuriad myself." I gave him a swift nod.

"Will you come down for breakfast, then?" he asked, and his brow creased in a hopeful expression.

"Are you kidding?" I told him, picking up my skirt. "It's moon sugar cakes day. I wouldn't miss it for the world!" I snickered.

He gawked at me, pleasantly surprised. "Oh, they're the best thing in all the five realms!" Millindrel said, leading me to the staircase.

"I can hardly wait to try them," I uttered, mindful of each step on our way down. "We didn't have those in the castle..."

In the middle of the last flight of stairs, Millindrel stopped. "A castle?" he asked, bemused.

Panic swept through me. Every inch of my body went taut immediately. "My mistress," I amended without looking back. "She lived in a castle."

The mage moved past me, reaching the landing. Standing in front of me, he squared his shoulders and took his inked hands to his waist. Millindrel bobbed his head. "Sounds like your mistress and the Fae Council have quite a lot in common." He leaned closer, seeking confidence. "Stealing from the likes of them is like plucking a hair off a rabbit." A chortle escaped him.

I tittered nervously, clasping my hands tight.

"Come on," he said, showing me the way into the dining hall. "Lads! Look who's finally awake!"

I'd not stepped inside the room a second when Romni gave a loud sigh of relief. "At last!" the mage said. "Gods, I'm starving! Can we please dig in?"

"We may." Leander walked inside from a door a few feet away from mine. In his hands, he carried a silver tray topped with countless piles of steaming cakes. At once, the delightful fragrance of cinnamon and sugar permeated the air. My mouth already watered, and I'd yet to see these delicacies up close.

"Have a seat, Snow." Essgard dragged out the chair next to the head of the table. A privileged spot, right in front of where the breakfast tray had landed.

I thanked him with a graceful nod, then pinched

my skirt and spread it wide, the silk billowing as I lowered on the seat.

"I'll get that for you, lass." Thuriad stretched an arm across the table. He grabbed the tray and pulled it towards him. "You want to eat these while they're still warm." He stabbed a fork into a pile and slipped it on a dish.

Romni appeared behind him, fork in hand, ready to snatch a pile of cakes for himself. "Man, will you hurry up?" he groaned, tapping a foot on the floor.

"Aye..." Thuriad growled. "Snow, catch these before he does, will you?" he grumbled, handing me the dish.

My eyes twinkled at the sight of this heavenly meal. I wasted no time, and carved a slice of the wobbling tower, then jabbed it into my mouth. The cakes melted against my palate, their taste sweet and buttery. "This is exquisite," I praised with my mouth half full. I chomped down and swallowed. "Who does the cooking around here?" One by one, I swept all faces at the table. I couldn't help noticing the one face missing.

"That would be Leander," Romni said, seated behind three scrumptious cake towers that covered his face up to his nose.

Leander slipped into the head seat beside me, slouching back with a satisfied glare.

My gaze cut to him. "You're truly talented in the kitchen," I told him.

"Ah, I appreciate that." Leander nodded, burying a smile.

"Please, don't encourage him," Essgard added in a nonchalant tone. "He *already* considers himself exceedingly gifted." He dragged the tray to him and filled his dish with a stack of cakes.

My lips parted in a grin. But the smile began to fade as I remembered. "Where's Brindel?" I asked, creasing my brow. "How is she this morning?"

Soon, I realized this was not a table where one could strike a conversation. The men chomped down their cakes and gulped freshly squeezed orange juice, caring for little else.

Finally, Thuriad took pity on me. He gestured towards the window with a cocked eyebrow and a tilt of his head. My gaze angled there, and I saw Brindel walking in the garden with… Ash. The fairy was slipping a hand around his brawny arm. Gods! It stung to see that. Oh, but why should it? Ash owed me nothing. My stubborn feelings only irked me more. I chewed roughly on the cakes in my mouth and forced myself to tear my eyes away from the window.

"She won't talk to us," Leander added, pouring himself a cup of dark brew. "Fortunately, she talks to *him*."

Against every shred of will in my being, I looked at the garden once more. Brindel had her arm locked around Ashton's now. Oh, the blood in my veins boiled at that. It made me even more angry at myself for the bitterness swelling in my heart. "She's walking," I forced myself to say. It would take all my royal breeding to put on my best face, and then some. "That's a good sign, isn't it?"

"Aye," Leander said under his breath. "Brindel's healing faster than I would have expected. That kind of improvement goes beyond any spell. It must be the work of friendship, I guess."

I clenched my jaw. "Of course," I said, stabbing my cake pile as my lips thinned into a minor grin. Oh, for all the gods, why couldn't I take my sight off that blasted garden?

When Ash strolled by the window, his gaze set on mine. In a flash, my stomach dropped to the floor, making me regret every mouthful of this breakfast.

Ashton's brow creased. He tilted forward. "Snow," he soundlessly mouthed from the other side of the glass, before starting towards the door.

Oh, gods of the Netherworld! I pushed back the chair in sheer panic. "Thank you for the lovely breakfast," I mumbled hurriedly, rising from the seat.

The mages exchanged wary glances, confused.

"But Snow," Millindrel began, "you've not tried

Leander's special glaze." He glared at me, deeply concerned.

I opened my mouth to apologize when Romni cut me off with, "More for me, then!" He reached across the table and yanked a jug.

"You're leaving, child?" Akron asked, carefully setting his fork and knife on the table.

The front door creaked open. Ashton's heavy footsteps drew near. I couldn't bear seeing him, much less listening to whatever he had to say—which, after all of our rough encounters, could add up to no good.

"Yes," I told the mage. "To my room." I pushed the chair forward, then walked around the crowded table. "I forgot…" I pursed my lips. "Something."

In an instant, all heads swung my way. The men gawked at me with inquisitive eyes, relentless until I spoke.

"*Women's business.*" I forced a smile.

The mages stirred into a tumult in their seats. Some blushed, while others harrumphed and buried their stares into their dishes, murmuring nervous words of endorsement. "All right, all right…" they mumbled. "Do your things. It's no concern of ours."

I immediately regretted putting them through such an awkward time. Although I would have found myself amused, had my pulse not throbbed hard with apprehension.

Out of the corner of my eye, I saw Ash as he approached the doorway. I scurried to the one I'd come from before, cutting straight into the hall.

I rushed upstairs, eager to escape Ash. He could only want one of two things as he pursued me, I decided. None of which interested me. If he meant to scold me again, guided by his misconceptions, I would not hear it. And if he meant to confide to me his love for Brindel, then I'd rather lock myself in that room for days. Either way, I wanted nothing to do with the man.

When I reached my room, my heartbeat thudded hard in my throat and ears.

The door snapped shut behind me. Immediately, I loosened a heavy sigh. Then, gently, I banged my head back against the door and winced. "Gods! What a mess!" I all but hissed with my eyes tightly closed.

The knocking on the door froze my blood.

CHAPTER SEVENTEEN

Again, someone knocked. No, not *someone*. I knew who it was. Ash was standing behind the door. But why? What could he possibly want? He hadn't revealed my identity to the mages. Not yet, anyway. Perhaps he meant to disclose my secret and was here to offer me fair warning. As I caught my breath, my fears grew stronger than ever.

"Snow," he uttered. "Will you *please* open the door?"

I halted at the coolness of his voice. What was I thinking, running away from him as if this were a castle with guards at my door? The slab of wood between us would only get me so far. But then, I hadn't actually expected he'd chase me all the way up to my room.

"We *need* to talk," he added, and his tone was final.

Unease rolled through me like an icy, dark wave. "I guess we do." My voice drifted into a hushed whisper. I faced the door, and swallowing hard, I gently turned the lock.

The moment he appeared behind the crevice, my breathing hitched. I chewed on my lower lip and stole a look at him, so tempting in brown fitted trousers and a crude white shirt. Unaware of my spying, he sighed and smoothed a cautious hand on the door, but did not push. "May I come in?" he asked.

I lowered my chin, staring at the doorway like it was the gateway to another realm. A realm of nightmares. "You may," I breathed, and gathering my hands on my lap, I stepped back.

He stood there, tall and straight. His bearing, almost royal. Devilishly handsome, chiseled muscles rippling beneath his shirt... Charming indeed.

I watched him warily as I sat on the bed. "Ash," I began, sheathing my feelings. Every minute of this meeting was absolute torture. I longed for it to be over.

He stepped inside and locked the door behind him. "I noticed you came down for breakfast," he said, moving closer.

"It's moon sugar cakes day," I mumbled in a

mellow tone, regretting each word as it rolled off my tongue. My cheeks burned. I had to look away.

"I… uh… brought you something." When Ash stood before me, I noticed the bundle in his hand. He dropped down beside me, facing me. "I believe these should fit." He set the most exquisite sword aside on the floor and a pair of leather boots, then offered me the neatly folded pile of clothes. "They belonged to Galhöe. She was…"

My gaze cut to his. "The seventh," I uttered, too astonished to stifle my reaction. I quickly softened my outburst with a stern, "Thuriad mentioned her."

"Oh," Ash said in a low voice. A glint of uncertainty flickered in his hazel eyes. He quickly recovered, though, gathering his poise again. "Then you know I'm not a mage." He spoke the words with unshakable resolve and absolute gallantry.

"I know," I managed, unable to unlock my tightly clasped hands for fear that he'd notice them shaking.

He flinched, clearly puzzled by my answer. Perhaps he expected harsher words. But how could I hold this lie against Ash when I myself had lacked all candor towards him from the start?

"What happened to her?" I asked, driven by an impulse of curiosity.

A muscle tensed along his jawline. "She's gone." He sounded curt, abstracted.

I took the clothes and set them aside. With narrowing eyes, I leaned forward. "Do you know who did it?" I searched his countenance for an answer. "Who killed the seventh mage?"

Derision and sympathy tangled in his glance. "An evil sorceress did." Ash rushed to his feet and sat on the bed. "Her name is Roslyn."

"Roslyn?" I blurted in full dread. A wave of apprehension coursed through my veins like freezing waters.

Ash loosened a long breath. His gaze turned vacant as his hands glided down his thighs and reached his knees. "Snow," he whispered, swinging his head towards me. "I saw your face when Brindel spoke of the monster that attacked her." His dark, unfathomable eyes bored into mine.

The air chilled in my throat. "It was a shocking story," I pushed myself to say. My lashes fluttered. My mouth went dry. "What you saw was my compassion for the poor girl." Forthcoming tears warmed my eyes.

Ash glided closer. "No, no," he breathed, shaking his head. "What I saw was *fear*," he corrected, slightly shifting towards me, where his earnest stare reached the depths of my soul. "Listen, I know we haven't been able to talk since…" The words drifted into silence. Ash licked his lips. "You are Maleath Snow,

Princess of Whitehaven. And the armor Brindel described—the blood rose on gold—that's Whitehaven's sigil."

One by one, the walls I'd raised came crumbling down like my castle's accursed tower. And with them, my tears fell, trickling down my warm cheeks. I pursed my lips tight to stifle the sobs that swelled in my chest.

"Snow, I..."

Finally, I turned to him. "Ash, I did not kill my father," I rushed to say, emptying my aching heart. My voice, hoarse with undiluted grief. I smeared the tears on my cheeks with the back of my hand and sniffed. "You *must* believe me!" At this point, I realized, I would do anything to convince him of the truth. Because it mattered to me, more than I ever imagined, that he knew who I was.

His hand folded in mine. "I believe you," he said with earnestness. The touch of his fingers shot a thrill that rippled through my limbs in warm, soothing waves.

I stared at him wordlessly, taken by sheer bewilderment. "You..." I managed. "You believe me?" Every inch of me went taut as his hand pressed mine. "I've not even explained..."

"You don't have to," he said with the same quieting voice as his long fingers interlaced with mine. "Snow, I was there." He paused. "I watched you flee from the King's Guard. I heard you mourn over your father's loss." His peaceful gaze was a soft caress. "No killer in the world could ever grieve as you did in that cave."

His tenderness surprised me as much as his words. "How do you...?" I barely spoke.

"I've watched you through it all," he continued. "And ever since then, your heartache is my pain, your fears became my worries." Ash tilted closer. His finger pushed back a stray lock of my hair. "Gods! When I think of how close you were to dying in the Black Forest..." His brow furrowed in dismay.

"What do you mean?" I asked, half in anticipation, half in dread. "My life was never in danger."

The corner of his lips quirked up. "Oh, really?" he whispered, lightly lifting his eyebrows. "The *barghest* that attacked you would beg to differ."

Gooseflesh shot up my arms merely from remembering. Nevertheless, I argued, "But the barghest never had a—" I halted. It then dawned on me. "The barghest?" I asked, wrinkling my nose. "Ash, I never told you about it. How could you know? I was alone in that forest." I frowned. "Well, it was me, that infernal hound, and a..." My expression slackened with the shock of discovery.

Ash stared at me knowingly.

"A white owl," I mumbled.

He cracked half a smile, then shrugged.

I gasped. At last, it all made sense. "Your arm," I told him, reaching a hand to his shoulder. Fortunately, he recoiled fast from what would have been a painful blow. "The hound bit the owl's right wing."

"It did," he conceded with a subtle nod.

"But then..." I started as another revelation struck me. "Last night..." My lips moved, but no sound came through. I shook my head. "That was you, in the window?" The pitch of my voice shot higher than what I would have wanted.

Ash bit his lower lip. His hand, steady on my own.

A blush spread over my cheeks. "So, you're a shifter," I said, coming to terms with the truth as it became more real when I pronounced the words. "*That* is your curse."

He bowed his head. "It's been my curse for years," Ash admitted. "A parting *gift* from Lady Roslyn."

Ice skittered down my spine. Queen Roslyn's evil met no bounds. She'd destroyed not only my life, but so many others. Wrath sizzled in the pit of my stomach.

"A parting gift?" I asked.

"Long before she met your father, there was *another* king in Lady Roslyn's life," Ash said. "It was her first attempt to destroy a kingdom. But her plan failed." His face was full of strength, beaming with steadfast conviction. "Mere weeks before her marriage to the king, I exposed Lady Roslyn as the wicked sorceress she was. The king banished her from Thornwood Hall on that same day." His gaze drifted, hollowed by painful memories. "But just as she was crossing the kingdom's gates, Lady Roslyn cast one last incantation. A curse against the one who shattered her ploy." He loosened a sigh. "My price to pay." A bitter smile tensed his lips.

"You saved your king," I assured him, trying to ease his suffering.

He watched me, wounded and doubtful. "Did I?" he said.

"What happened then?" I asked, eager to learn the full story.

"When I discovered the nature of my fate," he said, "that I was damned to become a beast night after night for the rest of my life, I fled the kingdom. I would spare my father the pain of losing his crown's sole heir to the burden of this curse." His eyes shuddered with uncertainty. "Soon, I learned my absence had taken a great toll on his health." He swallowed with difficulty and found his voice again. "My father fell gravely ill. He died within a fortnight."

"Oh, Ash..." I breathed, tilting my head. His pain

touched my own. I only realized then that the night he'd spoken of betraying a father's love, he wasn't speaking about me. He spoke of himself.

Endless words of comfort whirled in my mind. I could have said how much his loss pained me, that his story cast dark ripples in my soul... But somehow, all that came out was, "You're a... prince?"

His lips curled with faint amusement. "I used to be," he said, giving me a wistful look. "Prince Ashton of Thornwood Hall." His posture straightened as he pronounced his title. Not with pride, but cherished nostalgia. Then, relaxing once more, he exhaled. His gaze drifted to the window. "I've caused great pain and dishonor to my family, to my kingdom. I can never go back. Thankfully, the Seven took me in as one of their own. I've strived to make them proud every single day since."

"Ash," I whispered, smoothing a hand along his strong jaw. Slowly, I tugged until he faced me. "You are not a disgrace to your kingdom or to anyone." Longing filled me to the brim. "You saved my life." All this time, I'd thought him harsh and judgmental. How wrong I'd been.

Determination glinted in his eyes, feverish, as they lazily roved over my face.

My heart hammered in my chest, racing with anticipation.

Swift and violent, Ash cupped the sides of my face and pulled me to him. He stopped, leaving us a breath apart, and stroked my cheek gently with his thumb, stoking the fire that burned between us. Then, inching closer, Ash breached the unbearable distance, and his mouth claimed mine with a ravenous kiss that belied his outward calm.

The sole touch of his lips sent a shock wave through my being. But when his tongue forced through the slit of my mouth, blows of ecstasy rumbled in my core. Helpless as I yielded to his arms, I moaned. Never before had the blood coursed through my veins this strongly, like an awakened river.

"Snow," Ash purred into my ear, shooting lightning through my limbs. "We can stop..." A stuttered breath sailed through his lips. "If you want to." His stubble grazed my cheek as he brushed my face with the sweetest fondness.

"The Evil Queen wants my heart," I confessed to him, and at this, sheer dread flickered in his countenance. "She's already sent a huntsman after me. I do not know how long I have to live... But I do know that I want you."

Transfixed with dismay, his hand eased to the back of my head. "I won't let him touch you," he breathed, and pressed his lips against my brow. "I promise you, I won't." His kiss descended and reclaimed my mouth with renewed passion.

My fingers glided on his firm chest, tugging on his shirt to make it come undone. Divine ecstasy, the touch of his hands as they traced my frame. Unable to resist a minute longer, I pulled his sleeve.

"Ow!" Ash winced, holding his right shoulder.

As the fabric glided off his arm, I saw the wound. The barghest's fangs had carved deep marks into his flesh. And even though he'd almost fully healed, such injuries promised painful days ahead.

"I'm sorry," I uttered in the lowest of voices. My fingers glided on his arm, careful to avoid the tender wounds. The bravery of his owl form against the vicious hound brought tears to my eyes. "I'm sorry for everything." I looked away.

"Hey," he said warmly as he caught my chin. He lifted it gently, leveling my stare with his sultry hazel eyes, alight with magic. "I'm not."

When his mouth sealed mine, his kiss sang through my veins. My weathered soul hopelessly melted into him, longing for the peace that rested in his hold. Gently, he eased me on the bed. His firm hands dived beneath my gown and boldly climbed my thighs, skimming my hips.

We shed more than our clothes. No more secrets lay between us. No more mysteries. And the freedom of that truth raised my spirit soaring into unmitigated bliss.

As morning light danced on our bare bodies, I sought to learn him by heart. I took in his dreamy eyes and chiseled nose, the set of his mouth, his sculpted chest and strong arms corded in muscle. I wanted to seize everything and keep it in my heart, and cherished every moment of his nearness, for it could well be the last.

His bold touch roamed over my flesh, tracing each curve, wakening my senses to undiscovered delights. I writhed beneath him, eager to feel his firm body against mine, longing to be full of him, when, with quiet conviction, Ash took my hand to his chest, enticing me to explore him. He took my fingers lower, to the ripped muscles of his abdomen leading to an expanse of taut skin.

Shivers of delight rushed through my being as he slowly descended over me. My chest caved in with undiluted relief. Skin on skin, we were as one. I moaned in the sweetest agony as he sheathed himself inside me. I melted into him and the world was filled with him.

With restless hunger, Ash swept me in his arms and pulled me to him. My frame curled into the curves of his body naturally as we rocked together in exquisite harmony. Waves of pleasure tried my senses, shooting thrill upon thrill that shocked me breathless. In his arms, I soared higher than ever before. High into fathomless bliss, so much so that the thought of such abandonment almost frightened me.

Tears prickled beneath my eyelids as I skimmed the peak of ecstasy. My breath came in long, stuttered moans. At once, a flood of light and sensation burst behind my eyes and shattered in my core.

Ash cried out for release, his fingers burning into my flesh, adamant and demanding. He crushed me to his heaving chest, panting with pleasant exhaustion. His body shuddered and his embrace tightened, while shocks of pleasure ebbed and flowed inside me still.

He glided me on the bed, and as he did, Ash kissed my lips, my cheeks, my nose—all this with infinite devotion. He lay beside me, whispering sweet words of love into my ear, and I learned then what the flooding of uncontrollable bliss could be.

"You, my lady, are neither princess nor handmaiden," he managed between panting breaths, taking my hand to his lips.

My brow lifted slightly. "Oh?" I said in a mellow tone. "What am I then?"

His burning eyes held me still. His widened pupils, fathomless pools of enticing darkness. "You are a goddess," he purred, "and I'm the luckiest man to worship you."

A shudder of delight swept through me. "And you, my lord, might not be a mage," I replied, cupping the side of his face, "but you've bewitched my heart and soul just the same."

A smile bloomed on his lips. I curled against his chest and listened to his quickened heart. Ash wrapped his arms around my midriff and hauled me over him. And I laughed, savoring the feeling he'd left inside me.

As I lay in the comfort of his hold, my gaze drifted to the window. Dark clouds gathered outside.

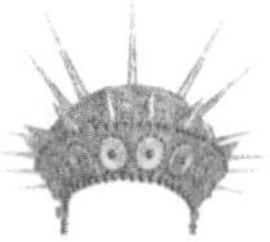

When the morning was spent, Ash and I made love again. This time, with unhurried passion, pacing ourselves as we learned and fed each other's pleasures. He was a warm and giving lover, but also tender and sweet.

As I lay in his arms, I sensed his uneven breathing on my cheek. Ash fondly caressed my bare arm with his fingers, raising tingles in my limbs with each velvety stroke. "Yesterday, while you were sleeping," he began, tigerish hazel eyes looming over my arm, "I found a new home for the pixies." His tone was full of promise, and something else.

I started, pleasantly surprised. "Really?" I said, rolling towards him until our brows kissed. "Where is it?" I bit my lower lip, eager for his answer.

"In a clearing, high in Hilgard Mountain." His

voice, deep and sensual, shot a ripple of awareness through me. His fierce eyes fixed in mine while his thumb glided along my jawline. "Do you want to see it?" His outright sternness tempted me beyond reason. Whether this palace rested in the highest mountain or the lowest valley, I would've agreed to anything he'd asked.

"How long will it take for us to climb this mountain?" I said, hopelessly subdued.

He flashed me an alluring smile that pierced a charming dimple in his cheek. "We don't have to climb the mountain," he assured me, pulling back a stray lock of hair behind my ear. "Leander keeps a portal glass in his room. We can use that."

I tilted my head, yielding my face into his firm hand. "A portal glass?" I breathed, narrowing my eyes. "Does it work like the stones on the hill?"

Ash pursed his lips, unable to conceal his delight. "Come," he said, sitting on the bed. "I'll show you." With one quick swing of his arm, he gathered his clothes from the floor and started to get dressed.

I matched his enthusiasm with my own, beaming as I stared at my new set of clothes. A white woven shirt, a spotless pair of brown leather boots and cream stockings, a dark green wool hooded cloak, and brown fitted breeches. "I've never worn trousers before," I confessed shyly.

A low, resonant laugh rose from his throat. "I think you'll like it," he said with a husky voice. He then slipped on his shirt.

I did like it. The mage's clothes were comfortable, the fabric light and airy. I stopped in front of the mirror and watched my new attire with unmitigated wonder. It crossed my mind then that the former owner of this outfit was now dead. I scrunched my face at that. I shook my head, driving those bleak thoughts away when Ash appeared behind me, half a head peering above mine. His hands smoothed on my arms, his chin lowered to my shoulder. "So, you approve?" he whispered in my ear. "We'll fetch you new ones in Port Bree if you do."

I turned to face him. "I'd like that," I said, excited by the prospect of venturing into any endeavor by his side.

Ash raked back with his fingers the locks of golden hair that drifted to his face. His free hand fastened mine as he inched closer. "Are you ready then?" he purred in his bedroom voice, stirring a whirlwind of emotions in me.

I blushed helplessly and agreed in silence.

The house was oddly quiet as we roamed across the bedroom hall. Perhaps another raid was taking place.

We halted at the end of the hallway. Ashton's hand folded on the doorknob.

"Wait!" I hesitated and inched closer. "Won't Leander mind that we're using his room?" I whispered, looking over my shoulder as if the mage himself would suddenly materialize behind me out of thin air.

Ash creased his brow in sheer disbelief. "Have you met the man?" he asked, amused. "His room is practically town hall." He snickered, pushing the door open.

My jaw slackened when we stood inside Leander's chamber. A clutter of precious oddities crammed the room. Treasure chests lined the walls, their lids ajar, revealing sumptuous riches. I saw many jeweled swords, a dozen twinkling crystal wind chimes hanging from the ceiling. A small writing desk set squeezed against the wall by the fireplace, laden with piles of scribbled and rolled parchment.

The penetrating scent of frankincense permeated the air. I sucked in a deep breath, filling my lungs with this delicious perfume. I then twirled around the room, trying to capture every detail. A poor decision, as I tripped and stumbled to my knee.

"Are you all right?" Ash said, catching my arm.

"I am." I buried a smile. As I got on my feet, my gaze swept the walls, dressed in black silk tapestries embroidered in gold thread. A string of gold inscriptions festooned the wooden doorframes, mysterious glyphs of magic.

"It's this way," he added, leading me to the wall that faced the hearth.

We stood before another silk tapestry sewn with colorful flowers and butterflies. Ash grabbed the edge of the exquisite drapery and swept it to the side, unveiling a tall black mirror hanging on the wall.

"Is that the mirror?" I asked, seeing no reflection at the moment.

"Mm-hmm." Ash slipped his hands into his trousers pockets. "It's made of black glass," he told me in the gravest tone.

"Black glass," I murmured, lured closer as I glimpsed the outline of my image. "I think I've seen this before." The memory escaped me, but the powerful sense of familiarity was real. I sharpened my focus, and gradually made out my details in the mirror. Only, it wasn't me.

Ash held my shoulder. "Be careful," he whispered in my ear. His gentle nudge startled me awake from the daze. "If you stare long enough, you might not like what you see."

A strong feeling of foreboding washed through me. My head swung to him. "How so?" I asked, intrigued.

"The mirror shows the darkest pieces of your soul," he said simply.

Gooseflesh shot up my arms. I swallowed hard. Drawing a step nearer to him, I asked, "Have you seen yours?"

Ashton's expression stilled and grew serious. "I have," he said with a subtle nod.

"Weren't you afraid?" The words rolled off my tongue.

He leaned towards me, his eyes cold. "Why would I be?" he said, perplexed. "It's only me."

His answer puzzled me beyond belief. And I would have asked what he'd seen, had the mere thought not filled me with sheer black fright. I decided then I'd rather not look into the mirror, after all.

"Now, let's open this door, shall we?" Ash said with renewed spirit.

I nodded dubiously, my awareness growing sharper by the second.

"Take my hand," he said, gesturing the offer, "and don't let go."

I did as he said. When our fingers intertwined, Ash stepped forward. He took his free hand to the glass and pressed it firmly, locking his stare on it. Out of the corner of my eye, I glimpsed movement inside the mirror. My gaze parted from him, briefly. And there, I saw my outline grow alight; my shape, trapped inside the black glass. The details surfaced in a flash. I wore golden armor, shimmering in sunny daylight. A spiked headdress was my crown. I gripped a sword in my right hand; the blade, smeared with blood, dripping on the edges.

"Snow," Ash uttered, pulling me to him as he walked into the mirror. "Look at *me*."

"Yes," I managed, baffled, as I watched him passing through the glass.

"Hold on tight!" he said, swinging an arm around my shoulders, sweeping me inside the magic portal.

Stepping through a portal was much like taking a plunge into the Dark Sea, I'd learned. Freezing darkness embraced us, numbing my senses. I held my breath as long as I could, bearing the oppressive feeling. My heart raced beyond control, rattling in my chest like a caged beast.

"Ash," I said in a thin voice. "I'm frightened."

"It's only a walk," he replied in a casual tone. His grip grew firmer, warmer. "We're almost there."

Ashton's confidence raised my own. He waltzed into darkness without a care in the world. And then, I understood. Ash dealt in light and shadow. He was a creature of both worlds, trapped in a shifter's curse. No wonder he did not fear his reflection in the black mirror.

At last, a sliver of light cracked the darkness. When Ash dipped his hand and swept away the black veil, I sighed in relief. Fathomless gratitude washed over me when my skin touched the thin, fresh air. I sucked in a long breath, taking into my lungs the sweetness of lilacs and honey that saturated the room.

I turned to find we'd walked out of a replica of Leander's mirror.

"Welcome to the pixie's new realm," Ash said, standing proudly next to the portal. He tugged on the black silk drapery, covering the glass swiftly.

Our footsteps echoed on the smooth quartz floors. The rooms differed from anything I'd ever seen, with curved vaulted ceilings and sinuous walls, organic lines that flowed as we meandered further. Sculpted leaves and vines hugged the pillars of a long corridor, lined with tall windows, colorful and reminiscent of human stained glass.

We arrived at a parlor. Very few items hung from the walls, mainly portraits and royal emblems. I sauntered closer to the landscape painting of a castle raised in precious amber, surrounded by giant twigs and lavenders. My brow gently creased. "Is this the...?" I uttered.

"Ash!" a voice called. Delicate steps quickly approached.

His lips eased into a devastating grin. "Your Majesty," Ash said with a gallant bow.

A tall and slender woman stood in the doorway, dressed in the lightest gown with a cape that seemed to float when she sauntered near. As the distance between us grew shorter, I noticed her larger eyes and the pair of pointy ears half concealed under her long mane of blue hair. A headdress made of shimmering black latticed twigs crowned her head. Her skin reflected the palest blue shade, and darker streaks of the same color hugged her neck and arms.

Trapped in a daze by the woman's beauty, I tilted closer to Ash. "Who is she?" I whispered in the lowest of voices.

"She's Queen Marioth," Ash murmured back without parting his eyes from her.

I started. "That's impossible," I told him, awestruck, as I realized what I had mistaken for cape were in fact the most exquisite black and blue butter-fly-like wings springing from her back. "I've seen her, remember? Her height was merely a couple of inches. This woman is tall!" I all but hissed.

"We're the ones who shrunk," Ash said through his tight teeth, holding his smile. "Now please, stop talking about heights. They don't like that."

Queen Marioth locked her hands over her gown, watching us with the kindest patience. "You've brought a friend," she said, noticing me. Her voice was full of grace and dignity, smooth and warm.

"I have," Ash said. His shoulders squared, a closed hand resting on the hilt of his sword. "This is Snow. You met her in the Red Forest. Perhaps Your Majesty remembers?" His eyebrows arched softly as he leaned forward.

An easy smile played at the corners of my mouth. It delighted me to glimpse Ashton's royal manners as they surfaced. I bit my lower lip, imagining Ash as the prince he used to be. I fancied him cleanly shaven with a trimmed hairstyle, garbed in fashionable dark fitted breeches and a royal blue coat with cuffs and collar embroidered in gold thread. Quickly, I decided I preferred his grazing stubble and long hair, the roughness of his hands as we made love, his everyday look in a casual shirt and trousers... Some men cleaned up well, but Ash dirtied up even better.

"Of course I remember," Queen Marioth replied.

Indeed, how could she forget about the human woman who'd destroyed her *last* home? My cheeks burned. "Your Majesty," I curtsied. "I'm so sorry about what happened that day. I didn't mean to..."

The queen broke from all protocol, stepping close until she stood in front of me. Her delicate hands fastened on mine. They were cool and hard as marble. "Nonsense, my dearest," she whispered, tightening her hold with sincere affection. "This is our home now, and you're very welcome here."

Calmed by the queen's earnest reassurance, I gazed into her glittering blue eyes. "Thank you, Your Majesty," I breathed.

"We're the ones beholden to you," Queen Marioth said, gliding a hand to Ashton's arm. "We're delighted with our Amber Palace, Ash. It's more beautiful and peaceful than we could ever dream." Her eyes glazed with sadness. "Let us hope they do not find us here."

"They?" I uttered, confused.

"The Fae Council, child," the queen said in a sullen tone. "We used to live in harmony in the Red Forest. But ever since the high fae lord Raathiel Ivasaar took the council's oath, he's made it his mission to sweep us off this realm." Her expression darkened.

"Queen Marioth and the pixies supported the Seven during the years of the rebellion," Ash added quietly.

The queen clasped her hands once more, noticeably shaken. "The council's treatment of our mage brothers was far from fair," she said, determined. She stepped back and paced in the room, screening the walls as if searching for an answer. "Everyone knew that. But no one dared to speak out and call the injustice for what it was."

"No one but you," Ash told her. He faced me to add, "And because of it, the council banished the pixies from their Lost Realm. They took their lands, as they did to the Seven."

I drew in a quick breath of sheer astonishment. "So it's true," I murmured. "The Lost Realm. It really existed."

The queen's wings slowly fluttered as she stopped by the window. "It did." She heaved a heavy sigh, thinning her lips bitterly. "And it was formidable."

"Surely, Leander will speak with Lord Raathiel and reach an agreement," Ash hurried to say, courteous and eager to comfort her. "He will clear this up, Your Majesty. You deserve to live in peace. We all do." His voice strained with concern.

The queen whirled around, her gown and wings swaying like passing clouds. "I'm so grateful to Leander," she managed. Her interweaved fingers clenched tight, whitening her knuckles. "But I'm afraid Raathiel will *not* be easily persuaded."

Ash parted his lips, willing to ease the queen's disquiet.

"Which is why I've set up an encounter with an old friend," she continued, and for once, hope burned in her blue eyes. "My friend holds a respectable influence over the council. I believe my kingdom might still be saved."

Ash stepped forward, lowering his head. "May I offer my service as your escort?" he asked with exemplary chivalry. I could not expect less from him.

The queen's long fingers set on Ashton's chin and slightly lifted his gaze. "That will not be necessary, my dear friend," she told him. "I thank you." Queen Marioth straightened. "We're meeting in a few minutes. I must go on."

"Of course, Your Majesty." He bowed.

Thunder rumbled above us. The parlor dimmed with scurrying shadows.

Queen Marioth glided a hand over the amber windowsill. "A storm is coming," she said, her gaze drifting to the giant garden outside. "I hear rumors of a human huntsman spreading death in the land." A wary look darted towards us over her shoulder. "We best be careful. Dark days lay ahead of us."

Her silence pricked the sticky air and made it bleed. My lips parted, wordlessly. *Yes*, I wanted to say. *There is a huntsman in the land, and he's come for me.* With shuddering eyes, I met Ashton's stare, calm and reassuring as he slowly shook his head, aware of my intention.

"Well," the queen said, agreeable now as she stood before us. "As long as you're here, you must see the

Night Garden." Her voice dropped into a joyous whisper. "It's absolutely stunning."

Her attention suddenly shifted, as if her hearing had picked up something neither Ash nor I could. "You must forgive me. I absolutely *must* go on." She pursed her periwinkle lips. "I'll send Arathne to find you with two spiced honeysuckle brews."

I inched closer, intrigued. "Spiced?" I asked.

"With pixie dust," Ash murmured in my ear. A thrill rushed through my limbs at the huskiness of his voice.

Queen Marioth nodded proudly. "A true delight," she said.

Displeasure thinned my mouth in an instant. "Oh, no," I uttered, much to my dismay. "You see, when mixed with wine, it can be..." Ashamed of my rudeness, I kept the rest to myself.

"*Human* wine?" the queen asked, narrowing her eyes. "My dearest, that's no good at all! Probably toxic." She wrinkled her nose, a fading gesture as she held my hand, leading me to a set of double doors. "Our honeysuckle brew is simply divine. You can ask my dearest Ash. It's his favorite."

Ash rose behind the queen. He scratched his nape and looked away, suddenly flustered.

"Very well," she added, stifling a laugh as she opened the doors. "You two have fun in the Night

Garden. I'll see you soon, I hope." Her smile widened in approval and her wings flitted joyfully.

"Fun?" I turned to Ash, entirely bemused as I scrunched my face into a scowl.

"Your Majesty." Ashton bowed, and slipping a hand around my arm, he ushered me through the doorway.

CHAPTER NINETEEN

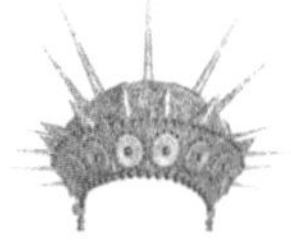

"This isn't a garden," I said, my awareness increasing as my gaze swept our surroundings. The place did not remotely resemble any palace garden I'd ever known. I saw no flowers, no shrubberies. No fountains or mazes. Dark paper-thin amber walls enveloped us like an exquisite fishbowl. A vast central hearth kept the room warm and the flickering lights dim, while music, loud and lively, filled the air.

Ash eyed me sidelong. "No, it's not." He did his best to stifle his amusement, but the beginning of a smirk betrayed him. He suddenly waved, greeting his pixie acquaintances from afar. His smirk broadened into a grin when he turned towards me. "Come," he said, and his hand found mine, gripping it with excitement.

He led me through the jostling crowd to the carved amber counter that encircled the tall stone chimney. A pixie woman stood behind the bar. Stunning, with braided locks of light blue hair and streaks of gold. Gleaming rings pierced her ears and nose. When she leaned closer, I couldn't help noticing the light gold freckles scattered on her cheeks.

"Hey there, Ash," she casually said, serving a brass mug.

"Arathne." He gave her a courteous, quick nod.

The woman's plum-tinged lips quirked into half a smile. Her clear blue eyes angled towards me. "Snow?" she asked, raising an eyebrow.

"That's me," I told her in a quiet voice.

"Two spiced honeysuckle brews," Arathne said, pouring another mug with the golden, foamy beverage. "Her Majesty's treat." She slipped the drinks across the bar. "Enjoy." She winked at me wickedly, and tossing a red cloth over her shoulder, Arathne whirled back. Her fluttering black and blue wings glinted with gold dust. Hovering a few inches above the ground, she drifted to a pair of pixies waiting for their drinks.

Ash folded his arms over the counter, and gliding on the bar, he spoke in my ear. "Gods, I'm dying to kiss you." His voice, laden with desire, spread a tingle through my being.

As he drifted away, I grabbed his muscular arm and hauled him next to me. "Why don't you?" I dared and snuggled close to him, pouting my lips.

He threw a wary look over his shoulder. I traced his stare to the guards standing by the entrance. The armed pair was eyeing us disapprovingly. My gaze strayed to the pixies that surrounded us. The young couples sitting at the long table behind us were glaring at us. Glaring at *me*.

Ash glided his thumb along my jawline, turning my face towards him until our stares locked. "I would ravish your mouth in a heartbeat," he purred with a stern expression, while his free hand slithered closer to mine on the bar, "if it didn't mean spending three months away from you… *locked in a dungeon*." Our fingers barely touched, but that was enough for me to feel the intensity building between us.

A scowl washed over my countenance. "A penalty for showing affection?" I mumbled.

He nodded gravely. "I'm afraid so," he said with a shrug.

I flashed him a candid smile. "Then maybe we should leave," I teased. Or did I?

His lips twisted in a lopsided grin. "Not yet." He looked me over with seductive eyes. Then curling an inciting finger, he wordlessly said, *Drink up.*

My cheeks hopelessly burned. I grabbed the mug

and brought it to my mouth. The promising sweetness of its floral fragrance filled my lungs. At once, I tipped the drink and took a swig, delighted by the frothy texture coating my palate. No less pleasing was the drink itself, fresh and tasty.

I lowered the mug, watching Ash dead in the eye. "This. Is. Remarkable." I spoke with such conviction that a hearty laugh roared out of him. His laughter made my heart sing.

I licked my lips, savoring the yummy dregs. "It has all the sweetness of honey," I added, peeking into the mug, stirring it with a light shake, "with a dash of vanilla, I think." My eyes squinted pensively.

Ashton's ripple of mirth faded. "I'm glad you approve," he told me, dragging his mug near.

"It's wonderful. Not unlike this place," I said, glancing past the hordes of merry pixies, spotting the small stage where the musicians played. A great platform, raised in maple wood, framed with crimson velvet drapes. "A tavern in a palace..." I knitted my eyebrows. "Imagine that."

"It wouldn't be the pixies' palace without one." He gave me a knowing look, and satisfied with his statement, he gulped down one more swig of honeysuckle brew.

I listened with bewilderment. What was *that* supposed to mean? A deeper furrow creased my brow.

I said nothing, just stared at him blankly, holding my brass mug.

Ash tilted his head, watching me in disbelief. "Have you not heard the stories?" he asked, brushing my hand again with his fingertips. A shiver of delight shot through my core at his touch.

He slid his tongue over his lower lip and snuck closer, his body molding to the curves of mine. His nearness made my senses spin and turned my thoughts into complete mush. And still, I welcomed it wholeheartedly… Oh, I longed to be crushed in his embrace and seal his mouth with mine.

When Ash parted his lips to speak, the melody abruptly changed. Flutes and crumhorns tangled with the spirited beats of tabors and castanets. At once, the pixies' interest shifted away from us as they stirred in an uproar, bursting into song and cheer.

"What stories?" I asked with my best charming smile.

Ash took a long draught of his brew, then slammed the mug on the bar. At last, he turned to say, "The ones that claim the pixies are the finest dancers in all the five realms." He stalked away from the counter, keeping his sight on me at all times.

"I bet we can teach them a thing or two," he challenged, beaming as he threw his arms open, tempting me to join him on the dance floor. And I did, meeting no resistance, because I was completely and madly in love with him.

We danced and drank for hours. I'd never once experienced such limitless bliss as I did now. Not even when I'd lived in a castle, the heiress to the wealthiest kingdom in the realm, whose every whim were met in an instant.

Gradually, the fire died, the hordes dispersed, and the music petered out into the mildest croon.

A gentle harp played, nothing more. Ash and I lingered in the empty dance hall, locked in each other's arms, barely moving to the melody's slow beat. In this stillness, all my worries disappeared. It was just him and me, and that was more than plenty, for nothing in the world could rival the peace of resting in his hold.

"I've had the most wonderful time," he purred in my ear. His breath was a soft caress that swept me in a gentle cloud.

"And I as well," I breathed, pressing my cheek against his firm chest. But for all my joy, the words drifted with wanting. I'd yearned for hours for him to kiss me. At this point, it felt like my entire being was filled with waiting.

His hand cupped the side of my face. A thumb under my chin raised my stare to meet his. "Snow…"

he whispered, holding back the eagerness mirrored in his untamed hazel eyes.

Before I could say a word, Ash gently released me. He gathered his hands and removed a ring from his index finger. I bit my lower lip, hesitant as I inched closer, studying the garnet mounted on the golden band.

Ash exhaled a stuttered breath, fiddling with the ring for an instant. "I want you to have this," he told me, offering me the precious jewel.

My stomach dropped. "Ash…" I managed, not knowing what to think.

"Take it," he insisted.

When he placed the ring in my palm, I struggled to keep my knees from buckling. "Ash, I… don't understand." I swallowed hard. My pulse shot sky-high.

"When the time comes," he continued, smoothing his hand over mine, "I'd like you to use this." Ash then took the ring and pinched the crimson gem between his fingers. With a quick twist, the stone swung to the side, revealing a small compart-ment filled with… *red dust?*

"What is it?" I asked.

"Venom," he said plainly.

I flinched in dismay. "*Use* this?" I uttered,

suddenly more anxious than seconds ago, when I'd assumed this was a promise ring. "How?"

"Dust your sword with it?" he said in the gentlest plea, slipping the ring on my thumb. "Even the slightest scratch will become deadly if you do." A touch of apprehension tinged his voice.

"When the huntsman comes, I'll be ready," I assured him.

"I know you will." He gave me the hint of a smile that faded all too quickly.

"It pains me to say it," he added, tugging a stray lock of hair behind my ear, "but we must go home."

I nodded in agreement, delighted as his fingers glided between mine.

We walked out of the Night Garden with sluggish steps, enjoying the tranquil nightlife that scurried through the palace's amber halls.

Soon, I recognized the path leading back to the portal.

"Ash," I began as we turned into the final corridor. "You said you found the pixies' new home yesterday while I was sleeping."

"Uh-huh," he uttered.

I started. "So, you're telling me the pixies built all this in a single day?" The words came out in a blurt. I had to ask. The building was much too precious and grandiose. How could they have raised a palace within such a tight timeframe?

We stopped at the doorway. "I helped," he told me in a cool voice, proud as he leaned against the jamb.

I tittered. "I'm sure you did," I said, delighted by his charm. "But still, it makes no sense at all."

He flashed me a smile, stabbing that sensual dimple in his cheek that made him so irresistible. "It really doesn't." He snickered, pushing the door open.

His reply was hardly satisfying. The beginnings of a scowl wrinkled my face.

"They're pixies," he explained with the sweetest disposition. "Their magic puts in shade their splendid beverages." His hand swung away from the doorknob and landed between my shoulders, gently gliding down. A shiver of delight skittered down my spine.

As he led me across the threshold, his fingers curled in the small of my back. My breathing stalled. I entered the room and stood stalk still, my widened gaze shifting from the burning hearth to the veiled black mirror.

The door snapped shut. In two quick strides, Ash came up behind me and seized my waist, pulling me to him violently. He flipped me in his grasp and pinned me against the wall. My heart turned over as his face inched closer, ready to claim my lips. I quivered at the intensity of his gaze, the roughness of his hands gliding along my jawline.

"Snow," he whispered between panting breaths, his chest heaving against mine. "It's been torture, waiting to kiss you. I'm not waiting one more minute." His sultry eyes raked boldly over me.

My hands sailed over his shirt, riding the curves of his chiseled chest. "I'm not stopping you," I managed, my lips burning for his drugging kisses.

"Oh, gods…" Ash breathed, and his mouth captured mine, forcing it open with a thrust of his tongue. His kiss quickly turned darker and demanding, and I wouldn't have had it any other way.

CHAPTER TWENTY

emerged from the black mirror, laughing at the silliness of a joke. The joke itself was not half as amusing as Ashton's poor skills of delivery. "I've found your greatest flaw," I told him, my cheeks flushed with wondrous intoxication. "The one the mirror showed you." With a quick pat of my hands, I dusted my sleeves from the glitter shed by the pixies' wings.

"You cannot jest to save your life! At last, I'm satisfied." I grinned.

No words came in reply. Not an outburst of wounded pride, nor one of Ashton's infectious laughs.

A flicker of apprehension seized me. I whirled on my heels and realized I was alone. "Ash?" I called, ambling closer to the portal.

I stared at the glass, desperate to catch a glimpse

of him when, inside, a silhouette gradually emerged. I caught the glint of golden armor, the bleeding sword gripped in my hand. Just as before, I was wearing the gold spiked crown. Victory was mine. I rose at the edge of the crumbling tower. My father stood beside me, inches away from falling to his death. And when his body sailed into the heavens, I watched myself smile.

"No..." I shuddered, hugging my arms. Appalled at the bleakness of those images, I moved away, clenching my eyes tight. It wasn't real, I told myself. It wasn't true. And yet, that crown could never rest on my head without my father's passing.

The air whooshed as Ash darted through the glass. Shaped in his owl form, he soared into the room with spread silvery-white wings.

"Ash?" I uttered with a frown. Confused, I wandered restlessly about the room, following him until he finally settled atop Leander's cluttered writing desk.

I stopped by the window. Nightfall had set in, and so had the storm. Black clouds smeared the sky. A steady deluge hammered the ground. I sighed. I hadn't thought we'd spent the full day at the Amber Palace.

My gaze cut to the white owl, to his amber eyes alight with magic. Sadness crept into my soul as I recognized in him, not my winged savior, but the man who'd stolen my heart. The unkindness of Ashton's curse wounded me deeply. The burden I carried could never match his.

I held back my forthcoming tears and, resolved not to spoil the fresh bliss that filled our hearts, I put on my best face when I said, "Well, then. I guess we should go meet the Seven."

The owl chirped and cocked his head. Mindful of Ashton's cautions, I tugged on the portal's black silk until it came rippling down, covering the black mirror.

When I stepped into the hallway, I picked up noises coming from the dining hall. I dashed to the stairs, and the murmurs grew louder. The bustle of an argument began.

By the time I reached the landing, chairs were screeching against the hardwood floor. The quarrel built up into a brawl. Growls and screams of protest came, too many to unravel each. Glass shattered. Loud thuds struck the walls. And then, silence.

I found myself holding my breath as I stood in the doorway, cautiously peering inside the room.

A feast lay on the long table. Roasted chickens, boiled potatoes, steaming cauldrons filled to the brim with fragrant broths. I saw freshly baked bread, a dozen platters of cheese and fruits so strange to me, despite my kingdom's extensive meal assortment.

It struck me as odd that the served dishes remained untouched, the cups of wine, brimming... And that's when I noticed the empty chairs turned on the floor, the smashed wine jars scattered in the room.

The Seven lingered in the chamber, their faces either paler than misery or flushed with the fiercest fury.

Leander passed me by, oblivious to my presence, too ensnared in his thoughts as he paced the dining hall. When he reached the hearth, he drifted a hand to his mouth. Something had shaken his usual collected self, and whatever that was, it had unleashed a flitting pandemonium.

Even though the air had thickened with the heat of the argument ended mere seconds ago, undeniable gloom dispersed in our midst. I clasped my hands tight until my knuckles whitened. The mages' somber stares and sullen mien stirred my old fears and uncertainties.

Essgard trudged across the dining hall. His tall black boots stopped near the head of the table. He crouched to lift the tumbled chair back up, then dragged it along with him as he made his way to the fireplace and set the chair against the stone wall.

The mage plummeted onto the seat, sighing heavily. When he bowed his head, an instant ripple of glistening black hair concealed half his face. His inked fingers raked through the mane, sweeping it back, and only then did I read his maroon eyes. Inside them, I recognized the hollowness of grief.

Akron stood by the window, towering, with arms folded across his chest. His hands drifted to the sill and he let his forehead touch the glass. I turned to Thuriad, who was sulking in the corner, an inked hand rubbing across his brow.

They seemed… *defeated.*

Romni sauntered before them, carrying a dish crammed with steaming delicacies. Lazily, he picked up a chair from the floor, hauling it with him as he approached the dinner table. He set the dish and loomed over the meal, sweeping the feast with an appraising glance. "Mm..." he uttered, grabbing a bowl and spoon. "That broth looks promising."

"Rom," Millindrel groaned, standing next to his twin. "How can you eat at a time like this?" He glowered in disapproval.

But Romni paid no heed to his brother as he sat on the chair. The mage stuck a fork in his meat and took the carved chicken into his mouth. "Mil, even if the world as we know it is coming to an end," he finally mumbled, yanking a piece of bread, "that doesn't mean I can't have dinner." He dipped the chunk of bread into the gravy saucer, making sure he coated it fully, and shoved it into his mouth.

"And besides," he added, cocking up an eyebrow, "we'll need our strength for what's coming."

"*Nothing* is coming," Leander said through gritted teeth. "It's all in your head." His tone was final, his expression stern.

"A *monster* killed my sister." Brindel dashed out of the corner beside me. Her clothes had changed. She wasn't wearing her lacy gown anymore, but light wool trousers much like mine, a brown leather vest, and an airy ivory shirt.

She met Leander by the fireplace. As they stood face to face, their profiles gleamed copper by the flickering flames. "It was real," she breathed, and her gossamer wings faintly quivered, lustrous as they glistened in the warm light. "I was there." Her voice came low and mournful, tinged with soundless pain.

Leander startled in dismay. He tilted his head, heartbroken as his eyes met the fairy's. "That's not what I meant, m'darling," he managed.

"That huntsman and his ghastly hound kill for sport." Brindel leaned forward, narrowing the distance between them. Grief gave way to sheer conviction in her countenance. "They will *not* stop."

"Not until we stop them," Essgard uttered, stalk still in his seat behind them.

"Leander," Brindel continued, and her delicate hands folded on his, "you're a mage of the Realm of Fae. You *vowed* to protect us." The words sailed from her, not as a demand, but as the gentlest plea.

The mage's gaze drifted to the fire for an instant. "And I will keep that promise," he told her, tenderly cupping the side of her face with his hand. A bitter smile tensed his lips.

"What's wrong?" I finally asked, pinned to the doorway with growing uncertainty.

As I spoke, Ash soared above my shoulder, spearing into the room. Magic gleamed brightly from him, sweeping his white silken feathers, rippling through him like a beautiful, pulsing light wave.

My mouth twisted into a smirk. "Oh, you *had* to make an entrance, Ash, didn't you?" I teased, becoming instantly the cynosure of all eyes.

Unmitigated shock stirred amidst the Seven. I didn't know what alarmed them more, that I was wearing Galhöe's clothes or that I'd actually talked to my dearest owl.

Ash stalked to the chimney mantel and perched up there, scrutinizing each face in the room.

"So, you've finally told her." Rom shoved aside his dinner plate with a sweep of his forearm across the table. A mischievous grin curled the corners of his mouth. His fingers eased around the stem of his glass and, raising the drink, he said, "Well done, my boy!"

"Some good news for a change," Thuriad uttered in a darkened voice. He sauntered to the hearth and stood by Ashton's side. Taking his hands to his hips, he straightened, watching Ash proudly. "I'm glad to hear it." He nodded.

"What's going on?" I asked, studying the turned-up room with a glance as I ambled towards them.

"There's been another attack," Brindel said with a vacant stare, her burdened mind wandering miles away.

I stopped by the hearth, scarce feet apart from them. Brindel's marred expression eased when her stray gaze found me. Her long blonde lashes fluttered as she drew nearer, compelled to inspect my face as close as possible. *Too close.* I could feel her cool, minty breath brushing my skin.

I'd once heard tales of the fae's fascination for humans. In those stories, such an enchantment often spurred the beginning of trouble. Brindel's sweetened disposition as her fingers glided through my heavy locks of black hair made me think of the last time I'd seen a puppy. The same fondness filled her sad eyes as her hand glided away, the locks slipping from her fingers and bouncing off my shoulder.

"Marioth, queen of the pixies, has been slain," she breathed.

"Queen Marioth?" I echoed, my desperate gaze turning to Leander. He said nothing. "No. That's impossible. We just saw her. Ash and I, we—" The air froze in my throat. I pushed myself to speak. "We were at the Amber Palace and…!"

My eyes brimmed with tears.

Leander drifted closer. "I'm afraid it's true, Snow," he said in the gravest tone. "The pixies found her in the Red Forest."

A whimper escaped me. "Who would do such a thing?" I managed as a shiver rushed down my spine.

"That damned huntsman, that's who!" Thuriad growled. He pounded on the table, making the wine and cutlery jitter in a dissonant clang that echoed through the ensuing silence.

The huntsman. Sheer dark dread washed through my being.

"Such viciousness. Such unwarranted violence against our kin..." Brindel spat the words. Rage and suffering tangled in her strained voice. "Why is he doing this to us?"

My breath stalled. I knew the answer. My silence had caused immeasurable damage. If I didn't speak now, more lives would be lost. I could not bear it. I could not hold my tongue any longer.

I bowed my head as my lashes dropped heavily. I tried to shun the hurt and failed. I summoned a deep breath, holding it in while my pulse throbbed hard in my chest, pounding in my throat. "It's my fault," I said at last, fixing my eyes on Brindel's. "The huntsman in the woods… He's come for me."

The fairy's expression slackened.

"For you?" Leander said, and his voice was sweet as honey. His brow slipped into a frown. "What business could a huntsman have with you, a runaway handmaid?"

The white owl screeched in disapproval. My gaze cut to his, warily, as my cheeks burned with unmitigated shame. I slightly shook my head. The time had come to tell the truth. I should have been honest from the very beginning.

"Leander, everyone…" I began in a grim tone. "I've lied to you all." Raising my hands, I hugged myself. "I'm not a handmaid, or a thief." I watched as painful disappointment surfaced on their faces. It made my stomach churn. However, I couldn't stop now.

I straightened and said, "I'm Princess Maleath Snow of Whitehaven. And the huntsman, the monster who committed these heinous crimes, was sent by the Evil Queen." It took all the strength in me to carry on, but I did. "He's come to take my life."

Unbearable silence lingered in the room. I'd said my piece, but the weight pressing on my chest became no lighter. Unease rolled through me like a dark, chilled wave.

"So, it's true then?" Thuriad said, folding his burly tattooed arms across his chest. The mage's green eyes stared me down with stern derision. "You killed the king, yer own father?" He scowled.

"No!" I said, the sound rushing from my throat like a restless plea. "It was all *her* doing. Queen Roslyn."

"Roslyn?" Essgard snapped, uncrossing his legs. He jolted upright in the seat and leaned forward, wearing the severest glare. "What has she done?" The question gave no room for stalling. It came as a demand.

Lightning flickered in the window. The thick, dark clouds expelled an angry rumble, shaking the house to its foundations. The storm was far from over.

I brushed a hand under my nose and sniffed. I'd never spoken about it before. Not as openly. It proved to be a challenge.

"The night she married my father, Queen Roslyn tried to kill me." My vision dimmed, flooded with vivid memories. "My father saved me and met death in my stead." A warm tear glided down my cheek.

"He was good and kind, and the most just of kings." I bit my lower lip as the bitterness of our last quarrels came back to haunt me. "Queen Roslyn claimed my father's throne. She's cast me off my land into a life of exile." I paused to garner my resolve. "The Evil Queen will not rest until I'm dead. She's made it quite clear."

Essgard's jaw clenched tight. He jolted off the chair and marched up to his friend. "Leander…" he told him, and the name became a warning. "Do you see what she's done, the harm that she's done?" A leery look speared towards me over the mage's shoulder. "How many more lives must she ruin before you make up your mind, man?"

A shadow of misery fleeted across Leander's countenance. His head swung to the mage, subdued like a wounded beast. His glistening blue eyes begged for mercy.

Akron and Thuriad exchanged furtive glares. Romni and Mil whispered in the lowest voices, their expressions wrecked with ruthless outrage.

I should have expected no less from them. I deserved their disdain, having barged into their lives, bringing death and desolation with me. But even then, it tore my spirit.

"She's out of control," Essgard added vehemently, searching for Leander's stare. "Gods! It hurts me to say this, but..." The crudest pain flickered in his eyes. "She must be stopped!"

"Not now, my brother..." Leander breathed as calm as he could be. He pressed a hand on Essgard's shoulder and locked eyes with the mage. "*Please*. Not now."

Brindel halted between us, her stormy eyes spearing me with a glare. "So, you're the one the huntsman wants," she said through clenched teeth. "*You're* the reason my sister's dead!"

"Brindel. Don't," Leander urged, holding an appeasing hand in the air.

The fairy fluttered her wings, soundless, as she hovered swiftly above the ground. She winced in mild pain, and within seconds, stood before me. "Cindary and Marioth are dead because of you!" she hissed, flashing her fangs.

Panic swelled inside me. I took a hand to my throat. A fairy's wrath was a fearsome thing to behold. "I never meant to bring my troubles with me," I blurted, stepping away in sheer instinct.

"But you did, girl!" she spat, dropping her hands to her sides, clenching them into tight fists. "And as long as you're in these lands, we're *all* in danger!"

"That's enough, Brindel," Akron said with stern authority as he ambled towards her.

"No," I managed between quickened breaths.

"She's right." I stopped in the doorway. "My sole presence has unleashed darkness in these lands. Queen Marioth, Cindary... their deaths are mine to bear." One more step.

My frantic gaze stumbled through the bare hall. "I'm sorry I did this," I whispered, tears blurring my sight. "I'm so sorry." In a flash, I darted to the door and threw it open to the harshest winds. Cold seeped through my cloak and made me shiver.

"Don't do it, Snow!" Leander called behind me. "It's dangerous!"

Ash soared into the hall, restless.

"Calm yourself, lad!" Essgard struggled to contain him, but to no avail. Ash fled his grip, shrieking a loud bark, grating with despair.

I bit down on my lip, sinking into the rawness of my feelings. Torn as I renounced not only the truest friendship I'd ever had, but Ashton's steadfast affection. I quickly dismissed all hesitation and pulled the hood over my head. And as I took the first step outside, I knew there was no going back.

CHAPTER TWENTY-ONE

I needed to run. I had to escape, to leave the Seven's secret lair behind. My boots met mud and mossy stones as I trudged the way uphill. I could not stop the tears from spilling. I'd found no comfort after admitting my guilt, and abandoning Ash worsened the pain. *How many more must die?* Essgard had said. Leaving was the only way to spare them from the huntsman's wrath. And with that thought in mind, I moved forward.

By the time I reached the portal on the hill, my chest was heaving with heavy breaths. Heartache and exhaustion were taking the greatest toll on me yet. I tumbled against the stone, slipping my back on its firm surface. And there I rested for a little while, garnering my strength after the steep climb.

I looked down at my waist, where my sword

should be cinched. It wasn't. I winced. It must have slipped off while I trekked up.

Below, I glimpsed the Red Forest, tangled in the dark, its dense foliage outlined by the fluttering lightning. Instant regret filled my spirit. I wished I'd been more open with the Seven. I longed for those brief days of peaceful living, the warmth and kinship that ruled the mages' lair. And Ash... Oh, Ash. A sudden bitter thought, the grim desolation that lay ahead of me.

"This is the only way," I murmured, and with renewed resolve, I strolled to the ring's center.

I whirled, my wary gaze sweeping the seven sarsen stones. Their hazy shadows leaned over me like a fearsome portent. I was standing in the right place. So where was the magic door? Frustration caught up with me fast. I slammed my hands on my legs, spattering rainwater around me. A string of curses dripped from my lips.

I let out a harsh breath and bowed my head, ready to give up, when my stare angled to the ground, distracted by a rapid pulsing light.

The gleam came from my left boot, from the blue stone that embellished it. Scrunching my brow, I crouched and inched closer. My fingers glided on the stone's smooth surface. I wondered if I tugged... The stone came off. But not only that. A hidden dagger unsheathed with it.

"This must have been Galhöe's," I mused in awe. As my hand closed in its grip, the blade's luster dimmed. Leander had used a similar dagger when he'd opened the portal in the well. Perhaps enough magic lingered inside this one, and I might tear the veil between both lands.

When lightning struck again, the earth quivered. The stones' shadows grew larger, twisted, and disturbing. An unfamiliar shade stretched on the grounds. My breath hitched. The hairs on the back of my neck tingled. I couldn't shake the feeling that I was being watched.

As my heart throbbed harder in my chest, I turned.

All was well. I was alone. My worries steered away as the fresh breeze scattered the heavy clouds above, revealing the full moon for the first time in the evening.

I girded myself with resolve. My grip tightened on the blade. I stretched my arm, willing to repeat Leander's movements as I'd witnessed them in the Black Forest. There wasn't much to it. A simple vertical slash, and a circle around it.

My hand trembled with cold and uncertainty, knowing myself unworthy of wielding the blade's power, fearful of the fate that waited for me on the other side. But I pushed through my uncertainties and swung the dagger skywards. A glint of magic twinkled in the stone. And for once, I felt true hope.

"This might actually work," I mumbled. And as my arm started its descent, a golden gauntlet seized my wrist, its frightful hold so tight that the magic blade slipped from my grasp.

I froze. In a heartless move, the gauntlet came thrashing down and brought me to my knees. Rattled to the bone, I raised my shuddering eyes and glared at my attacker.

His body was all shadow. Silver moonlight spilled behind him, bleeding the grim outline of his towering figure. Lightning flashed, and I caught the gleam of golden armor, grimed and worn. Another burst of light revealed a haunting blood rose chiseled on his breastplate.

A whimper escaped my lips as fear, stark and vivid, swept through my being like never before. "The huntsman..." I cringed, pinned to the ground by his mighty weight.

In a ghastly flash, the storm's flickering play of lights exposed the huntsman's face. My lips parted to scream, but no sound came through. Panic had seized my throat. I wished to all the gods my eyes had never seen such horror.

His was the face of death, pale and rotting.

Moldering flesh shed from his cheek, exposing putrid muscle and raw bone. His eyes blazed with a fire of the darkest magic. And as he glowered down at me, I watched the scar that crossed his monstrous features and dragged a twisted smile on his chapped cerulean lips.

At that moment, I learned what the deepest fright could be. A man whom I'd despised and believed to have perished had somehow risen from the grave with a ferocious thirst for vengeance. He'd slain many a man and woman before, and creatures of magic after his death... I knew then he'd kill again, and *I* was his next victim.

The earth rumbled beneath me with a roar of thunder, casting disturbing quakes into my already broken self. What was this thing? Its sole existence defied all reason and crushed me with anguish. My mind whirled to understand it.

It was devastation and chaos. Darkness molded into flesh. The undead walking with the living. It was... "Daron Blackstone," I managed, feeling my face slacken at once. Even as the captain towered before me, my mind refused to accept it. Daron was dead. I'd seen him fall!

The undead captain dropped my wrist begrudgingly as his hand swung for his scabbard. Between panting breaths, I scrambled my limbs and hauled myself back until my spine met cold stone. And there I watched in full dread as Daron's sword came free.

Across mud and grass and stone, he dragged the blade, marching towards me with dull, heavy footsteps, like a broken puppet missing most of its strings.

Daron's murky sabatons stopped inches away from me. A chilly, black silence sailed between us. I released a stuttered breath, slowly looking up.

The captain's gaze ignited in sheer fury. In one ruthless swing, his sword slashed down, although lacking strength and precision. Driven by a reckless impulse of survival, my gloved hands seized the blade, successfully forcing it away. At once, Daron's golden blade slipped from his grip. He growled in frustration. And as he trudged to retrieve the weapon, I rose to my feet, barely managing an escape.

With quivering limbs, I staggered to the next stone when my knees buckled and pulled me to the ground. I gasped, taken by a shiver of panic when, out of the corner of my eye, I glimpsed Daron's burly frame picking up the blade. My mouth went dry. My heart thudded hard in my throat and ears as each quickened breath burned into my lungs.

Raw instinct prompted me to crawl behind the massive stone, and there I curled my legs against my chest. Even as my grip tightened around my knees, I shuddered. My mind fluttered away in anxiety when the sharpest pain pulled me out of the daze. I held up my left hand and discovered the slash on the black leather and the pink flesh drenched in blood underneath. I choked back a cry.

Stamping a foot on my cloak, I ripped off the trim with my good hand. I wrapped the soaked linen around the wound and fastened it tight, praying to all the gods for a quick escape.

At last, the storm began to wane. The rain reeled back into a drizzle and moonlight spilled atop the hill. I sighed quietly, welcoming the scant light as a favorable omen. But my relief was short-lived as a howl clamored in the distance.

Ice flitted down my spine at the gruesome sound.

"Come out, come out," the captain chanted, his voice hoarse and hollow. Not of this world.

I cringed. My body shuddered through and through, swept by fear, helpless as a child. I slapped a hand over my mouth to stifle my sobs.

"Where are you, girly?" Daron crooned, his staggering footsteps blundering nearby. The sweep of sharp metal grazing stone prickled my nerves into alertness.

I held back the tears that burned my eyes. A blurry vision was the last thing I needed. Had there been more light, I would have made the run downhill. But shadows swept the land, the fickle moonlight ever shifting. I sharpened my gaze and screened the moors before me, meeting rocks and trees and mud... and something else.

My eyes widened. The hand drifted from my lips as I saw the man skulking behind a boulder several feet away. A painful distance. He raised his open hand, calling for absolute stillness, his dark eyes taking a stab at my own.

"Essgard," I breathed. My lips eased into a brief smile of relief. The mage had followed me here. I wasn't alone.

Essgard pointed to the side, to the stump of a fallen tree. Loose strands of flowing red hair loomed over it. Slowly, the man's face emerged up to his nose. Thuriad watched me with fierce eyes, and suddenly, he winked. When the rest of his head appeared, I saw the snarky grin etched on his lips.

Lower on the hill, I noticed Akron, Romni, and Millindrel making the climb to join the others.

"Did you hear that howl?" Daron taunted in the same gruff voice. "It's the barghest. He wants you too." He lurched closer, spurting all my fears to feed his amusement.

The undead captain growled, mimicking the barghest's eerie shrieks. Gooseflesh rippled up my arms. "My eyes aren't what they used to be," he complained.

"Oh... I bet," I breathed from my hiding place, shuddering beyond control.

"But the hound's scent is deadly sharp," he spat, swinging the blade in the air. Daron cleared his throat. "Between the barghest and me, girl, I'd say the choice is clear..." His voice drifted away.

A wave of Essgard's hand called my attention. The tense lines on his face relaxed, and he nodded, pointing to my side.

"You want *me* to kill you, girly. Not him," Daron added.

My head swung to where the mage suggested. A stack of boulders swathed in the thickest fog. Hope bloomed in my heart again when the man skulking behind the rocks emerged. Tendrils of dark hair swayed in the breeze and stroked his cheeks. His piercing blue eyes narrowed as he raked the land with a glance.

"Leander," I managed.

I recognized a flash of steel in the mage's hand. Leander knelt, pressing the blade against the muddy grass. And in one quick thrust, he shot the sword towards me with such strength that it scurried to my side.

It was Galhöe's blade. Instant comfort swept through me as my hands clenched tight around the blade's grip. Ashton's advice resounded in my mind.

At once, I twisted the ring's stone, swiftly sprinkling its venom on the sword.

"She wants your heart. That's easily done. I'll do the rest for my enjoyment," Daron sneered. "Arms or legs. I *do not* care what my sword meets." His footsteps drew perilously close.

"Perhaps I'll slice open your neck and leave it at that," he scoffed, wielding his blade in the air, "like I did to your rotten father." Vicious laughter blasted from his throat.

I seethed with mounting rage. Dread yielded to spurred fury, and in an instant, I shot to my feet and faced the captain. "I'll take that arm first," I hissed out the words contemptuously, unwavering in my conviction as I braced myself for an imminent fight.

Daron's lips curled into a crooked grin. "We'll see about that," he growled, amused.

In a flash, the monster lunged at me, his blade swung high. When the sword came down, I blocked it with my own. Steel against steel. My frail frame hardly stood a chance against him, so I slipped on the muddy ground to dodge his massive self, and braced myself again.

The howling returned. More than one beast this time.

An unsettling chortle rumbled in the captain's chest and echoed in his throat. "They're coming for you, girly!" he said, whirling towards me. "But don't worry, *princess*. I'll send you to your father first." He lowered his chin and charged against me like a wild beast.

I strengthened my grip. My left hand throbbed with undiluted pain, but I pushed through. Again, my boots glided on the ground, avoiding a lethal slash. "Not... yet," I breathed. And rising beside Daron, my slim blade flashed in a practiced arc. Its cold steel bit into his arm with savage fury, chopping off the putrid limb in a single blow, as if mud had replaced bone.

A heavy thud struck the ground when Daron's golden gauntlet fell. His vicious sword dropped with it, too. Not a shriek of pain came from his throat. The captain didn't blink or cower. I shuddered at his numbness and stumbled back, absolutely horrified.

A bank of fog scurried through the land, enveloping us in a cold, blinding cloud. My breaths quickened with increasing apprehension. I remained utterly still, dreading the instant when the maimed creature would emerge from the dense white mist. Each of my senses sharpened into alertness... And then, the growls began.

Howls and hissing surrounded me. I grounded myself in the ring's center, sword in hand. A cold knot clenched my stomach as I watched a dozen flaring red eyes burn through the mist. My attention narrowed on the creature that stalked forward.

The barghest emerged from the veil of fog, a harbinger of death flashing lethal fangs. The creature's unhinged snout shed rotten flesh, and so did its hind legs.

"Gods of the Netherworld..." I stammered, shaken by the shock of discovery. It was real. The barghest from the Black Forest had risen from the dead, and its ruthless maw now claimed me with unscathed hunger.

"Now, lads! Now!" Leander said in a call for battle. "Take them all down!"

The fog shifted, swallowing the barghest. I froze in the fiercest dread while, desperate, I gazed into the mist. I didn't know which I feared more, Daron or the monstrous undead hound.

With a whoosh of air, an axe swung past my shoulder. A loud whine shrieked in my ear, and when I turned, I saw the axe carve a red ruin out of the barghest's chest. Instants away from sinking its keen fangs into my neck, the beast dropped to the ground, lifeless.

Out of the mist, Thuriad appeared, darting past me fast. He crouched over the barghest, reclaiming his weapon from the beast's limp body. His axe swung down and chopped the creature's neck as easily as cordwood. "Keep your eyes peeled, lass!" he warned me as he rose, twisting his mouth into a lopsided grin.

Cries of war and wails of death scattered in the wind while, beyond the heavy mist, I glimpsed a bleeding sky. I tightened the grip on my sword's hilt. The blade thirsted to kiss Daron's neck. "Where are you?" The memory of my father's murder triggered a roar from me. "I killed you once, Daron. I'll do it again!"

As the fog cleared, the crimson sun appeared. The sarsen stones rose tall and imposing. I stood before the largest one, when all this time I'd thought I'd been standing in the ring's center... When a gold blade glinted out of the corner of my eye, the stone suddenly shifted. My stomach turned as I realized this was no sarsen stone, but the undead captain standing inches away from me.

His gauntlet swung at my face with no warning. My head dodged the blow, but his fist caught my shoulder, sending my body flopping to the ground.

I sat up and groaned, wincing in undiluted pain. A tendril of horror seized my chest as I watched my sword lying far from my reach. The clang of Daron's armor set my nerves on fire as he marched closer.

Blackstone rose before me within seconds, his lethal blade glinting in the morning light. It was hopeless. I was doomed. The words flitted across my mind. *This is how I die.* I shut my eyes and prepared myself to see my father again, and my mother.

A slash and a thud shook me into alertness.

"Snow!" a familiar voice called.

Beyond the scurrying mist, I glimpsed a man. The sun's radiance spilled behind him. He was riding a white stallion, clutching a hand on the reins, the other on his blade.

Ashton's sword swung into a flawless arc and slashed the barghest attacking him. The beast dropped dead in a flash of silver. "Let's finish this!" he told me, shaking the gore off his blade as the stallion whinnied, prancing from side to side, restless for battle.

"Ash," I cried. But my relief quickly withered as a dark shadow splashed over me—Daron, crawling on his knees, wounded and howling in savage anger.

"Up here!" a woman called. "Take it!"

My head swung to meet Brindel soaring over me. My sword slipped from her grip. I caught it fast.

"Together!" Ash said, holding his blade up as his stallion galloped nearby.

He charged against Daron from the side, sword ready to slash his neck in silver fury. I wielded my blade to match his. Death spurted from the wound as both swords crossed in Daron's neck. The savage blow beheaded the captain in an instant.

My body went limp with immediate exhaustion. The crimson blade dropped from my hands. A ripple of numbness swept me whole.

Ash leapt off his ride. He rushed to me, his knees gliding on the mud. His sturdy hands cupped the sides of my face eagerly. "It's over, my love," he whispered as his thumb stroked my cheek with fondness. He wrapped me in his arms. And I broke down in his hold, weeping in silence.

"You're safe now," he breathed, pressing his lips against my brow. "Let's go home."

CHAPTER TWENTY-TWO

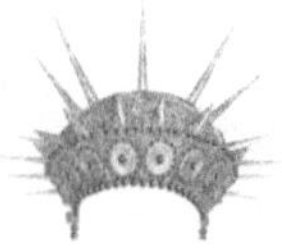

I'm lying on a bed of grass. The song of morning birds wraps me in a gentle croon. Rose petals drift in the breeze, smooth as they spill on my cheeks. Their sweetness fills my lungs. I dig my hands in the thick grass and rake small pebbles with my fingers. Their warmth stirs a tingle as I press them into my palms. I blush in the radiant sun. My lips ease into a pleasant smile.

Slowly, I rise. I find myself sitting on top of a hill. Whitehaven Castle's silvery turrets gleam miles away. I've never seen the spires so clearly. The reason hits me quick. Winter does not swathe the land in its hazy hold as it has for centuries; its frosty storms, so unremitting, they gave Mother reason to name me Snow—even if Father favored Maleath. In the end, I kept both names.

I tilt forward, taking in the precious view of sun-kissed trees and blossoming fields that stretch before me. All this time, so much beauty has lied dormant beneath layers of frost and snow...

"Maleath," a woman says behind me. "It's time to come home."

My expression slips into a frown. "I don't want to." I pout, shaking my head. "I like it here."

A delicate hand glides over my shoulder. "The queen, my love..." the voice whispers, the mildest warning in my ear. It rings loving and true. So terribly familiar.

I snap out of the daze. "Mother?" I breathe, whirling back. My gaze sweeps through the surrounding forest. I search for her, *any* sign of her, to no avail.

"She wants your heart," Mother reminds me. Her voice drifts in the distance. "You must be brave, my dear. She's coming."

A flicker of panic washes through me. In a brutal shake, the ground breaks beneath me and I plunge into fathomless darkness.

I'm sitting on solid stone. My hands clutch what feels like icy armrests. At the first ray of light, I glimpse the long hall, lined with ancient mirrors, the crooked chandeliers swinging in the freezing air, the tattered golden carpet, tarred with ashes.

I'm sitting on the White Throne.

A rippling pool of shadows lies before me. From this pond, a most menacing figure rises. Daron Blackstone, drenched in thick tar, dripping darkness as he stands. His mouth slackens in a silent shriek that rattles my nerves to the core. He drags a foot forward, and suddenly, the captain collapses to his knees and melts into a puddle of mud that flows towards me.

Within seconds, Daron's shadows bleed into my feet. The sludge climbs the throne, slow and viscous, fastening my legs, gluing my hands to the marble stone.

I writhe in the grip of darkness, useless, as the tar grasps my shoulders and tightens my chest. It clutches my throat, and seals my mouth shut. My eyes open wide in terror as a scream slices through the fog of my brain.

"*Snow,*" a man calls. The voice is remote, but clear.

My breath stalls. I can't move. I can't breathe.

"*Wake up, lass,*" he says. This time, closer.

I JOLTED AWAKE ON THE BED, MY HEART quickened into a wild gallop. A blur of wood furnishings and stray sunbeams meshed before my shuddering eyes. The sharpest apprehension tightened my chest.

"It's all right," the man said in a low, soothing voice. "I'm here, m'darling. No need to worry."

My frantic gaze cut to my side. And there I met Leander's pale blue eyes, twinkling sapphires in the room's twilight. His firm hand folded over mine and gave it a light pat. "You were having a nightmare," he told me with the sweetest demeanor before easing back in his seat.

I sucked in one long breath and caught the fragrant whiff of apples and cinnamon. "A nightmare," I echoed, my thoughts whirring in fading stupor.

One by one, the memories took shape. I rushed my wounded hand to eye level and found no bandage, not a trace of Daron's sword etched into my palm. "But I was..." I uttered, unable to construct another word.

"I healed your hand," Leander added with limitless patience. He leaned forward, offering me a steaming cup of tea. "The bruise on your shoulder will take a while longer."

I looked down at my clothes. A crude ivory nightgown, fresh against my clean skin. "What happened after we got home?" I breathed, taking the warm cup in my hands. Holding the mug alone comforted me greatly. I wondered if this was not part of the mage's spell. My brow furrowed. "I can't remember..."

"You had a fever, Snow," he told me, shuffling in his seat to make himself comfortable. "Ash took care of you while you were ill."

"Ash." His sole name lifted my spirit. "Where is he?" I asked, hopeful to see him, since sunlight spilled inside the room.

Leander eased his elbows on the armrests. He gathered his hands, steepling his fingers. "I sent him downstairs," he confessed. "The lad's hardly eaten since..." The words sailed into silence. Leander pursed his lips. "He'll be back soon." He cleared his throat. "Drink your tea."

I took a swig. The beverage's pleasant warmth soothed my restlessness at once.

"Leander," I began, tilting forward, "what happened on that hill was not natural." I licked my lips, savoring the dregs of spicy cinnamon. "The huntsman who murdered Marioth and Cindary, I knew him to be dead. Yet he walked the same earth as you and me." No dread clung to my words. They rolled out of my tongue in sheer calmness. I drew the mug close to my lips and took another sip of tea, enjoying the instant coziness that spread through my limbs.

The mage folded his brawny arms. When his

linen shirt shifted, I glimpsed several arcane symbols inked on his chest. "Mm..." Leander uttered with a stern frown, slowly nodding in agreement.

I flinched at the mage's certainty. "How is that possible?" I asked, sensing a wave of apprehension as it rolled into my soul.

The same restlessness glinted in Leander's eyes, suddenly darkened like ominous thunderclouds. A muscle tensed along his jawline, and he lowered his gaze. "Death Magic," he whispered, curt and detached. The mage swallowed hard. "I should leave you to your rest." He exhaled sharply, and slipping his hands over his knees, he straightened.

I mouthed soundlessly, completely bewildered, as I watched him leave. How could he, after uttering such terrible words?

"Leander," I told him as his hand folded on the doorknob. "She wants my heart."

The mage remained shockingly still. A long, brittle silence sailed between us. "Who, m'darling?" he finally asked. And although he strived to sound mellow, his voice strained in dismay. However, he did not look back.

"Queen Roslyn," I told him, quickly biting my lower lip. "She wants my heart. She said it herself the night my father died." The air in my throat froze. It pained me to remember, but I pushed through the hurt. "She's robbed me of all I ever held dear." A stuttered breath escaped me as my eyes brimmed with tears. "And yet, she would have more." I paused. "Has she not taken enough?" Pain gave way to anger as I spoke the last words.

Leander slightly looked over his shoulder. His face was stern, with a tight crease on his brow. The mage rubbed a hand across his mouth. He loosened a long sigh before facing me once more.

"Snow," he said, and my name on his lips sang like a warning. "There's something you should know about Queen Roslyn." He ambled closer, with slow, pensive steps.

"I know she's an evil sorceress," I hurried to say, suddenly swept by anxiety. "I've seen the fire of magic burning in her eyes." *The same I've glimpsed in yours,* I wanted to add, but refrained. "It was her. She summoned the huntsman back from the dead, and the barghest too."

Leander stopped at my bedside. His hands dropped to his sides. Slowly, he sat on the bed, watching me with pleading eyes. "Yes, m'darling. She did," he whispered, wounded. "A sorceress she may be. But she's more than that." His expression tensed with increasing disquiet. "Queen Roslyn... is cursed."

"Cursed?" I started.

The bed squeaked as Leander shifted his weight.

He rubbed a hand on his nape, then eased both elbows on his knees and clasped his hands. His gaze drifted to the hardwood floor. "It happened a long time ago," he said with heaviness. "Queen Roslyn was a child back then, when a *truly* evil sorceress cursed her for all eternity."

I leaned forward. "What happened to her?" I asked.

"Evil most contemptible," Leander said, swept in his dire thoughts. "Fire and darkness have brewed inside her soul ever since. A devastating sentence that will someday consume her, swallowing all remnants of the woman, leaving behind only death and shadow."

Gooseflesh shot up my arms. I hugged myself. "Can a curse like hers be broken?" I whispered, but my thoughts turned to Ash and the magic spell that tied him to the bleakest fate.

The mage straightened. His stormy gaze angled towards me. "There is one sure way to end any curse, lass." The corner of his lips curled bitterly.

"Tell me how," I breathed, invested more than ever in our conversation.

"Why, destroying the one who cast it in the first place." He shrugged at a truth glaringly obvious to him. "Assuming the sorcerer refuses to lift it, that is."

"Then the queen must die," I whispered in the

lowest of voices. But the mage was immersed so deeply in his tale, he didn't even hear it.

"Queen Roslyn's curse, however, requires a different remedy," he amended, rising from the bed. The mage dipped his hands into his trousers' pockets as he strolled to the window. *A royal heart, the fruit of love... Become a queen and rule the dark.* " Leander's words came drenched in such gloom that a shiver skittered down my spine.

"A royal heart," I repeated, taking a hand to my chest. The flash of a stark memory assailed me. Queen Roslyn's icy dagger pressed against my cheek. I shuddered, finally glimpsing the truth.

"But why take *my* heart?" I begged with quivering lips. Tears brimmed my eyes. "Why not take the life of the witch who cursed her?"

Leander smoothed a hand over the windowsill. "That," he said thickly, "I do not know."

The door creaked open. A gasp sailed through my lips as the height of anxiety spurted through me.

"I heard voices," Ash whispered, pushing the door all the way through. "Has she wakened?" With light footsteps, he treaded in the room.

The tension in my face immediately thawed when I glimpsed him. His gleaming hawkish eyes narrowed as he swept the bed covers, searching for my face. Relief thinned his lips when his gaze found me.

"Come in, lad." The mage stepped back. "She's awake. She'll be all right… and so will you." Although his lips curled in a smile, Leander's eyes dimmed with sadness.

"Ash," I breathed, stretching my arms, ready to embrace him, when a bolt of pain struck my shoulder. "Ow!" I winced, taking a hand to the tender spot.

"Don't move," he whispered lovingly, gliding on the bed. Ash slipped his fingers between mine. His hazel eyes hunted my own. A flicker of delight filled his widened pupils when our stares met.

"You're here," I said, soaring in sheer bliss.

"Yes, my love." His firm hand eased along my jawline. I lost myself in his earnest eyes, and relished in the intoxicating freshness of his cologne permeating my lungs.

"I'll tell the others…" Leander stood in the doorway, a hand fastened on the doorknob. "They've been pestering me for hours in my room, asking for news regarding your condition." He paused. "They'll be happy to know you're back with us."

"Leander?" I said, peering over Ashton's shoulder. "Thank you."

The mage knitted his eyebrows, puzzled. "For what, m'darling?" he asked.

"For being there," I added. "And here." *For never forsaking me*, I meant to say, but words eluded me.

The mage half smiled. He gave me a quick nod and closed the door.

"I'm so glad you're—" Ash began, but my lips sealed his mouth before he could finish. He returned my kiss with sweetness, and parting from me gently, his untamed eyes roved my face. "Never leave me again," he pleaded, lifting my chin with gentle fingers.

"I won't," I breathed. "I promise."

Ash heaved a heavy sigh. At once, he pulled me into his strong arms, corded in muscle. Hopelessly, my body succumbed to the warmth of his hold. He gently eased us on the bed, and I rested my head against his chest, listening to his vigorous heartbeat, a steady song that silenced all my fears and slayed my uncertainties.

CHAPTER TWENTY-THREE

$\mathcal{A}$sh tugged an arm behind his neck and rested against the headboard. His free arm gathered me to him and held me snugly. I nestled my head on the slope of his chest. Through his disheveled shirt, I glimpsed the scar on his shoulder. A remembrance of the barghest's brutal attack. No more than the faintest line now.

In this nearness, I admired his profile, sharp and radiant against the day's golden hour. I noticed the firmness of his mouth, the set of his chin, the skin pulled taut over his cheekbones. His face spoke of power and ageless strength. It could be no other way. He was his kingdom's rightful ruler.

"Tell me about your home," I said, watching him intently, eager for his answer.

A slight curl surfaced on his lips. "You want to

know about Thornwood?" he asked, pleased. His eyes glazed with longing as he summoned back a distant memory. "Well, the castle rises on a hill. A vast grey-stone gallery surrounds the keep. From there, you'll glimpse evergreen fields that stretch as far as the eye can see." His smile broadened and pierced that all-too-familiar dimple in his cheek. "Mornings are chilly and so are the evenings. The citadel smells of freshly baked honey wheat bread. Children gather by the lake in the sunny afternoon to dip their feet into the rosy waters..." His heart sang with delight. "My people are kind and generous and take pleasure in the smallest things."

"I wish I could see it someday," I told him, swept in fascination.

"I'd like that too," he said, staring at me sidelong.

"Ash?" I whispered as my fingers skimmed beneath his shirt, carefully trailing the scar's fading path.

A shadow of wariness touched his face. His head swayed towards me. "Yes, my love?" he whispered.

I bit my lower lip, becoming increasingly uneasy under his scrutiny. My mouth opened in a flicker of hesitation. "I know a way to break your curse," I finally blurted.

"Oh?" he uttered, slightly raising his brow. Next thing I knew, Ash rolled to his side, drawing his full attention towards me. "What is it?" The question belied the disenchantment darkening his hazel eyes. Years of damnation must have consumed any hope his heart had dared to harbor. And despite all of it, he would satisfy my musings.

I straightened beside him, pushing down the cramped nightgown from my lap. And watching me with infinite patience, Ash inched closer.

Resolve hardened my expression as our stares leveled. "We must kill the queen," I told him, with no signs of relenting.

"Mm…" he mumbled, lowering his gaze, pensive as he drew in a deep breath. Slowly, he exhaled. "Kill Queen Roslyn." A moment of silence passed before a mirthless snicker sailed through his lips.

My expression twisted into a scowl. "Do you find my plan amusing?" I snapped, aggrieved.

Ash swiftly recovered his sobriety. "No. It's not that. Forgive me, my love. I shouldn't have…" He pursed his lips. His hand glided up my shoulder, gentle fingers fiddling with the laced trimming of my gown's neckline.

Smothering his vacillation, he added, "For the past three years, I've done nothing but invest my time in such deliberations." A frown creased his brow. "I've struggled to unearth the answer to escape my fate, diving into the world of magic, learning its boundaries and the workings of its spells." His warm hand climbed the slope of my neck and rested on my jawline. "Killing Queen Roslyn to recover my freedom is something I've considered many times." His voice broke, subdued with pain.

His suffering moved me to tears. My hand quickly covered his. "And what's stopping you?" More passion tinged my voice than I would have wanted.

Ash licked his lips. "Two things, really," he told me, shedding the gloom from his handsome face.

"And they are?" I said, narrowing my eyes as I slid closer.

He tugged his free arm behind his neck and stared forward. "The first, that Queen Roslyn is now a powerful sovereign, with all the perquisites the title entails, which to you and I are so familiar." His eyebrows shot sky-high as he gave me a knowing look.

I conceded with a nod. "And the second?" I asked, intrigued.

"Ah, the second..." Ash heaved a sigh, then sucked at his teeth. "It's the fact that it cannot be done," he said with unbearable aloofness.

I scrunched my face in disapproval. "Why not, Ash?" I whined, but I didn't care. His life, his freedom, was at stake. I would do anything to see him conquer his curse. "You owe her *nothing* but retribution!" The words rolled off my tongue in a roar of frustration.

Ash stared at me, stunned by my enthusiasm. "It's not that it *shouldn't* be done, Snow," he clarified, lowering his arms. "I have no sympathy for the woman. There's just no way for us to kill her." His voice was firm and final.

I gasped, deeply dissatisfied. "I don't understand," I mumbled, shaking my head.

"Allow me to explain," Ash added, leaning closer. "Queen Roslyn wields unfathomable power. Have you not seen what she did to the king's guard, to the barghest?" His voice was an urgent plea. "My love, she brought them back from the Netherworld!"

I listened to him with rising dismay, but I refused to lose hope. Especially now.

"Ash," I managed, fighting through the tightness of my throat, "Queen Roslyn has taken everything from us. She's stolen our loved ones, our kingdoms, our freedoms, and even our names." My vision blurred with forthcoming tears as my hand cupped the side of his face. "You're the best thing that's happened to me since." His eyes widened, alight with magic. "I will not have her steal our future from us, too." My jaw ground tight. "I will fight *to the death* before that happens."

His expression hardened with stern determination. "Then I will fight by your side," he replied, and then moved his mouth over mine, devouring its softness.

"And so will I," a voice said, just as committed.

Startled, our heads swung forward. My brow slipped into a frown when I saw the man standing at the foot of the bed. I saw his fiery braided beard and long locks of red hair, and his mischievous green eyes that narrowed as he grinned.

"Thuriad!" I cried, my eyes widened in shock. "You should've knocked!"

Shedding from all formalities, Ash threw back his head and laughed. His laughter was warm, rich, and resonant.

"You should have closed the door, lass." The mage shrugged, flashing his palms.

I grabbed my pillow and tossed it at the devious mage. And even when my aim had speared flawlessly, another pair of hands intercepted it.

"You *really* should have closed that door." Essgard twisted his lips into half a smile as he clutched my little pillow.

"I thought it *was* closed." I stabbed him with a playful glare. "Anyway, I'm sure you're quite lost. This isn't Leander's room." I stifled a chuckle.

"Aye, he's had enough of us, the poor soul." Thuriad snickered.

"It's good to have you back, Snow," Essgard added, throwing the pillow back at me. I caught it and swiftly held it against my chest.

"Lads, come meet us downstairs," Thuriad said, easing his way back into a grave tone. "We have guests."

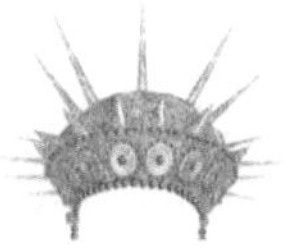

CHAPTER TWENTY-FOUR

Ash and I leisurely descended the staircase. The new attire he'd given me was lighter and fitted me better than Galhöe's. I strolled down in comfortable mahogany breeches, an airy white shirt with a wine doublet layered on top, and brown leather boots that were sturdy yet snug as slippers. The outfit's fine tailoring did not go unnoticed by me. When and how had he come across these? I began to wonder if there was anything Ash could not accomplish.

"What happened to my other clothes?" I asked, out of plain curiosity.

He watched me sidelong with wary eyes. "We... burned them," he hesitated to say. "I'm sorry, but they were beyond salvageable." Ash cleared his throat, slightly furrowing his brow. "Do you not like your new ones? The seamstress who sold them to me said—"

I held his arm, drawing his shifting gaze towards me. "I like them just fine," I assured him, secretly relieved to know I'd never have to wear the dead mage's clothes again.

While we moved on to the last flight of stairs, the tension in Ashton's expression softened but mildly. "You're probably missing your lavish gowns, huh?" he mumbled, his stare once more adrift with uneasiness. "Like that Lathiriua silk one. Which, by the way, I should mention..."

"You burned as well?" I finished, shooting up an eyebrow.

He pursed his lips and bowed his head in silent admission.

I halted on the last step when Ash reached the landing. My grip tightened on his arm, and feeling the pull as he moved forward, he whirled back. Now that we stood face to face, I eased my hands over his shoulders and clasped them on his nape, boring my eyes into his. "You could burn all the gowns I left in Whitehaven, and I wouldn't mind," I told him. But my stare shot skywards as the realization struck me. "Gods, you could burn off the clothes I'm wearing, and I *still* wouldn't be crossed with you." When I looked at him again, I tittered.

Ash charmingly flustered. The corner of his lips quirked up.

"The thing is," I continued in a more serious tone, "if I'm being completely honest, I don't miss any of it." My cheeks flushed. "I'm perfectly happy as I am. And I think you should know that."

His firm hand was tender as it glided along my jawline. I tilted my head towards his palm, yielding to the warmth of his touch that hopelessly made every inch of me tingle in delight. I could stay like this forever, in his company, enjoying the stillness of this house... My expression slowly slipped into a frown.

"What is it?" he whispered.

"Where is everyone?" I asked, looking over his shoulder. Not a sound sailed from the dinner hall. Not the faintest movement stirred.

Ash held my hand, sustaining me while I stepped off the staircase with the caution demanded by the most hazardous move. "Well," he said under his breath. "Thuriad said we had guests." A flicker of apprehension fleeted across his countenance.

"What's wrong with that?" I asked, soaking in his unease. Dull and disquieting thoughts instantly reeled in my mind.

"We *never* have guests," he uttered, his voice rough with suspicion. "We've had friends over, yes.

But guests?" He winced doubtfully, then shook his head. "You're the exception."

"Do you know where they might be?" I managed.

"I can think of one place only," he mumbled, caring little to conceal his bemusement.

Ash led me around the staircase. We stopped at a set of double doors. They swung open to a long gallery with hardwood floors dressed in rich burgundy carpeting. A vast array of tapestries and paintings hung from the stone walls, dressing them almost completely.

At the end of the hallway stood another pair of doors. I was imagining what mysteries could lie behind them when Ash halted midway through.

"What's wrong?" I breathed.

"We're here," Ash said, tugging aside the tapestry beside him. His hand smoothed along a wooden panel on the wall, and with a light push of his fingers, a hidden door triggered open. "Come."

I followed Ash down a narrow staircase that delivered us to a broader landing. Blazing torchlight spilled a warm amber gleam upon the imposing black stone archway rising before us. As I looked up, capturing the details of this gateway, I couldn't help thinking back on the forest's well. The same mysterious inscriptions ornamented the glistening rocks.

"Protection spells," Ash whispered in my ear as he caught up with me.

"Is this..." I wavered, my mouth suddenly dry. "A portal?" The gods knew I did not enjoy crossing through those. Secret passageways I could handle—we had plenty in Whitehaven Castle. Magic portals? Not so much.

Ash moved ahead and stopped under the archway, waiting for me. "It's just a tunnel," he said, dipping his hand into the shaft's pitch darkness.

I sauntered closer and peered inside. The passage ran so deep it might deliver us to the building's foundations. The air was cool and moist. Not particularly welcoming, though.

Ash leaned closer. "This place is heavily guarded by the Seven's magic," he assured me. "No matter who's in there, it's safe." He offered me his hand. "Do you trust me?"

I silently agreed and glided my palm over his.

Who were these mysterious guests? Why did their visit call for the mages' highest protection? My thoughts stumbled upon another, quickening my fears, as we moved further in the tunnel. By the time I glimpsed the end, my heart pounded hard against my chest, swept in sheer anxiety.

We arrived at a spacious vaulted room with a wide blackstone round table in the center. Tufted black velvet armchairs surrounded the magnificent piece, embellished with gilded flourishes. The chamber's walls were of gold veined black marble, engraved with golden arcane symbols like those tattooed on the mages.

The room's splendor defied the lair's modesty. This was hardly the makings of a dinner table or an ordinary cellar. I turned to Ash, awestruck. He looked back at me, quietly satisfied, and narrowing his hawkish eyes, his gaze shot skywards, persuading me to do the same.

Bemused, I did as he suggested, instantly stunned at the marvel my stare met. The ceiling over our heads, ribbed in gold, was a massive dome through which I glimpsed the clearest evening sky, laden with myriad titillating stars, and multicolored trails of condensed vapors that reminded me of my land's December fire serpents.

A soft gasp escaped me. "We're in a cellar in the middle of the day," I managed, caught in a daze. "It's impossible."

"It's magic," he spoke in my ear, pleased.

"Ash," I said, awestruck, as I faced him. "What is this place?"

"Welcome to our council room, lads," Essgard said, dragging a chair away from the table. The mage eased into the seat with the same carelessness as if he was upstairs in the dining hall. Once settled in the chair, he slipped a foot over the grand table.

"Where did *he* come from?" I asked Ash in the lowest of voices. "Was that magic too?"

Ash pointed a discrete finger towards the wall ahead. Chiseled on the black marble was a subtle archway, similar to the one we'd walked through earlier. It framed no tunnel, however, but a large pane of black glass, like the one in Leander's room.

"Now *that's* a portal," he said.

"A big one," I mumbled, immediately picking up distinct voices approaching. Startled, I swept the chamber with a glance, struggling to trace their source, but to no avail.

"I've already told you..." Romni walked into the chamber through the black mirror, vexed as he looked back to continue the argument. "I know what I saw!" Flustered, he raked his fingers through his long, straight hair.

It didn't surprise me when his brother, Millindrel, emerged from the portal after him. A scowl twisted his features. "Rom, are you sure about this?" he asked, his face marred with worry. "You can't be joking about these things."

Romni growled in frustration. In a desperate attempt to escape from his brother, he strolled to Essgard and exchanged a few words with him.

"I saw them too," Akron uttered, his presence so imposing, even the glass shuddered as he marched through.

Millindrel heaved a sigh. "Oh, gods..." he woefully said, rubbing a hand across his brow. "Then, it's true."

"I'm afraid so." Akron nodded gravely.

At once, Romni whirled on the ball of his feet. "*Him*, you believe." He scoffed, slamming his hands on his breeches.

Millindrel's arms flung open towards his brother, flashing palms. "Oh, come on!" he begged. "Don't be like that. You're always teasing me. I never know when you're being serious, is all..."

"Do you like it?" Thuriad said. His voice was low and collected. He was crossing the portal mirror alongside Brindel. The mage carried himself with sternness, his green eyes scouring her face for any signs of disapproval. "I know throwing daggers isn't your weapon of choice. But I saw these, and I thought..."

"They're very well made," she conceded with a nod, eyeing the knife in her hand. The polished blade sparkled as she turned it. "Where did you get them? The market in Port Bree, maybe?"

Thuriad harrumphed. He stroked his beard, restless. "Uh... well..." he uttered, stopping by the portal.

"They were a gift from a high fae lord who's recently passed."

I wasn't sure I believed that story.

The mage folded his arms over his chest, quickly recovering his aplomb.

"I'm sorry for his passing," Brindel said, sheathing the shiny dagger into her belt.

Thuriad's sharp stare cut to mine. Briefly, but enough to startle me. "Uh... yeah." His focus returned to Brindel. "Me too."

The mischievous mage pulled a chair and offered it to Brindel. She refused him with a light hand wave, lingering by the mirror expectantly. Only then did I notice her attire. Brindel was clad in armor. Not steel, but leather, thick and well-trimmed. She wore dark brown bracers and pauldrons, and laced greaves. Even her fawn hair looked different, gathered back into a sleek braid.

At the sound of forthcoming voices in the portal, her countenance hardened with icy resolve. Brindel squared her shoulders and straightened, slightly lifting her chin. The heel of her delicate hand eased on the hilt of her sword, cinched to her waist, resting in its scabbard.

Leander appeared through the mirror. He was not alone, but escorted a fairy woman into the council room. The gown she wore was delicate, adorned with small golden chains that crisscrossed her svelte figure. Her wings seemed tailored in the sheerest gossamer. Locks of silvery hair tumbled carelessly down her back.

The fairy's cheeks were of rose and pearl. Her eyes, a vivid shade of blue. Her countenance was pale, but proud. And through the loose tendrils of hair that softened her quiet, oval face, I glimpsed her pointed ears.

At the fairy's presence, Essgard jolted upright. I read no signs of alertness on his face, however. At least, that was encouraging. The mage peered through the group as they assembled at the table, locking stares with Ash and me.

"Lads," he mouthed the word, curling a finger to call us near.

Ash and I stalked around the room. When we reached the black mirror, Brindel tugged on a golden chord, dropping a heavy black velvet drape over the magic gateway. She stood guard next to the threshold, while we remained on the other side, keeping watch over the assembly from a distance.

CHAPTER TWENTY-FIVE

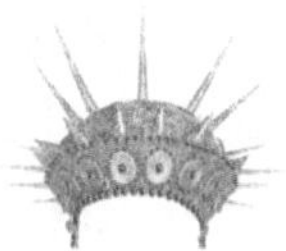

"We're pleased to welcome you to our lair, Inoue," Leander began, the only one standing in front of his seat. "It's been a long time since we last shared a conversation." His softened blue eyes steered from the mages to the fae stranger. "I will remind you, at this table, we bear no titles, no medals, or crowns. You may speak freely, and thus you shall be addressed." He paused. "Do you agree to these terms?"

The fairy bowed her head. Her pride, unscathed.

"Who is she?" I asked Ash in the lowest whisper.

Ash leaned closer and spoke into my ear, "Inoue Erzabelle, Fairy Queen of the Diamond Court."

"Fairy Queen of the Diamond Court," I echoed.

"Well, then," Leander breathed, easing into the chair. "You may state your business."

"*My* business?" The faintest wrinkle etched on the queen's brow. "This isn't about me or my people's interest," she clarified, and her voice was cold and exact. Not an ounce of emotion disturbed her flawless countenance. But I quietly observed as her long-fingered hands stretched over her lap while she consciously held a strict upright posture. "I'm here to discuss a most grievous fate that brews on the horizon."

The mages stirred in hushed discomfort.

"Our realm faces great peril," Queen Inoue continued, addressing each of the mages at the table. "It suffers the awakening of dark magic summoned by the Evil Queen." She paused, building up her resolve. "This moment has been fast-approaching. And now, time has finally caught up with us." Her piercing eyes stabbed Leander with a knowing look. "Evil cannot endure. Evil *must not* prevail."

"What do you propose we do?" Leander asked in a dispassionate tone, steepling his fingers over the table.

"There's but one thing left to do," Essgard intervened, quick and unwavering.

"War," Thuriad spat, slamming a hand on the table.

"War is not the way," Akron softly said, his brow creased with wariness. "In fact, I'm certain Leander disapproves of the entire notion. Don't you, brother?" The chair squeaked and strained under his heavy frame as he turned to the mage. "I, for one, trust your judgment."

"Nobody questions Leander's judgement," Essgard explained, holding high an appeasing hand.

"*I* question it often," Thuriad grumbled.

"Forgive me, brother. But you must accept," Essgard continued, facing Leander, "you will never see things for what they truly are." He held his breath, pain twisting his features. "Not in this instance." The passion in his voice withered. "Akron, you know this to be true."

"Leander?" Akron said, hopeful as he faced him. "What say you to all this?"

Leander shifted in his seat as silence, heavy as a summoned sin, fell upon us.

"There's an army marching through our land," Romni said in a blurt.

"Rom!" Millindrel glowered, shooting his brother a venomous look.

"An army?" Leander echoed, pivoting his body to the pair.

"I saw them too." The words left Akron's mouth begrudgingly.

Leander's concerns drifted to the queen. "Is that your army?" he asked her with urgency.

"Leander?" she mumbled, taken aback. For once, genuine sentiment molded Queen Inoue's features, and I glimpsed as unmitigated shock flew through her being.

Leander's jaw clamped tight. "Is that *your* army?" he insisted in a harsher tone.

"No!" the fairy stammered with shuddering eyes. "Until this moment, I'd not heard a word of it. I promise you, my people have nothing to do with this. Don't you see? This is the Evil Queen's doing!" She drew up a shallow breath, her stare angling towards Romni. "An army, you say?"

"A *troll* army," Akron added.

"Trolls?" Ash gasped, and his face lost all color.

"What's so terrible about them?" I asked, disturbed merely by witnessing his reaction.

Unwillingly, we attracted all eyes. Queen Inoue watched us with unveiled interest. Without moving from her seat, she raised her chin ever so slightly and tucked a long, loose strand of hair behind her ear.

"*What's so terrible,* she says," Romni said under his breath, his eyebrows shooting sky-high.

"There's a reason an Iron River splits the Realm of Man from the Realm of Fae," Essgard patiently told me. "Trolls are a significant part of that reason."

A shiver skittered down my spine. I daren't ask anything further.

"We spotted them this morning," Akron continued, puffing out his chest as he spoke. "A battalion of a thousand trolls, led by a gray goblin. They were heading south."

Thuriad cursed. "Excuse me, ma'am," he amended, addressing the queen with deference. "Darned troll traitors." His hands clenched into tight fists. "We should have destroyed them long ago when they ratted us out to the Fae Council!"

"South!" Essgard rose from the seat, gripping the table's edge, as if otherwise he might stumble. "Leander, do you see what she's doing?" He stiffened. "The Evil Queen…" The words sailed into silence.

A soft breath drifted from Leander's lips. He shut his eyes, crushed and burdened. "She's gathering an army," he mumbled, his voice broken in dismay.

"She's preparing for war!" Thuriad exploded, leaping off the chair so fast the seat fell behind him.

I clutched a hand to my chest, which had unwaveringly grown tight with trepidation. "Gods of the Netherworld," I managed. "The Evil Queen would do all this to seize my heart?" Haunting images of her vicious troll army seeped into my restless thoughts.

"I think it's gone beyond that now, lass," Thuriad said, calmer as he picked up the chair from the floor. He pressed a firm hand on the table, fierce green eyes fixed on Leander. "The clock is ticking. Queen Roslyn will soon succumb to her curse." He swallowed hard. "Death and desolation will follow. She will not stop. Not until she's burned us all to ashes."

"She cannot win!" Essgard blurted with ardent conviction.

Millindrel rose to his feet. "We will never allow it," he said, slipping a hand over his twin's shoulder. "We *must* prevail. For our brotherhood, for our realm... For our people." He nodded gravely. "We fight for them."

"No," Leander said in a groan of grief. "I will not have any more bloodshed. Surely, Queen Roslyn can be persuaded into the light once more."

Grunts and murmurs of discontent rose amid the Seven, the sounds escalating into a cacophony of objections and restrained fury.

The fae woman stood. "I'm afraid there's no other way, Leander," she mournfully said. "We have no choice but to fight." She pursed her lips, hesitant to say more. "Do you not know? Queen Roslyn has unleashed the Force of Death. A war will be waged whether or not any of us wants it."

"The Force of Death?" Leander breathed, heartbroken. "No..." His eyes shimmered with suppressed tears.

"What is that?" I asked, shedding from all shyness as I stepped closer.

Brindel joined me near the table. "The guard you killed was not the only one Queen Roslyn had risen from the dead." She turned a wary stare to Queen Inoue, waiting for a sign. Upon the queen's swift nod, Brindel carried on. "As of this moment, throngs of undead warriors stand guard outside the citadel, protecting the Evil Queen. Her Red Army, she calls them. The people in Whitehaven have become hostages, fearful of their own sovereign."

I shuddered in sheer black dread.

Leander jolted off the seat. "That's impossible!" he objected with a ferocity I'd not glimpsed in him before.

"Dare you imply that I'd lie?" the fairy queen glowered. Her voice's inclination showed all the signs of rage, and yet, not a trace of emotion had ruined her countenance.

"Your Majesty," Leander bowed his head. "That is not what I meant. Forgive me."

"Now..." Queen Inoue began in a terse tone. "I've expressed these concerns to Lord Raathiel Ivasaar, who holds great influence over the Fae Council." She addressed Leander. "He has assured me your intervention in this matter will dissolve any grievances between you." She paused, eyeing me over the mage's shoulder. "Given these newest reports, I'm afraid we must act fast."

The queen placed a hand over the mage's muscular forearm. "Fight with us against this darkness, and your crimes shall be pardoned. You and your brothers will be welcomed into the Council of Magic once more."

Leander's features hardened, drawn in agony. His gaze swept the room, searching for his brothers' faces, each of them nodding as they met. "Looks like it's already decided," he whispered, stepping away from the table. "You shall have my brethren's loyalty in this fight… and mine."

"And what about the sons of Man?" the queen asked, narrowing her bewitching eyes on Ash and me. "Where do *their* allegiances lie?"

Standing before her, I straightened. "I'm Princess Maleath Snow of Whitehaven." Fury rushed through my veins like wildfire. An army of the undead plagued my kingdom into heartless ruin as we spoke… I would not stand for it. "My allegiance belongs to my people," I told her. "I will crush the Evil Queen and take back the White Throne."

"A princess," Queen Inoue said, subtly arching an eyebrow. "Of Whitehaven, no less." Inscrutable, she regarded me. "I expect the cause that now brings us together will join our kingdoms in fraternity and peace when you are queen."

"As do I," I answered with no inclination.

"And what about you?" the fairy queen asked, turning to Ash. "Where do you stand on this issue?"

In a single stride, Ash stood between us. A shadow veiled his face. "Queen Roslyn destroyed my life and my kingdom," he said, his voice laden with grief. "To this day, Thornwood suffers the consequences of her evil." His hazel eyes met mine, subdued. "My sword is yours," he told me with steely resolve.

"The sword of Thornwood Hall, my *prince*?" the fairy queen asked with icy shrewdness. If she knew that much about Ash, then she must have known full well of his exile. Why torture him with such a question?

"I answer for myself alone," Ash told her curtly.

"The lad's as good as twenty men, if you ask me," Thuriad intervened, and closing a hand around his shoulder, he gave it a light shake.

"That should break us even," Romni mumbled, stopping near the mage. He tilted his head, and added, "For you're as bad as twenty, Thuriad." His mouth twitched with amusement.

"Maybe more," Millindrel teased, sharing a mischievous snicker with his twin.

No ripple of mirth washed over the redhead mage.

"You have our full support, Your Majesty,"

Essgard interrupted, still and serious as he broke through the pair of rascals. "May the gods' will prevail."

Queen Inoue curled the corner of her lips. "May they smile upon our victory," she said, clasping her hands over her graceful gown. "I'll leave my captain to relay to you the details of the council meeting." She glanced at Brindel, and turned away, lithe as a feather drifting in the warm breeze.

When my gaze followed her to the portal, beyond the glass, I glimpsed a dozen fairies waiting, armed with long swords, crossbows, and daggers. The queen's royal guard.

As Queen Inoue stepped into the glass, Leander joined her, leaving the chamber in the bleakest silence. A portent of war and cruel times to come.

"Snow?" The silken touch of Ashton's hand easing on my forearm startled me awake.

"I want you to know I meant what I said," he whispered, drawing me away from the others. "You have my sword. On this day, I vow that when this dreadful night falls upon us, I will walk with you to the depths of darkness. I will pave with a thousand fallen the road that leads to the White Throne." His gentle eyes bored into mine. "I will be your knight. Your champion. But please, take heed of this: only *you* can slay the dragon."

A brief gasp escaped me. The sole mention of a firebreather sprung my nerves into painful alertness. I cared little to hear about dragons—even in the context of allegory. "What do you mean?" I breathed.

Ash leaned forward, narrowing the distance between us. "Many are the fates at stake upon this hour." He paused. "You must not lose sight of your destiny, my love. In the end, this is *your* fight. *Your* kingdom. *Your* crown... if you will claim it."

A shiver of awareness rippled through my being. "I will," I told him, determined.

He nodded, and easing his hand on the back of my head, he pulled me to him. Ash pressed his smooth lips against my brow, holding me in a tender embrace.

"So..." Thuriad said in a casual tone. He glided an elbow on the table and took his fist to his cheekbone. "When's the killin'?" A flash of a charming smile shot to Brindel.

The fairy's countenance lit up with shocked amusement. In that moment, I trusted something might actually happen between those two in the future... if we had one.

"That's for the council to decide," Brindel said, ambling towards him. She stopped a few feet from the mage's seat. "They gather tomorrow."

"We'll meet them then," Thuriad replied with fierce conviction.

Brindel's smooth brow lightly furrowed. Her hand folded on the back of the chair next to the mage. "You cannot attend the Fae Council's convention," she told him in a quiet tone, dragging the seat away from the table. Slowly, Brindel seated. "Your punishment still stands. No member of the Seven is allowed inside the Marble Hall."

"Surely, that can't be true." Akron whirled towards the pair, bemused. "Brindel… We need eyes and ears inside that chamber, a voice to represent us!"

"We already *have* someone who will speak on our behalf," Leander interrupted. As he strolled towards the group, his firm voice echoed in the vaulted chamber. "Queen Inoue and I have determined this just now."

"Who will you send?" Ash asked, carelessly resting the heel of his hand on his blade's hilt.

Leander stopped in front of him. "I'm sending you, Ash," he said matter-of-factly.

"Me?" Ash whipped his head back, confused. "Why on earth?" He pouted.

"I'm sure I do not know," Leander said with a shrug. "The Marble Court… they've asked for you, my lad." His gaze cut to me. "And Snow, too."

"That *is* strange…" I mumbled.

The mage drew closer, seeking confidence. "Be wary of these high fae lords," Leander told us in the lowest of voices. "They're guileful creatures. Despite their fearsome beauty, mercy does not beat in their hearts." He stopped, waiting for a sign of our acknowledgement.

I gave him a swift nod.

"We'll be careful," Ash whispered.

"Good." Leander swept a hand along Ashton's arm. And though the gesture was warm, the mage exuded extreme tiredness. "You leave tomorrow."

I stretched my back and shoulders, strained by the journey on horseback. We'd parted at the break of dawn, cutting our travels in half with the help of the Seven's portal. But the way to the high fae lands was far from breezy. Even though evergreen woodlands shaped our scenery, the road up the Mighty Mountain was sinuous and challenging.

"I know a song that tells of the fae Marble Hall," I told Ash, eager to assert some knowledge of this realm. I longed to impress him in the way he struck me as a worldly man.

He whipped his head towards me, his eyes glinting with delight. "Do you, now?" he said, stroking his horse's neck. "Well, let's hear it." A flash of a smile. "Since neither of us has ever set a foot in their palace, I'd appreciate any report."

My cheeks flushed at the purr of his voice. "Valathüre, Valathüre..." I declaimed, facing ahead. For otherwise, I'd lose my frail confidence. "Your walls are made of ice. Your Marble Hall, an empty den feeding on humans' demise."

Frail silence broke between us.

Ashton's eyebrows shot skywards. "Whoa," he uttered, tilting his head. "That's um... quite a song." Leaning forward, he patted the horse's neck.

"Yes, I guess it's a bit gloomy." I gnawed my lower lip, trying hard not to burst into nervous laughter.

"I'd say so." He cleared his throat. "May I share with you the accounts as *I've* heard them?"

"You may," I told him as renewed heat of shame spread across my face.

"Valathüre Palace rises beyond this mountain," he began. "It has five white limestone towers, crowned with spires glazed in white gold that prick the sky like gleaming needles." He stared at me sidelong, pleased, as he tugged the reins.

His words cast a vivid impression in my mind's eye. I'd been brought up to believe no kingdom in all the realms could ever rival Whitehaven's grandeur. But the more I learned of the Realm of Fae, the more my misconceptions became glaring.

"You've been here for the past three years." I could not stop myself from pondering. "You've met with other fae before... Why have you not met them?"

"The people of the Marble Court mostly keep to their own," he replied with complete openness. "Which is why it surprised me to hear of their summons."

I squinted. "It's strange, isn't it?"

"Maybe not," he dismissed with half a shrug.

I flinched. "Please explain," I told him, lowering my chin as I shot him a glare.

Ash snickered. "What I mean is..." He dug his teeth into his leather finger and peeled the glove away. "Why *wouldn't* they want us?" He cracked a lopsided grin.

With a flick of a finger, Ash opened the saddlebag and slipped his hand inside. "I'm sure they've learned by now you're the Princess of Whitehaven," he added offhandedly. An enticing red apple came out of the bag. "And, I'm Prince of Thornwood Hall... or whatever." He took a bite.

My brow slipped into a frown. "What good are those titles when we're both exiled from our kingdoms?" I couldn't help sounding sour. I gazed down at my white mare, who shook her head in disagreement.

"Snow," he said, reaching a hand across until it covered mine. Our rides halted. Ash waited until our gazes met. "You and I care little for these titles because we've been around them since infancy. But the high fae lords of the Marble Court are frivolous creatures. They adore shiny new things."

The crease in my brow deepened. "We're the shiny new things..." I mumbled, uncertain.

Ash leaned forward on the saddle, wrapping the rein in his right hand. "May I speak candidly?" he asked in a cautious tone.

I bristled at the insinuation. "I wouldn't have it any other way," I blurted, suddenly crossed. My sycophants remained in Whitehaven, surely not so keen now on the treacherous runaway princess.

Ash gave his luscious apple one more bite. Oh, that I was that apple... My temper simmered down at the thought.

"I suspect they've called us merely to indulge their curiosity," he confessed. Then, throwing me a knowing stare, he pursed his lips and rubbed a hand across his chin, hesitant to say more.

After a minute, he added, "One quick look at us, and they'll realize we're not as pretty as them, and they'll send us back home to convey the delightful news of their allegiance." He let out a harsh breath.

With a swift tug at the reins, my horse began to walk again. I forced myself to straighten my expression. "Mm..." I uttered pensively. "I'm not as pretty as the fae, huh?" I gave him a hard stare, arching one eyebrow.

Ash started in dismay. "Gods, no!" he stammered, more flustered than ever. "I would never—" An appeasing hand in the air. "I did not mean…!"

I threw back my head and let out a great peel of laughter. When he found himself caught in my game, Ash simply shook his head.

Regaining his aplomb, he resumed. "You're the fairest creature I've ever laid eyes on." His sweetness met no equal. I could only handle so much of his tenderness without succumbing to the need for kissing him.

I watched him out of the corner of my eye, etching an impish smile while I gently rocked sideways on the saddle. "And I'm sure no high fae lord comes close to your good looks," I told him, amused.

At length, we reached the opening into the mountain. A long dark tunnel carved in the stone marked the threshold into the Marble Court.

"No guards…" Ash mumbled as our rides strutted through the bleak passage. "That's odd."

We made the crossing in wary silence until light shone ahead. Compelled, I pushed my mare to chase it. And within seconds, we halted at the end of the tunnel. As I glanced at the landscape spread before us, the air fled from my lungs in one slow exhalation.

"Valathüre Palace," Ash said when his horse caught up with mine.

I blinked twice, gawking at the dreamlike view.

Behind this treacherous mountain lay hidden the most whimsical valley. Scintillating sunbeams skittered on a peaceful ocean and speared through the dense gardens that hugged the glaring citadel. Myriad blooming white roses hung from its imposing walls. And beyond its silvery gates, a road lined with towering marble effigies led to the palace itself, where the five magnificent towers rose, their gold spires breaking into a thousand shimmering stars, almost blinding.

We continued the ride down the mountain along a steep, sinuous road.

"It's just as you said," I breathed, swept in fascination.

"Oh, gods..." Ash uttered, jerking the reins so fast his horse shifted restlessly. Startled, the beast whinnied and reared. "What is that?" Sheer terror hung from each word. My heart jolted into a gallop at the terrible sound.

"Ash?" My brow furrowed.

Without saying a word, he grasped my ride's reins and tugged them, steering our horses into the mountain's woodland.

Ash dismounted fast, and with the same haste, he

hitched his ride to a tree. Then, taking a finger to his sculpted lips, he urged me into silence.

I did as he asked and hitched my mare next to his. With a quick hand wave, he signaled me to follow him deeper into the woods. After a few steps, Ash called for stillness with an open hand, slowly crouching near the edge of the cliff, taking cover behind a large bolder.

My mouth dried. Instantly, I slunk behind him. "What is it?" I whispered in his ear.

"Look." He spoke in the lowest of voices. "There," he said, pointing at the citadel's gateway.

My shuddering eyes focused ahead. On the palace's silvery bridge, standing on each side of the gates, two figures stood guard. They seemed like ordinary men, though taller than usual. Their long manes of braided sunny hair swayed in the warm breeze, glistening with a sublime light that spilled on their taut muscular bodies. Wide, deep-blue streaks branded their chests and faces. They wore light silver-plated armor and carried threatening long swords and burnished shields, crimson-splashed from recent battle.

"Who are they?" I managed in a quivering voice.

"Trolls," Ash said in a grim tone.

He slowly got to his feet. I mirrored him. "I thought Akron said they were moving south," I told him as undiluted wariness washed through me.

"I know," he whispered. His expression slowly darkened.

"But trolls are supposed to be ugly and dim-witted," I whined, attempting to ward off the horror rushing through my veins. These were far from dull creatures, but seasoned soldiers. "The stories said—"

"You've been listening to the wrong stories," Ash dismissed, withdrawn in his own thoughts. After a minute, his gaze found mine. "Mind you, trolls are just as vicious as what they seem in the flesh." He paused, endless thoughts racing through his mind. "They're fearsome warriors, sworn enemies of the fae."

I straightened my shirt and took a hand to my quickened heart. "Then why are they here, in their palace?" I asked.

Ash shook his head, and heaving a sigh, he dragged his fingers through his mane of tawny-gold hair. "I honestly don't know." He pursed his lips. "I don't like this, Snow," he said, stepping back. "I think we should go home."

"*A 'fàgail cho luath?*" a gruff voice said.

A shiver scurried down my spine.

Shadows spilled on Ashton's face, his eyes glistening white with undiluted terror.

In a flash, something snatched my arm with

harshness. Next thing I knew, the forest swept from underneath me. Everything was a blur.

"No!" Ash roared. "Let her go!"

And then I realized someone hauled me on their shoulder. With incredibly long strides, the creature moved through the woods, reaching my mare within instants. Swiftly, he tossed me onto her back and bound my hands and ankles.

"*Siuthad!*" another said. The voice's sharp accent came almost as a growl. "Take them to the palace."

CHAPTER TWENTY-SEVEN

Icy stone chilled my cheek when the soldier dropped me on the floor. The brazing ropes that bound my wrists were tight and unforgiving. A groan sailed through my lips as I gently swung my head and glimpsed the rows of pristine marble columns that lined the majestic central nave.

As a child, I used to dream of visiting the Marble Court's palace, but being treated as a criminal was definitely not what I'd envisioned for my welcoming.

I need to rise. I must carry myself with some dignity, I told myself. But my tied hands and ankles whispered back, *no.*

I took a peek above. An impressive round dome rose above our heads, the likes of which I'd never seen, embellished with revetments in glistening gold and blue lapis lazuli. Sunlight spilled through its central glass eye.

"Snow," Ash whispered.

I rolled towards the voice, instantly relieved when I met his sparkling hazel eyes. He was kneeling beside me, the ropes tangled in his wrists and legs as grazing as mine.

Sheer concern twisted his features as he looked down on me. "Are you all right?" he asked.

"I've been better," I told him, curling my lips into a wry smile.

An earthy fragrance, rich and exotic, filled my lungs. It was subtle and woodsy, infused with alluring spices. It mildly soothed the disquiet brewing inside me.

"Untie them," someone said. His voice resounded in the majestic hall. The place reminded me of White-haven's old cathedral, just as grandiose and humbling. A skeleton of a building, nonetheless.

The guards' footsteps echoed on the sleek marble flooring as they hurried towards us. I felt the harsh tug at the ropes and heard the clean sweep of a blade as it slashed through them. I was left sitting on the floor and rubbing my wrists. My fingers tingled as the blood flow renewed properly through them.

I took a hand to my nape and massaged it. Every inch of my body hurt from the rough ride to the palace, but I couldn't think of it now. A dozen mighty troll soldiers stood guard behind us, armed with long swords, ready to come free from their scabbards at our slightest provocation.

Ash slipped a gentle hand around my arm, nudging me to my feet. As I slowly straightened, my gaze locked on him. Warmth and sternness etched his expression. With that alone, Ash gave me all the reassurance I needed.

We stood in the middle of the great hall, surrounded by the fae court. An army of fae soldiers clad in silvery plated armor held a safety line between us. Although judging by the wariness that shaped the court's faces, I doubted they'd even attempt crossing. Their restless whisperings reached my ears. Their shuddering eyes swept us with sheer scrutiny.

A dais rose in front of us. Steps carpeted in gold embroidery led to a white marble throne ornamented with silvery gold foil. My eyes narrowed on the figure sitting in the royal chair. Surely, he must have been the king. It was most puzzling to me he'd chosen not to wear a crown. However, he carried himself with pride and unquestionable noble bearing.

Sunshine spilled on the fae king's platinum hair. It hung from his head in long graceful curls that spilled below his shoulders. Pointy ears loomed between the fair strands. A black leather single pauldron sleeve was his only armor, leaving bare his muscular chest. His hand, beautiful, long-fingered, and strong, smoothed on his knee as he slumped back in the seat, suddenly throwing his leg over the armrest. The movement had been agile and feline.

Owning this attitude, the fae king's gray-blue flecked eyes raked me top to bottom. Ice skittered down my spine at his shameless fierceness. He was not the ethereal creature I would have imagined, but a hardened warrior, grounded and sensual.

"I demand an explanation," Ash said, planting himself beside me. "We were summoned by the council!"

The fae king held his tongue. Twisting his mouth into a sneer, he turned his gaze to Ash and studied him with a derisive glare. "The council…" he uttered. A mirthless laugh followed. "There is no council anymore."

Ashton's eyes darkened, the fire in him stifled by the king's revelation.

"You lie!" I spat, furious at the fiend.

The king's face brightened with amusement. "Oh, I'm sure I do not," he told me in a low, velvety voice. And leaning forward on the throne, ominous like the flicker or lightning, he added, "I know because... *I killed them.*"

A stuttered gasp escaped me. The blood chilled in my veins.

He sank into his chair. "What good were they? Pesky sycophants," he mumbled. "They relinquished their power to the king years ago... That's why I finished him, too."

Silence fell heavily upon us.

"Do I scare you?" he asked with feigned concern. "Mm... I'll do whatever it takes to make my court rise from the failure of reigns past. Killing royalty is nothing new to me. I've slain many nobles and kings... and even a queen." He paused. "That troublesome Marioth."

My expression slackened. "You killed Queen Marioth?" I breathed. Fear and anger knotted inside me.

"Aren't you relentless like a lion on the hunt?" a woman said.

The sole voice shot gooseflesh up my arms.

The fae king's attention shifted behind me. Once his stare settled on the newcomer, he growled at her provocatively. His eyes hooded with immediate hunger, tracing the woman's figure as she sauntered towards him.

When she strolled past me, her long crimson velvet cloak slithered along the marble floor. I couldn't see her face as she stopped on the dais, a few feet away from the fae king.

The king grinned in fathomless delight, flashing his fangs like a shameless braggart. Satisfied, he slouched in the throne, and swept a hand under his chin, contemplating the woman.

"You were right, Raathiel," she told him, pulling down her hood. At once, heavy locks of blonde hair tumbled down her back. "Fooling them was easy." The woman whirled on her heels. A sinister smile stretched her carmine lips. She wore crimson plated armor, engraved with emblems of dark magic. Fearsome spikes stemmed from each pauldron.

Slowly, I lifted my gaze and faced this soulless devil, this woman who unleashed tragedy in every kingdom unfortunate enough to suffer her presence.

"Queen Roslyn..." I managed, despite the dryness in my mouth and my heart's quickened beat.

King Raathiel waved a dismissive hand in the air. "They're all yours," he told her. A cold edge of irony sharpened his tongue.

The queen wasted no time. With swiftness, her delicate fingers undid the latches of her cloak, setting the heavy garment free at once. The cloak flopped to the marble floor, allowing the queen to saunter my way while stabbing me with the glare of her incandescent eyes.

"You!" Ash all but hissed. Driven by restless fury, he lurched towards the Evil Queen. A useless attempt, as the troll soldiers only tightened their restraint on him.

The heavy lashes shadowing the queen's cheeks flew up. "Oh, my..." she uttered, seemingly surprised. "Fancy meeting *you* here, Ashton." She swept him with a look of indolence, and once satisfied in her curiosity, her attention shifted towards me again.

"Don't you dare touch her!" The words rumbled out of Ash's throat. He fought against the guards' grip, but to no avail.

Queen Roslyn met his accusing eyes without flinching. "Poor Ash," she said with deceitful grief. "Always picking battles you cannot win." The queen tisked. All compassion dissolved from her face as her features slowly became rigid. "Now, please. Shut your mouth." With a snap of her fingers, Ashton's lips sealed tight. Nothing, save muffled noises of struggle, came through.

The Evil Queen strut forward and halted inches away from my face.

The air caught in my throat, and when I exhaled, it came out in a series of short breaths. Inside, every inch of me shuddered. For I'd witnessed first-hand the queen's dark might. However, I held my bearing. And grinding my jaw, I summoned the courage to say,

"I'm not afraid of you." My quivering hands curled into tight fists.

Her countenance darkened. "You will be," she told me in the lowest of voices, cold and determined. "I want your heart soaked in dread when I snatch it from your chest."

A whimper sailed from my mouth.

The queen's crimson lips eased into a sinister grin. She looked at King Raathiel over her shoulder. The fae monarch matched her smile and nodded in solemn approval.

Pure black dread washed through me at their silent exchange. No good could come out of their allegiance. Against paralyzing fear, I pushed myself to move. I stepped aside, facing the ruthless king. "Why are you doing this?" I begged him, appealing to a shred of goodness in his nature. "Can't you see she's evil?"

King Raathiel's smooth brow barely creased at the beginning of a frown. He bit his lower lip, watching me keenly with fierce eyes. He then stooped in the chair, like a lion ready to pounce on its prey. "Aren't you the woman who killed her own father?" he asked with vicious intent. "Tell me, Maleath Snow, *who* is the villain in this story?"

His pernicious words unleashed a weight upon my chest that robbed me of my breath. If this was indeed his magic, it was the vilest kind. Unconsciously, I took a hand to my throat. "I had no other choice," I stammered, helpless and broken.

"I loved your father!" Queen Roslyn said in a roar of grief, flustered and swayed to the verge of tears, like the truest widow in mourning. "My one chance at happiness is lost because of you!" Unmitigated hatred drenched each word.

I scowled in utter disbelief. "If you'd truly loved him, he wouldn't be dead," I managed in a low, doleful tone.

I stepped back when a sudden jolt of pain throbbed in my hand. The ache quickly grew louder, inescapable, like a portentous scream.

"How dare you—?" the queen spat.

"Snow," the fae king interrupted, deliberately disregarding my royal title. A gentle finger softly pointed at my hand. His eyebrows tangled in fictitious woe. "You're… *bleeding.*"

I held my hand at eye level and watched in terror as a crimson drop scurried from my leather glove and splashed on the pristine floor. My face slackened in dismay. With haste, I peeled off the glove. A tendril of panic shot through my being when I realized the wound carved by Daron's blade had reopened. Fresh blood gushed out of my palm in lazy rivulets that trickled down my hand.

Ash groaned in protest. Out of the corner of my eye, I watched him fight the pair of trolls until he became free, earning a blow to his stomach that immediately winded him.

The pain in my hand worsened. It shot up my arm and spread through my being like a flash of lightning, weakening my limbs. At once, my knees buckled, and I crashed to the floor.

The queen pressed a hand to her mouth, stifling her wicked giggles. "Raathiel, you fiend..." She looked at him with amused wonder. "I absolutely adore you."

When a bout of rich laughter blasted out of the king's throat, not a soul in court joined him. I took my focus off the wound, deeply unsettled by the court's behavior. That's when I saw the quiet despair that paled their faces.

Swift as it had struck, the pain washed away. My gaze cut to my hand again. I started. The wound was no more. Not a trace of blood stained my palm or smeared the floor. It had all been... an illusion.

I glared at the fae usurper with shuddering eyes. Raathiel Ivasaar was not only king of the Marble Court. He was also the King of Deceit.

"Shall I wrap them for you?" he purred to Queen Roslyn.

"You may keep the shifter boy," she told him. "I only want *her*." A crooked finger targeted me.

Ash growled, unable to voice his rage. At once, the guards crushed his shoulders with mighty hands and pinned him on his knees.

For the first time since I'd met him, the fae monarch rose from the throne. "Throw him into the dungeon," King Raathiel said in a dispassionate voice.

"No!" I uttered, too damaged to rise to my feet.

Ash resisted the guards yet again. His defiance cost him dearly.

"Like it or not, you're coming with us," a troll guard said. At those words, his fist swung down and punched Ashton's face. A crimson drizzle spotted his shirt when his lip burst open. Ash groaned. He winced and shook his head, fighting to stay alert.

"*Please*!" I begged. "*Please*, stop! Don't hurt him!"

It shattered me to see Ashton's body give out, his head hanging low as the guards dragged my love out of the hall. I did not know if he was conscious, and that only increased my pain.

My throat clenched tight. Through teary eyes, I saw the queen stroll towards the fae usurper waiting for her on the dais. He welcomed Queen Roslyn with an extended hand, aiding her as she climbed the remaining steps to meet him.

With the Evil Queen by his side, King Raathiel snapped his fingers. "Servant!"

A fae footman drew near. He was tall and well

built, with fair long hair that seemed white as sunshine spilled on him. He bowed begrudgingly, and when his head swung up, I glimpsed the deep scar that split his face, from his brow to half his cheek. The mark crossed the fae's glazed left eye. His right, however, was cobalt blue, and turned its hard stare on me.

A shiver skittered down my spine.

"Give me that cloak," the king ordered his steward with unwavering nonchalance.

The scarred fae ground his jaw. With no attempt to conceal his displeasure, the servant swept the garment off the floor, and gathering it to his arms, he offered it to the king.

King Raathiel curled his lips in vicious amusement. "Now go," he told him.

The servant obeyed. And as he marched down the hall's central nave, the king's harsh stare followed him.

"Leave," he commanded, his voice thundering in the hall. "All of you!"

Massive doors cracked open in unison, casting echoes that shook against my chest and tangled with the racing heartbeat throbbing inside me.

Gradually, the crowd dispersed. Within minutes, only the three of us remained, along with the monarch's personal guards.

The King of Deceit paced around Queen Roslyn,

stopping to ease the cloak over her shoulders. "I've kept my promise," he whispered in her ear with a lover's voice as with gentle fingers he latched the garment back in place. "Will you keep yours?"

The Evil Queen flushed. "Raathiel Ivasaar," she managed, "you'll get your crown."

The fae king smoothed his cheek against hers. He closed his eyes, and taking a quick inhalation, he relished in the perfume of her skin. "Stay tonight," he purred, his hand locked on the queen's wrist.

Her lips tensed with the subtlest pleasure. She heaved a sigh. "I'll leave tomorrow at daybreak," she whispered.

My blood boiled with fury. Only minutes ago, the queen had professed nothing but the purest love for my father. And now, she would frolic with the fae usurper.

Not in the least disturbed by my presence, King Raathiel's gaze angled towards me. "What shall we do with her until then?" he asked the Evil Queen. "I can lock her in the grey tower..."

"No," she said, watching me sidelong. "Put her in the dungeon." She paused. "Use the cell closest to the shifter boy."

"Very well, my queen." Raathiel slowly stepped back. He descended the dais and moved towards me, locking me in an unshakable glare.

I wanted to scream, but my voice seized up. I tried to rise and run, but my limbs refused to listen.

The King of Deceit ambled closer. Upon his nearness, I picked up again that soothing fragrance… It reminded me of the red woods after the summer rain. The perfume filled my lungs in constant, appeasing waves.

"You're exhausted, Snow," he spoke without moving his lips. *"You want to sleep."* His voice was enticingly lulling. Even then, a numbed sense of alertness stirred inside me.

The fae king was in my head. This was bad.

Instant drowsiness took over me. "No," I breathed in a dull voice, struggling to keep my eyes open.

He stopped inches away, looking down at me with indolent, stormy eyes. Within seconds, invisible fingers seized my throat, diving deeper and tighter.

"Let go," he whispered in my mind. It wasn't a suggestion.

My vision blurred.

Everything went black.

My eyelids fluttered gently, like a newborn butterfly's wings. I cracked open my eyes and squinted at my surroundings. A flaming torch flickered nearby. Scant amber light outlined the bars that imprisoned me. I lay on an icy stone floor with a thin layer of scattered straw that neither offered warmth nor comfort.

Slowly sitting down, I rubbed the drowsiness from my eyes and sucked in a deep breath. The air was musty and bitter. How many hours had passed? I did not know. Wrath simmered in the pit of my stomach as reality came crashing hard: I was a prisoner of King Raathiel the Usurper.

A chirp startled me fully awake. I looked up. Inside the cell in front of mine, I found the snowy owl, restless, flapping his wings. At once, Ash lifted in flight, silken feathers glistening with pulsing magic.

He darted towards the door, determined to glide between the bars. They were wide enough. And when he came close to managing this feat, a shock of lightning beamed off the gate and shot him flying backwards.

My lips parted in dismay. "Oh, Ash!" I gasped, getting on my knees. "Are you hurt?"

The owl hooted. Once more, he set in flight. And again, the cell's magic repelled him. I feared if he insisted, the damage might be too great. "Ash," I told him, in as collected a voice as I could manage. My hand reached towards him, though touching the bars was unthinkable. "It's all right. Everything's going to be all right." I knew well it would not. Soon, the sun would rise, and the Evil Queen would send her guards to fetch me.

My words touched him. His owl form stopped struggling.

The warmth of forthcoming tears rose to my eyes as I realized these would be our last moments together. These would be the last words he'd hear me speak. I strengthened myself with the conviction that I wouldn't have his last memory of me be that of a fearful woman, broken and weak.

"Do you remember the day we met?" I whispered,

brushing a hand under my nose. "I thought you were the proudest man I'd ever come across." A brief laugh escaped me. "And I've met my fair share of arrogant men, believe me." My brow lifted sky-high, my lips easing into a sour smile.

The owl flapped his wings. He moved closer to the gate, keeping a safer distance this time.

"You proved me wrong so quickly," I managed through my tightened throat. I swallowed hard, fighting back the ripple of heartache that washed through me. "And that day at the Night Garden?" I pursed my lips. "I'll never forget that last dance…"

Suddenly, his wings became alight with radiant magic, stronger than I'd ever witnessed. So much light beamed from him that I had to shut my eyes and look away. But compelled, I shielded my brow with my forearm, and squinted through the flood of magic. The light was expanding into a man's figure. Pristine feathers stretched into long fingers. Wings reshaped into muscular arms... From this perfect pool of light, my love emerged. His sculpted body, bare and shuddering with cold.

Unable to hold back any longer, I wept in silence, covering my mouth with a hand to stop myself from sobbing.

Ash grabbed his clothes from the ground and slipped them on. And when his sweet hazel eyes found mine, they were shimmering—not with magic, but in the crudest pain.

"I have failed you," he said in a low, mournful tone. "Forgive me, Snow." A dark cloud settled on his features.

"But how have you failed me?" I asked, moving closer.

"I should have acted faster," he managed through gritted teeth. "At the first sign of danger, I should have turned back..." The words sailed into silence. "I jeopardized your safety and exposed you to this evil!" His brow creased in unmitigated sorrow.

"Don't do this to yourself," I breathed, slipping my fingers through the bars. A tingle shot up my hand. "No one could have foreseen any of this."

"*I* should have," he replied, shutting his eyes. And as he lowered his head, he rubbed a hand over them. "Some hero I turned out to be..." A mirthless laugh drifted out of his mouth.

"What are heroes if not rebels with a bit of luck?" I told him.

Ash slowly raised his head, his expression stricken with wonder. "You're absolutely right," he said, slipping a bold hand between the bars. A flicker of light burst when his grip tightened around one, but nothing more. "This isn't the end." His voice carried unwavering resolve. "I'll make my own luck. Snow, I promise you. I'll find a way."

The corner of my lips curled. "I believe you," I said as newfound confidence bloomed in my spirit.

Heavy boots stomped against the stone. The clank of a bucket kicked on the floor resounded in the dungeon.

"The guards," Ash stated.

"I know."

Within instants, a towering troll soldier stood before my cell. The hilt of his long sword glinted spectrally in the dim light. "Rise and shine, Your Highness," he said in a gruff voice, slipping a key inside the lock. "Time to go."

Panic rioted inside me.

Ashton's countenance stiffened in sheer fury when the soldier grabbed my arm, hauling me to my feet. A growl lingered in his chest. Against the violence of his feelings, he refrained from uttering a sound. Fearful of risking my safety, I assumed.

"Snow!" Ash finally said between quickened breaths.

I looked back.

"I love you," he said.

His words unlocked me, heart and soul.

"Let's go!" the guard roared, yanking my arm, all but dragging me out of the dungeon.

"Prove it to me," I told Ash as I walked across his cell, a grin stretching my crimson lips. And all the while, my mind spoke these words again and again: *He loves me. Ash loves me as I love him.*

Ash smiled back. "I will." His voice, terse and sincere, worked the truest spell. It stirred a breath of life into my frozen heart. It created something out of nothing.

Hope.

CHAPTER TWENTY-NINE

We rode across the Red Forest, leaving behind a blood-streaked sky, and headed towards an overcast horizon. The queen's cavalcade moved south, to the land that had seen me grow into a young princess. Grimly fitting that Whitehaven would also witness my demise.

Queen Roslyn's Red Army escorted the stately assemblage. The undead soldiers concealed their monstrous looks in scarlet plated armor with grisly spiked helms. I shivered when I glimpsed a flash of marmoreal skin, the unnatural gleam of violet eyes.

I looked away, clearing my mind as it tried to reconstruct the shocking image of their rotting faces. My shoulders dropped with a heavy sigh. I turned my thoughts to Ash. To the words he'd said as he professed his love, and the promise he made. He loved me. My lips eased into a smile.

"I don't like this one," a troll soldier told his mate. The voice came hoarse as a growl. "Look at her. The way she's smiling… It makes me shudder."

I stared down at the ropes that tethered my saddle's pommel to the queen's carriage. Escaping was unthinkable. A troll squad surrounded me, watchful and leery, as if I might destroy them with a puff of air.

"I'd wipe that grin off," the troll soldier continued, eyeing me sidelong. His unwavering hand glided to the dagger cinched to his leg. "But the queen said we can't touch her."

"It's the fae king's doing," the other replied, catching up with my horse from the opposite side. The trolls bounced wary glares between them, with me in the middle. "He plays tricks on their minds until they lose their wits. It's madness."

"Or she's a witch," the first guard cockily retorted, shooting up an eyebrow.

My jaw clenched tight. "Maybe I'm both," I turned to say, stabbing him with a glare. "A mighty witch with an unsound mind."

The soldier startled. A cloud of wariness set on his face. He swallowed hard.

"I'd be careful if I were you," I added in a cool voice.

"Don't look at her!" the second troll all but hissed. "And you. Shut up."

The queen's carriage slowed its pace. I watched ahead as the Red Army's captain raised a hand. The procession reined into a halt. At once, the horses became restless. They neighed and whinnied, strutting side to side, shaking their heads with agitation.

My brow creased into a frown. "What's happening?" I mumbled.

The eeriest stillness scattered in our midst. A murder of crows cawed nearby. The guards remained alert, sweeping the woods with sharp eyes.

It began with a tremor. At first, I thought it came from the disquiet brewing inside me, but as the rumble increased, it became clear to me that something terrible headed our way.

"It's an earthquake!" a troll guard announced.

"No," I managed, bracing myself. "It's something infinitely worse." I paused, locking my gaze between the trees. "And it's coming."

The furious tide swept through the forest in a blaze of darkness. A merciless horde of black unicorns charged against the caravan, ramming into the squad like a tempestuous storm. Within seconds, horses and riders flung off the ground, swept by the galloping swarm into a shadowy cloud of dirt and shrieking screams.

I tightened my grip as my horse reared and whinnied, desperate to flee. Queen Roslyn's carriage had escaped the unicorn's attack, and so had I. But luck had not spared us from their wrath. The unicorns closed in, encircling us in a wild gallop.

"Easy girl," I whispered to my unsettled mare. As her temper simmered down, I swept my tied hands along her mane of chestnut hair. "Easy there... Easy."

When the unicorn's mighty run came to a halt, a door opened from the queen's carriage. I watched as the Evil Queen descended, burdened with annoyance. Her golden locks bounced off her cloaked shoulders when her boots touched the ground.

"Pesky unicorns," she muttered, not in the least intimidated as she faced their dark muzzles. "I've had enough of you." She paused, glancing at the fearsome horde. "Go away now, before I curse you!"

The unicorns kept their bearing. They did not move an inch.

A neigh speared through the silence. Slowly, the menacing gathering before us parted, giving way to their missing member.

The glistening white unicorn emerged, strutting calmly into the road. Its magic beamed so brightly it swallowed the rider that came with it.

The creature stopped a few feet from the queen. Gradually, its light diminished, and the rider's silhouette appeared, soaked in radiance like a blazing deity. The man sheathed his sword fast and dismounted in a swift leap.

Never had I been so glad to see pale blue eyes.

"Leander..." I gasped. My heart quickened with hope.

As the dust slowly settled, five more riders emerged from the horde. I recognized Thuriad's piercing green eyes, Akron's fair hair swaying in the breeze, the scar on Essgard's face. Romni and Millindrel rode beside them.

The Seven. They'd come to my rescue.

The Evil Queen's kohl-rimmed blue eyes widened in undiluted shock. Her crimson lips slightly parted. The wind was stiff when it picked up. It gathered her red cloak and shook her royal banners.

"Leander." She spoke the name with contained fury. "What do you think you're doing?" Her leather gloved hands squealed as they clenched into tight fists. "Leave at once. Go back to your group of merry men!" A wry smile curled her mouth.

A roar of laughter burst from the remaining trolls. The Red Army, however, kept eerily still, waiting for their queen's command.

Leander took a step forward. "Let Snow go," he said. His voice was a gentle plea rather than a challenge. *I beg you,* his eyes told her.

Queen Roslyn flinched. "Don't be ridiculous! You *know* I cannot do that," she snapped, hatred hanging from each word.

Meanwhile, out of the corner of my eye, I caught the movement of a shadow. It stealthily stirred between the trolls.

Leander's expression slackened. "This is not the way," he said, holding an appeasing hand in the air. As if that gesture alone might ease the Evil Queen's ire.

A stuttered breath fled from the queen's lips. For a second, her confidence wavered. But she straightened her poise just as fast. And lifting her chin, she looked down at the Seven's leader. "You're wrong," she told him in a dispassionate voice. "It's the *only* way."

The shadow drew closer. Carefully, I peered to my side and saw the hooded rider flashing a silvery dagger in his grip. I couldn't see his face, as a dark scarf concealed it.

"It's too late, Leander." For the first time, Queen Roslyn lost all pretense as she spoke. And for the first time, as she bowed her head and swallowed her tears, I glimpsed her pain.

"Don't say that," Leander Sár whispered, warm and caring. He took one more step.

The mysterious rider stood beside me. With a finger pressed against his veiled face, he warned me to be silent. And I did as he asked, because by then I'd already recognized his gleaming hazel eyes.

Ash slipped the dagger between my wrists and slashed the rope in a single swing. He then cut the tether to the carriage and climbed on my mare, sitting behind me. His strong arms slipped under mine and hugged my waist. The comfort of his firm chest pressed against my back eased my apprehensions.

He leaned closer, tightening his grip, taking hold of the reins. And smoothing his cheek against mine, he whispered in my ear, "Don't worry, my love. We're getting out of here."

A thrill coursed through my veins. I longed to hold him tight and kiss him, and there would be a time for that. But for now, I simply nodded.

With a thief's agility, Ash began to steer the horse away from the caravan.

"We can still solve this," Leander told the queen with mellow softness. "Together."

Queen Roslyn ground her jaw, her eyes blazing with impatience. "We can't," she said in a choked voice. "Don't you see? My time is all but spent." She boldly met his eyes. "It's over!" And swinging her cloak away with a swift pass of her arm, she whirled towards her carriage.

"*Galhöe!*" Leander roared. "There's been too much

death already. You must stop this now!" His thunderous voice resounded in the woods.

Sheer shock flew through me. "Galhöe?" I turned to Ash.

His fierce eyes twinkled like precious gems. "We're leaving," he said curtly, and at that, Ash yanked the reins. The horse gave a loud neigh, drawing all stares upon us.

"Guards!" the queen howled, a crooked finger pointing at us. "Seize them! They're getting away!"

At the monarch's call, the Red Army drew out swords and mallets. But it was too late for them to act. Ash and I darted deep into the forest, heading to the clearing where the portal well waited.

CHAPTER THIRTY

When dusk set in, the sickle moon fled the sky, leaving behind a blanket of glittery stars. We gathered outside the Seven's lair, sitting by a roaring firepit. Leander lingered by the doorway, withdrawn and pensive. A few feet away, I glimpsed Ash in his owl form. He was watching us, perched up in the nearest tree. An impenetrable silence scattered in our midst.

Too many worries burdened my whirling mind. I was thankful to the mages for rescuing me, drained after suffering the fae king's captivity, hopelessly heartbroken by the painful distance carved between Ash and me because of his curse. Lowering my head, I heaved a sigh.

A cool breeze sailed across the land, smooth and comforting, sweeping up wisps of rose petals and leaves. A faint shiver scurried up my arms. I hugged myself and stroked them.

"Snow..." A warm voice spoke behind me. When I swung my head, I found Akron's gentle eyes. He eased a white woolen blanket over my shoulders and offered me a steaming mug. "Drink this, why don't you? It's getting chilly."

I gave him the hint of a smile, at once taking the mug off his hands and bringing it close to my lips. The delightful aroma of cinnamon reached my lungs, spiced with a pinch of ginger and clove.

The mage trudged back to the circle, and releasing an old man's groan, he sat on the sculpted tree stumps that served as our chairs. Sometimes I forgot these men were centuries old. Their youthful guise was too deceiving.

"Brindel is coming," Essgard mumbled, leaning towards the firepit with a stick in his grip. Cinders snapped when he poked at the fire, stirring charred logs off the fresh timber.

As the fairy captain sauntered down the maple-tree road, the wind picked up tendrils of her fawn hair and tangled them playfully. She cleared them from her cheeks with a brush of her hand and settled with us by the fire. While the flames' copper radiance bounced off her flawless countenance, a stern expression etched on her features.

"So, you've heard the news?" Millindrel said, slightly raising his brow. "The Fae Council has fallen."

Brindel nodded gravely.

Thuriad growled. He snatched away the fire poker from Essgard's hands. "Our cause is lost," he grumbled, giving the logs one quick stab. "No one will fight with us now. Not with Raathiel as king of the Marble Court."

"I hear he's being crowned soon," Brindel said in a dull tone.

"That traitorous vermin!" Thuriad spat, stabbing the firepit again. In a fit of fury, he tossed the fire poker aside and cursed.

I took a large swig from my mug. At once, the tea's warmth spread through my limbs, as comforting as a long embrace.

"What about Queen Inoue?" Romni asked quietly.

His twin turned to the fairy captain. "Will the Diamond Court fight against the Evil Queen?" Millindrel's brow furrowed.

Brindel lowered her chin. Her eyes glazed slowly, and without uttering a sound, she shook her head.

"Why would they go back on their promise?" I blurted, stricken with grief more than anger. It demolished me to know that as the bleakest shadow hung above my kingdom, I was powerless to spare my people from their doom.

"It's the council's raid all over again," Thuriad said in a smoother voice, yet no less harsh in the words of his choosing. "They betrayed us then. Why wouldn't they do it now?" He pursed his lips tight. "I'm sorry, Brindel. But you know it's true."

Brindel clasped her hands in silent admission. "My people are too frightened," she explained. "Raathiel Ivasaar is a formidable adversary as it is. This allegiance to the Evil Queen makes a devastating combination. A force too great to be defeated."

"What about the dwarves, the pixies... the blasted unicorns?" Essgard pressed, holding his mug with both hands.

"I've spoken with them for hours," she breathed. "They will not fight." Brindel slumped her shoulders.

"If not even the captain of Queen Inoue's Royal Guard can persuade them, then our cause is truly hopeless." Akron's voice was drenched in gloom as it speared through the stillness.

All eyes turned to Leander when he arrived. Silence enveloped us. A frail pane of glass, seconds away from shattering. And I knew that it would, because I'd be the one to break it.

"You called her Galhöe." The words rolled off my tongue, spiteful as they left my mouth. I watched

Leander with sheer scrutiny, unsure whether to make him out as friend or foe.

My focus shifted to Thuriad, who stood next to the mage's leader. "You told me Galhöe was dead," I challenged, narrowing my eyes.

"*Gone*," the mage mildly corrected. "Taken from us years ago."

Leaning forward, I rested my elbows on my knees. "If Queen Roslyn is Galhöe, and she was one of the Seven, then surely there was a time when she shared your views," I said without inflection, wearied in body and soul. "What made her change?"

Leander slumped in the seat. He smoothed his hands over his knees and exhaled a long breath. His brooding eyes swept the gathering, as if searching for approval. And when his gaze returned to meet mine, he pursed his lips. "Brace yourself, lass. It's a long story," he told me.

"I've got time to spare," I replied in a cool voice.

The mage sighed. "It happened five hundred years ago," he began. "Galhöe and I, we were *children in magic* back then."

My jaw slackened. Five hundred years. Merely contemplating such a period took my breath away. Considering Leander's lifespan would surely crush my mind. This man looked no older than twenty-three.

As difficult as it was, I shed those thoughts from my head and focused on his story.

"We were strolling through the Red Forest, heading home, when we came across an old woman in need." His ice-blue eyes fixed on the flames, as if pulling those vivid memories from the firepit. "Galhöe's heart, more generous than mine, compelled her to the woman's aid." A glint of magic flickered across his face. "'*Help me, child,*' the woman said. '*For I am hungry and I've lost my fruit basket. Age has stripped the sharpness from my poor eyes… Won't you find it for me?*'

"Galhöe promptly agreed, and I begrudgingly followed… At length, we stumbled upon an old cottage hidden in the woods. And sitting by the door, lay the woman's wicker basket." Leander's expression darkened. "Galhöe reached for the basket, but it was not what it seemed. The straw swiftly sprung wicked vines that wrapped around her ankles out of their own accord. Within instants, they bound her legs, her knees, and tangled higher, until the woman's fiendish trap muffled my sister's screams."

I blinked, barely able to restrain a gasp. I glanced at the faces surrounding me, picking up heartbreak, but no trace of the astonishment that swept through me. All along, they'd always known Leander and Galhöe were brother and sister… *Leander, Queen Roslyn's brother!* It was too terrible a thought.

Leander addressed my shock with a subtle nod. He then continued, "Icy fear twisted in my heart when the old woman shed from her guise and revealed herself as a powerful sorceress. *'Release my sister!'* I demanded with the fiercest fury. My zealous affection amused the sorceress greatly. A malevolent laugh rumbled in her throat. *'And why would I do that?'* she asked me. *'I need her youth to live. I will have her. Now go!'*

"*'Take me instead, foul witch!'* I hissed, stepping in her way. But my offer only spurred the woman's mirth. *'You are meaningless to me,'* she told me. *'The spell calls for an unspoiled maiden. I have what I need.'* The deceitful woman flung a hand in the air, casting me aside in a violent blow of magic.

"Lying on the ground, I watched her climb the steps to her front porch. Anger built up inside me like a disastrous storm. At the whim of my power, the air harshly shifted in our midst. Overcast skies darkened the land, flickering with the spark of lightning. The sorceress turned her wary eyes toward me. She knew then *I too* wielded unfathomable power."

Thunder roared in the distance. I pulled the blanket tighter around my frame as a shiver rippled through my being.

"*'Libera. Draconem. Mago','*" Leander whispered, his voice drifting into silence.

"Brother, don't..." Thuriad begged, all fury drained from his face as melancholy took over.

Leander held out his hand, asking for some leniency, which the red-haired mage cautiously granted. "My pride got in the way," he told me. "It fooled me into believing that despite my brief experience as a mage, I could defeat the vicious sorceress." He paused. "But I was wrong."

The mage hesitated to say more. It took him dragging a deep breath to garner the resolve to finish the story. I waited patiently.

"When my sister's bonds snapped, I sighed in relief. I welcomed Galhöe as she dashed to my arms, shuddering in dread. *'Let's get out of here,'* I whispered in her ear. *'Walk with me. Pay no attention to the old woman.'* We stalked away from the mighty witch, careful not to show our fear. For all creatures of magic are drawn to such emotions.

"The witch did not protest as we escaped. For all her lies, her blindness had been true. I considered ourselves lucky to walk away unscathed from such a perilous encounter. Relief found a way to my heart. But my reprieve was short-lived, as another eerie cackle burst from the sorceress' mouth. The sound expanded and increased, louder until it resounded in the woods, spreading dread across the land.

"I halted at the edge of the clearing. *'What amuses*

you so?' I demanded from the witch. Galhöe protested, but I would not listen.

"*'You do!'* the cunning sorceress said. *"'You think you've saved her? Take her, I no longer want her!'* The woman's words stirred turmoil in my heart. Swept by dread, I gripped my sister's hand. Her safety concerned me more than ever.

"*'You're a fool,'* the sorceress said, pointing at me with a crooked finger. *'You've cast the wrong spell. She would have had a better fate with me!'*

"*'Stop speaking to us in riddles,'* Galhöe muttered, curling her hands into fists. *'Tell us what you know!'*

"The woman turned her vacant eyes on my sister. *'Your sweet brother has damned you forever,'* she told her. *'Thanks to his enchantment, from this day forward, you will no longer be human, but a creature that shifts in the night. Each time you change the spell will eat away a piece of your human heart. And by the end of five hundred years, there will be nothing left. The beast will win over the woman!'*

"*'A beast?'* Galhöe stammered, her face pale with fear."

Leander stopped. He shut his eyes and turned away, consumed by pain and regret. "My hate was such that I threw myself against the evil sorceress, willing to destroy her with my bare hands. But Galhöe stopped me..." His eyes cracked open. "Even then, she pitied the old fiend." A bitter smile curled his lips.

"*'Yours is truly a generous heart,'* the woman told her, moved by my sister's gesture. *'You would spare me from your brother's wrath, and you would spare him from your rightful scorn.'* She paused. *'A royal heart, the fruit of love. Become a queen and rule the dark… Only then will you be saved!'* Having said that, the witch clapped her hands and disappeared into the ether, never to be seen or heard of ever again."

Leander exhaled. "So that is how I doomed my sister. Foolishly attempting to save her. The shifter's curse is the reason my dearest Galhöe fled the Seven's safety into the Realm of Man. And when she left, consumed with sadness, she took winter with her."

"That's why it's snowed in Whitehaven for five hundred years," I mumbled, awestruck. After a moment, I flinched. "But the sorceress said Galhöe would shift into a beast every night, like my sweet Ash…" My gaze cut to him for an instant. "And yet, I've met Queen Roslyn several evenings before. I've never known her to become a monster."

"I believe she's found a spell to delay the transformation," Leander replied. "But you see, it's been five hundred years since that day in the forest. Her change will soon become permanent, regardless."

"And so she wants my heart…" I turned to Ash,

peaceful in his owl form. A flicker of apprehension washed through me. "Will that happen to Ash, too?" I asked hurriedly. "Is he sentenced to becoming an owl permanently?"

Leander nodded painfully.

"Oh! My sweet Ash," I breathed, taking a hand to my chest. A thousand shards of glass stabbed my heart. "How can he bear knowing such a fate? He kept this from me, kept his pain silent all this time…!"

Twigs broke nearby.

At once, we jumped to our feet. Swords flung free from their scabbards. Our gazes sharpened, piercing the shadows, watching the figure that stirred in the undergrowth.

CHAPTER THIRTY-ONE

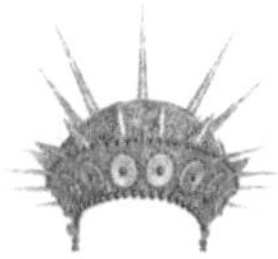

The stranger emerged from the dark. A tall man of a slender but sinewy build. Glistening tendrils of his long, fair hair danced in the humid breeze. He moved closer, stepping warily through the undergrowth.

I tightened the grip on my sword, my pulse throbbing hard in my throat and ears. Out of the corner of my eye, I glanced at the mages. The same heightened alertness brewed in the Seven, casting a most haunting stillness in the woods.

At last, the man reached the firepit's pool of flickering amber light. Without saying a word, he flashed his empty hands at us. Cautiously, he took one to the dark hood that cloaked his identity and dragged it back. I glimpsed his sharp blue eye, and the scar that grooved his other one.

"Put your swords away!" Leander commanded, holding an open hand in the air. "He's a brother fae." Swiftly, he returned the sword to its scabbard.

"I see no fae brother," Thuriad spat, swinging up his blade until its merciless edge kissed the fae's throat. Undiluted contempt stiffened the mage's expression as he leaned forward, green eyes flaming with furious magic. "His lot has sided with the Evil Queen." His voice hardened ruthlessly. "That makes him the enemy."

The fae's cobalt eye fixed its gaze on me.

I blinked. "Thuriad, please!" With a single step, I stood between them. My hand eased on the mage's forearm, the pressure persuasive enough that he finally lowered his weapon. "I know him."

Restless agitation stirred amidst the Seven.

I faced the fae trespasser. "You were at the Marble Hall," I hurried to say, hoping to allay Thuriad's concerns. "You're King Raathiel's steward."

A muscle tensed along the fae's strong jawline. Even as his brow creased at the onset of indignation, the sentiment did little to mar his chiseled features. "No. Not his steward," the fae said through clenched teeth, "but his slave." His breathy voice would appear soothing, but the tone was irascibly patient. It shot gooseflesh up my arms. "And Raathiel Ivasaar is *not* my king."

"I don't believe him." Thuriad shook his head. His weapon remained unsheathed, hanging loosely in his grip, ready to swing at the slightest sign of trouble. "Our friends alone hold the key to pass through the portal well." He paused, spearing the fae with a glare. "How did you get here?"

"I followed you to the portal and crossed the veil instants before it closed," the fae admitted with a shrug.

The answer proved less than satisfactory to Thuriad. He squinted at the intruder. "Are you the king's spy?" he demanded. "Did he send you?"

"Oh, Thuriad." Essgard tisked. "You think everyone's a spy," he mildly teased, patting the mage's tense shoulder. His dark stare cut to the fae. "Now, lad. You better start talking before my friend here loses his patience." Essgard's hand glided away from Thuriad's shoulder and slipped to the hilt of his sword.

"He's not a spy," Brindel said, ambling closer. Her face clouded with confusion. The fairy captain stopped inches away from the intruder. "He's Arthion Thamaris, younger brother to the fallen Fae King, and rightful heir to the Marble Court's crown." A subtle frown creased her brow. "Why have you come here?"

My shoulders jumped at the roar of thunder. Lightning cracked the darkened sky. No more stars twinkled above us.

"A storm is coming," Leander told Arthion. His hand warmly folded around the fae's arm. "Come join us inside. We can dine and drink, and then we'll talk."

"I'm afraid I cannot stay long," Arthion said hurriedly. "I've come here hoping I might serve our cause."

"Speak then, my friend," Akron prompted, settling next to Brindel.

"There will be a feast tomorrow at Whitehaven Castle." Arthion spoke in a hushed voice, his stare drifting towards the trees. "Excuse me, I... I've grown wary of the shadows." He hesitated. "Raathiel has kept a close watch over me ever since..." His brother's demise, I assumed, but the words trailed off into silence. "Queen Roslyn will hold a lavish ball in honor of Raathiel's coronation." He pursed his lips. "She will bring forth their grievous alliance into the Realm of Man."

The blood chilled in my veins. A stuttered gasp escaped me.

Arthion's focus lodged on Leander. "I've gathered a small battalion willing to strike Raathiel tomorrow," he said. "And I thought perhaps... we might..."

"Join forces," I added knowingly.

"Princess Maleath." Arthion bowed his head. "Our numbers are far from impressive. But the

Seven's magic and my brothers' fighting skills might just be enough to stop imperiling darkness from spreading through our lands."

I nodded.

"What's the plan?" Thuriad asked, finally gliding the sword into its scabbard.

"Whitehaven's keep will be open to the people for the coronation," Arthion told him. He slowly swept us with a glance, addressing each. "We will blend with the crowd. I will position my men at all points of entry." He paused. "At my discrete signal, they will seal the doors shut. And then…"

"We attack," Millindrel said with fierce resolve.

"Deal with Raathiel as you wish," Leander softly said. "But allow us to handle Queen Roslyn ourselves." He spoke not as the Seven's leader, but as an injured brother ensnared in grief and guilt. Who could refuse such a heartfelt request?

"Do you agree to this?" the mage added with a hopeful expression.

Arthion inclined his head. "You have my word," he told him. "No harm will come to Queen Roslyn from my court's hands."

"Good. When shall we meet?" Leander asked, his confidence rebuilt.

"Meet us at the castle's gates at sunset," Arthion replied.

"We will," Leander said. "Go now, my brother. Return to the Marble Court before you're missed."

Arthion Thamaris' lips thinned wryly. He stepped back, ready to begin his journey, when suddenly he halted and whirled on his feet.

"Princess Maleath," he said, snatching a small felt bag from his leather belt. "Take this!" With a smooth flick of his wrist, he tossed the purse in the air.

Startled, I caught it in my hands.

"For the prince!" Arthion added. "When the time comes. So that he may fight with us." A slight smile danced on his lips. He then pulled the hood over his head and leapt into the night, disappearing in an instant.

CHAPTER THIRTY-TWO

A stiff breeze lashed through the woods. The leaves stirred with violence, their rustle a most foreboding song. Cold seeped through my doublet, shooting an instant shiver down my spine. I tightened the cloak around my neck. My gaze angled skywards, to pitch darkness cracked with lightning.

"We should go inside," Akron said, whirling on the ball of his feet. Romni and Millindrel followed.

Essgard held out an arm, locking his stare on a tree. "Come on, lad!" he called.

The hoot of Ashton's owl form preceded his dive into the clearing. He soared to the mage's forearm, light and pristine as a falling white feather. "Let's get you home," Essgard told him, strolling back to the Seven's lair.

I turned around, ready to do the same, when

Brindel stopped me. She stood in front of me, holding a hand slightly raised. In silence, she asked me to stay. My eyes followed her as she moved past me and stood in the middle of the triangle drawn by Leander, Thuriad, and myself.

She exchanged glances with each of us wearing a hardened expression. "I will fight with you," Brindel finally stated with unwavering conviction.

Thuriad started. "Brindel?" he said with a wary frown. "You can't. You're the captain of the Diamond Army. Joining our fight would mean going against your queen's orders!"

The fairy captain's deep green eyes shifted towards the mage, sparkling with a glint of regret. "I failed you once," she managed. "I should have fought when the council stripped you from your lands." Her eyes shut, tilting her head away in shame.

As Brindel's eyes slowly opened, she met Leander's stare. "I will join you in this fight," she told him. "I will stand for what's right, come what may."

"So be it," Leander said, giving her a swift nod. He then looked over his shoulder, piercing blue eyes spearing through the night to where Arthion had vanished minutes ago. Instants later, he drifted towards the place as if summoned by the woods themselves.

"Where are you going, man?" Thuriad said in a blurt.

Leander did not look back. "I'm going for a walk," he said under his breath, his voice laden with exhaustion. He trudged further into the woods, keeping his head low, his shoulders slouching. The turmoil brewing in his heart was all but tangible. I could imagine his dismay. His only sister was a wicked sorceress. She'd take down an entire kingdom if it meant she'd become free from the curse he'd cast on her.

"There's a storm coming..." Thuriad added in a cautious tone.

"I'll be fine," Leander dismissed, before slipping into the evening's thick shadows.

I watched Brindel intently, then strode to the door.

"Snow," she said, quickly matching my pace.

"I appreciate your gesture," I told her curtly, folding my arms across my chest as I kept moving. "You kept true to your word."

"Snow," she insisted, gliding a delicate hand on my arm.

The first drops of rain fell as we stopped at the doorway. "I regret deeply my people's withdrawal from what will surely be the most decisive battle for both of our realms." Brindel lowered her head until our stares leveled. "Please, do not hold this against them when you are queen."

Ice skittered down my nape at those last words. Too much truth and too much horror hung from them. Never had an uprising like this taken place in the history of the five realms. Our fates and my kingdom depended on tomorrow's triumph. I could not help being bitter at the Diamond Court's betrayal. And yet, Brindel presumed victory would be ours. *When you are queen,* she'd said. Not *if.* Perhaps it was the commander in her. She sought to encourage my desire to take the throne from the Evil Queen's claws. But who was to say what kind of queen I'd become if the odds played in our favor? I myself had no answer to this. Her concerns were well-founded.

"No matter what tomorrow brings," I told her with quiet firmness, "I will always remember your loyalty. It will be an honor to fight by your side, Brindel." I paused. "As for your people..."

The door creaked open. "I'm off to bed," Akron said, pulling the door further. He turned and plodded to the staircase. "Don't stay up too late." The mage yawned, stretching his brawny arms as he climbed the first steps.

Brindel and I strolled into the hall. "We won't," I

assured him, if that would ease his worries. Although I could not guarantee I'd get an ounce of sleep tonight.

"As for my people..." Brindel whispered, standing inches behind me.

I faced her, grief and weariness marring my countenance. "I will seek no vengeance when all is said and done," I told her in reassurance. My hand folded on her arm. "*If* we win this war, I would not care to start another."

The captain's lips thinned into a smile of relief. "We will win," she managed with dazzling determination.

"How can you be so sure?" I urged in the lowest of voices, envious of her certainty.

Brindel leaned forward. "We will win this war," she told me in confidence, "because we have to. Darkness cannot claim this victory."

"Where's *he* off to?" Thuriad asked with a scowl, shutting the door close behind him.

"Oh, Thuriad..." Brindel told him in a soothing tone, easing her hand over his shoulder. "Let Akron be." When the fairy captain ambled to the dining room, her fingers trailed down Thuriad's arm. The mage's eyes almost popped out of their sockets at her warm gesture.

Thuriad caught my prying stare. He cocked up an eyebrow and nudged his head towards the captain, quietly asking if I thought there was a chance she'd be interested in him.

My brow slipped into a frown. *I don't know,* I mouthed soundlessly and shrugged my shoulders.

"I think so too," he whispered back. The mage's stare angled towards the dining hall. He cracked a toothy grin, and squaring his shoulders, he headed to the room with a confident strut.

My eyes flew open. "No, wait!" I all but hissed, going after him. "That is not...!" I halted at the threshold, nearly crashing into Romni.

"Careful there." The warning came in a mellow tone, while Romni swung away the tray in his hands. "Leftovers, anyone?" the mage asked. He carried a plate piled with slices of roast beef, cheese, and bread.

We shook our heads.

"Meh, suit yourselves..." Romni shrugged, setting the tray on the table. The mage dragged a chair near. "So, what's inside?" he casually asked me as he slumped into the seat.

"Inside?" I scrunched my nose, confused.

"The bag Arthion gave you," Millindrel clarified, picking a slice of cheese from his brother's tray.

I'd almost forgotten about that. "I don't know.

Let's see..." I dug my fingers into the felt bag and tugged until it opened. "How very odd. I've not seen anything like it before," I mused, pouring the purse's content into my palm.

A vial filled with a silvery liquid emerged.

Brindel inched closer. "May I?" she asked, offering me her hand.

I silently agreed. The fairy captain took the vial and studied it, rotating it slowly. When she held it against the hearth's flames, the liquid sparkled as if stuffed with pulverized diamonds.

The fae captain's eyes grew alight at a sudden realization. "I know what this is," she mumbled, awestruck. "Griffin tears. An elixir. It's quite rare."

"Rare indeed," Millindrel said, peering at the vial over Brindel's shoulder. "It's been centuries since I last saw one." With unchanged aloofness, he folded the slice of cheese between his fingers and jabbed it into his mouth.

"I'm sure Arthion paid a steep price for it," Essgard uttered, taking the seat near his favorite spot by the fireplace. "*If* he purchased it, that is."

"Why is this so rare and precious?" I asked, looking at the vial. It had no labels, no instructions. "What exactly does this elixir do?"

"What doesn't it do?" Thuriad said, raising his

brow. He'd been sitting in the corner, sharpening his sword, and dropped it on his lap.

"A few drops could revert Ashton's shift or even stop it for a day," Brindel said, returning the vial to my hands. "More than that could be lethal. For all its remarkable power, this poison should not be used lightly."

My gaze cut to Ashton's owl, perched up on the chimney's mantel. "What do you have to say about this?" I tenderly asked, showing him the small crystal vial.

The precious bird cocked its head. He leapt off his watching post and glided towards me, baring sharp claws as if chasing his prey. In a flash, Ash seized the vial. He gave one quick turn about the room and returned to the fireplace, soaring above Brindel's shoulder before settling again on the mantel.

"Looks like he's made his choice," I said, curling the corner of my lips.

Brindel nodded, wearing a thin smile.

"We're off to Port Bree, lads…" Millindrel said, sauntering to the stairway.

"Port Bree?" I flinched. "Now?"

"We'll take the portal," Romni added. "No need to worry. We'll be back in time to fight."

"Have fun, boys," Brindel said, waving them farewell. When she turned to warm her hands by the hearth, I realized Ash had twisted the tight braids that bound her temple's fawn hair. Faeries were so different from the high fae lords and ladies of the Marble Court. They had wings, and rounder, warmer features, and they appeared to be so much kinder.

On an impulse, my fingers reached to untangle her braids. Brindel's wings faintly fluttered as she startled.

"I'm sorry," I hurried to say, feeling my cheeks burn in unstoppable waves. "Ash tied up your braids when he flew by..." I pursed my lips, trapped in the most uncomfortable silence. "They're beautiful."

Brindel stared at me, amused. At least she hadn't found my words insulting. I considered myself lucky not to have sparked the wrath of the captain of the Diamond Court's royal guard.

"Beauty is hardly the intention," Brindel said, sitting on the table. Her brown leather boot quietly landed on a chair's empty seat. All sternness fled from her expression, taken over by a friendly disposition.

"The braids are part of a millenary tradition of my people," she explained, taking a finger to her temple. "Each braid you see here represents an enemy captain slain by my sword."

My expression slackened at her revelation. Countless braids twined Brindel's hair. More than ever, it became clear to me she was a force to be reckoned with.

"I believe you've earned a braid recently," she said, shooting me a knowing look.

I flustered at her remark. There had been neither valor nor merit in my actions that night at the Seven's portal. Giving Daron the final blow had been a last resort to stay alive.

"Beheading an undead captain surely deserves more than a single braid," Thuriad added, joining us by the hearth.

Brindel flashed him a smile. "I believe you're right," she told him.

"None of it would have happened without your help, Brindel," I said in a timid voice, humbled by her achievements. "Now that I think about it, I never even thanked you."

"Don't," she said firmly. "Never thank a fellow soldier in battle, Snow." Brindel's hand smoothed along her thigh, gliding down the straps that sheathed her throwing daggers. Her fingers moved swiftly and drew out the blade mounted on gold filigree, engraved with fae symbols.

"In times of war, we soldiers are one and the same," she continued. Her free hand found mine and dragged it towards her. Carefully, she turned it over. "No ranks exist on the battlefield. No heroes. For all lives are equal in the eyes of death." She slipped the dagger over my palm and gently closed my fingers around its grip. "Remember this, always."

I looked down at the beautiful weapon, unable to fathom the impact of her words. I inclined my head and accepted her gift, slipping the dagger into my belt.

"So, how many braids does Snow get?" Thuriad asked, leaning against the great oak table, a mug full of ale in his hand.

Brindel threw him a mischievous stare. "We shall see," she replied, a hint of playfulness in her voice. Her slender fingers dove into my hair, carefully unpinning it. Dark locks rippled down my back, which she carefully arranged into sections.

"I don't deserve them," I confessed, lowering my gaze in shame. "Back there, at the hill, I was not brave. Daron forced me to act. I had no other choice." I picked at my nails.

Brindel sucked at her teeth. "And what's bravery if not acting in the face of evil?" she asked, her voice smooth as velvet. "Darkness waits in the fight ahead, and it is such as none of us would ever wish to encounter." She paused. "But we will, because we must. We have no choice but to move forward."

"I think she's ready," Essgard said, resolve glinting in his dark eyes.

"Don't you think you should ask her first?" Thuriad snapped mockingly. "She could say no, you know."

My brow creased with worry. "Ready?" I asked. "For what?"

CHAPTER THIRTY-THREE

"What's all this secrecy?" I mumbled, shifting my gaze from one mage to the other.

Thuriad gave his ale a long swig and uttered a sound of enjoyment once he'd swallowed. "He should get one too," he told Essgard, tilting his mug towards Ashton's owl. His twinkling green eyes stared at him sidelong.

"Fine," Essgard replied, folding his arms, throwing Thuriad a smug glare. "You can do his tomorrow." He strolled to the cabinet by the entrance, opened the door, and peered inside. The mage slipped a hand on the top shelf and swept it, blindly looking for something.

"Me?" Thuriad snapped with a scowl.

"Aye... *you*," Essgard told him under his breath. He swung towards the mage, holding a wooden chest he'd recovered from the cupboard. "I'm not risking getting stabbed by Ash." The mage lowered his chin, spearing a dark look at Thuriad. "Accidentally *or* not."

Thuriad threw back his head and roared with laughter. After a while, he stroked the braids in his red beard, trying to regain his aplomb, but a snicker lingered in his mouth. "You're mad if you think I'd ever risk *that*!" he said between persisting chuckles, striding to meet the mage.

Essgard laid the chest on the table. I peered under his elbow as he opened it slowly. Out came a crystal flask filled with dark ink, along with a handful of gold needles.

A heavy sigh sailed through Essgard's lips. He sucked at his teeth. "We should flip a coin," he mumbled, his brow furrowed.

Brindel uttered a brief laugh, quickly covering her mouth with her fingers.

"What are they talking about?" I asked her with a frown. "I don't understand a thing they're saying."

The fairy captain's expression softened. "Brands, love." She spoke in my ear while she finished my last braid. "I pity the mage who brands our Ash." Her sharp green eyes drifted towards his owl form, resting on the chimney mantel. "He's not as tame as he seems now."

"Brands?" I echoed, still puzzled.

"Tattoos," she explained, amused by the mages' discussion.

"Watch your tongue, woman!" Thuriad whirled, aggrieved. "These are no ordinary tattoos." He pointed at the brand on his neck, the veins all but bulging as he spoke. "They're exceptional arcane sigils of protection. Each one tailored to our specific strengths and weaknesses. It's the highest privilege to carry one. No more easily earned than your braids, m'dear." The mage lowered his chin. His left eyebrow rose a fraction.

"All right, all right..." Brindel offered him a forgiving smile. "No need to get so snippy." Her hands glided on my shoulders. "There you are. Three braids make up for one nasty undead captain, I should think," she told me. "Now, go get your brand." A light pat on my back encouraged me.

I took my fingers to my temple, sensing the flawless twists of threaded hair, when my features slipped into a worried grimace. "But will these sigils work on us?" I hesitated to say. "Ash and I... we're no mages. We're just human."

"They will," Essgard assured me. The warmth of his smile reflected in his voice. He offered me his hand and led me to a chair. "And you've earned yours for a while now." As he dragged the ink and needles near, my pulse quickened a little.

"We face a powerful enemy tomorrow," I managed, shifting my focus to Thuriad. "It will be my honor to carry your brand into battle. I'm sure Ash agrees with me."

The owl hooted in complicity.

"Good!" The pristine chime of silver rang when Essgard flipped a coin in the air. "I call heads," he said, trapping it in his hand.

Thuriad leaned closer, looming as the mage revealed the coin. Brindel peered over his shoulder, whereas I had a front-row view of the scene.

Slowly, the mage retrieved his hand. Heads. At once, Thuriad groaned, stepping back. "Arg! You cheated. I'm sure of it." He glowered. "Essgard, you fiend. You know better than to use magic to your advantage!" He trod away, waving a righteous finger.

Essgard started. "Brother, you offend me," he said with steady conviction and a furrowed brow.

"Yeah, yeah..." Thuriad mumbled, waving a hand dismissively. He stopped by the hearth, resting an arm on the chimney mantel.

When Thuriad wasn't looking, Essgard gave me a mischievous wink. With a pass of his hand, the mage revealed the true face of the coin.

It was tails.

An unconscious smile curled my lips.

"Well, then…" Essgard pulled a candlestick near. He dropped into the chair next to mine. "You're one lucky princess, Snow," he told me, grabbing a needle and warming it in the flame. "My unshakable pulse and artistic nature make me the best mage for the job."

I removed my doublet. Essgard rolled up my sleeve and carefully laid my arm on the table.

"Don't you dare punch me tomorrow, lad!" Thuriad scolded the owl, swinging both fists to his hips.

Ashton's amber eyes flickered with the magic of his curse. An indolent chirp came in reply when his wings opened, resembling a shrug.

Undiluted laughter broke from us at his response.

"I guess he'll make no promises," Brindel said, stifling a chuckle.

That did not sit well with Thuriad. He stormed out of the room, crossed and muttering.

"I'll fix this," the fae captain said in an amiable tone, going after him.

"Good luck. The man's unfixable," Essgard mocked, failing to suppress a grin. "Do your best." He dragged the seat closer to me.

"The first jab is unpleasant." Essgard dipped the

needle in the ink, ready to proceed. "The rest will be easier. You grow used to the pain." He turned over my hand. With the other, he dipped a piece of linen into a flask with brown liquid and swabbed my wrist with it.

"Take one deep breath," he murmured, plunging the needle into my wrist. It pricked the flesh as lightly as a thorn. *That's nothing,* I thought, smiling inwardly. Then Essgard pushed the needle further, slipping the black ink into the deeper layers of my skin. That's when the *unpleasantness* began.

"It hurts," I said, not fully convinced I could stand the pain.

Essgard removed the needle and dipped it again in the bottle of ink. He stared at me sidelong. "Nothing worth having ever comes easy." His brows set in a straight line. "Shall I continue?" he turned to ask.

"Yes," I replied, garnering my resolve. "Go on."

"Good choice," he told me with a nod of satisfaction.

As the mage returned to the task, I blurted, "So the songs are true."

He frowned, refilling the needle with ink. "What songs?" he mumbled.

"The ones that say the Fae Council took your lands because you'd share magic with humans," I added, watching him keenly while consciously avoiding any glimpse of my wrist.

"Ah, yes..." He heaved a heavy sigh. "Each of us used to rule over our magedoms." His dark eyes cut to mine. "*Dukedoms*, I believe you'd call them." A furtive smile curled the corner of his lips. He picked up the needle and carried on with the brand. "It wasn't magic that we wanted to share with your realm," he explained. "What we wanted was to strike an allegiance with humans. Put an end to the distance between us."

"Oh." I gasped, transfixed. "I didn't realize..."

"When we learned the council disapproved," he continued, his eyes glazed with the distant memory, "we tried to take matters into our own hands." A mirthless laugh escaped him. "You know how *that* went." He shrugged his shoulders in mock resignation.

"I know what it's like," I told him, resting my chin on the heel of my free hand. "Having everything you had taken away from you."

"Mm..." he uttered, pursing his lips. "I bet you do."

"When we win this war, I will see to it that your land is returned to you." I spoke the words meeting no hesitation. This was my vow to the Seven. It was the least I could offer them after all the kindness they'd shown me. But above all, it was fair and right. They deserved justice.

Essgard's head swung towards me, a flicker of delight crossing his countenance. "Spoken like a true queen," he said, immediately returning to his work.

I flustered.

Minutes sailed between us in silence. Until the mage's work concluded.

"There we go," he said, putting his instruments away. "What do you think?"

My gaze drifted to my wrist for the first time. I couldn't help my jaw from slackening, if only briefly. The brand was a flawless thorn wristband with a rose embedded in the center. A wonderful piece of art. Words eluded me.

"Do you like it?" he asked, giving me a hopeful look.

"Like it?" I mumbled, turning my wrist towards the hearth's flickering light. "It's beautiful." Suddenly, a thought slipped into my mind. My eyebrows knitted together.

"What is it?" the mage said, leaning forward.

"Well, I..." I wavered to say more. "I thought you'd give me a bigger brand." I looked at the ones inked on Essgard's neck, his hands and forearms. The mage was covered in them.

He purred a soft laugh while putting the cleaned

tools back inside the chest. The mage closed the box and faced me, wearing a grin of amusement. "With your fiery temper, that's all the protection you'll ever need," Essgard said.

Our laughter resounded in the stillness of the great hall.

Ash soared about the room and landed on the table, inches away from my arm. "We should get some sleep," I said, smoothing my fingers through his silken wings. "We have a ball to attend tomorrow."

I shut my eyes and forced myself to sleep. After a while, I realized it wouldn't work. As I lay in my bedroom's twilight, I hugged my pillow. Restless, eager for tomorrow, I waited for the first beams of sunrise to break through the drapes when gentle fingers glided on my waist.

With eyes wide open, I rolled on the mattress. Immediate joy washed through me as I met gleaming hazel eyes. "Ash!" I breathed, my pulse quickening fast as lightning.

The sickle-shaped moon peered through the window. Had I somehow fallen asleep?

This was no dream. Ash was kneeling at the bedside. A soft smile tugged at the corner of his lips. Taken by sheer bewilderment, my hands reached his, tugging him closer. "Oh, I missed you," I whispered.

Without saying a word, Ash glided on the bed. I sat up at once and snuggled against his firm, chiseled chest. "How did you...?" I managed, parting enough to sweep his handsome face with a glance. "You used the griffin tears... But, Brindel said—"

My sweet prince wrapped an arm around my waist, hauling me close until his stubble grazed my cheek. "Is that really how you'd like to spend the evening with me," he purred, quirking up an eyebrow, "talking about what Brindel said?"

I shook my head, yielding to his warm hold.

"Mm." He nodded, pleased. "Anyway, I'm deeply grateful to whoever found this elixir."

A frown gradually creased my brow. "Do you not remember?" I asked, my mind reeling with confusion and sudden wariness. "Ash, do you keep any awareness when you shift into an owl?" I'd never dared to ask as I did now, knowing his curse could ultimately consume him and trap him into his shifter form.

I wished Ash himself would have told me the truth of his curse. But that wouldn't change a thing.

How much time did we have left? The question tormented me incessantly. But I swallowed my fears. In a few hours, I would defeat Queen Roslyn, and all dregs of her evil would vanish from this earth. For my kingdom, and my love. I could not afford to believe otherwise.

A flicker of magic glinted in his eyes. Ash turned away, avoiding my stare. He gnawed at his lower lip, then mumbled, "I do. It's just.... uh..." He wavered. "Lately, it's been a challenge." He pursed his lips, reluctant to say more. However, he pushed himself to speak. "When I come back to my human form, I remember some things. But others..." His voice came low, strained with pain.

"It's all right." My grip tightened on his hand in reassurance. "It was Arthion Thamaris," I told him. "He wanted you to have it. He's…"

His head swung towards me. "He's a friend," Ash eagerly interrupted. "Arthion set me free from the Fae King's prison."

I started. "What?"

He climbed on the bed and sat cross-legged close to me. "Minutes after you left Valathüre's dungeon, Arthion came to see me." His breath escaped in a swift exhalation. "He told me his story and revealed his plan to overthrow Raathiel Ivasaar. When he released me, he said he'd hoped the gesture might prove his allegiance to us." He stretched the last words for emphasis. "Arthion vowed to fight on our side with his army against the wicked pair of monarchs."

My expression hardened with resolve. "That's exactly what we'll do," I told him.

"Yes," he said knowingly. "The time has come, my

love. And I will keep my promise." His soft fingers slid along my jawline. "I will be your champion." Ash leaned closer until our brows touched. His lips found mine in one slow, meaningful kiss.

We drifted apart, barely, when he added, "Now, let me look at that brand." Ash carefully took my wrist and lifted it to eye level, inspecting the tattoo. "Does it hurt much?" A shadow of concern fleeted across his countenance.

"It doesn't hurt at all," I admitted, still astonished by the fact.

His smirk broadened into a handsome grin. "Ah… The perks of magic," he said, satisfied. "It's a beautiful sigil."

"You're getting yours in the morning," I warned him in a teasing tone.

His face lit up as I spoke. "So I hear," Ash mumbled. "And I *also* hear Thuriad is the lucky mage to do it." A grimace of mischief surfaced on his face.

"You must not punch him," I taunted, quirking up an eyebrow.

He gave me a lopsided grin. "I'll see what I can do." Ash tightened his hold around my waist. Gently, he eased me on the bed, molding his sturdy frame against my back. "Sleep well, my love," he whispered in my ear. "This time, I'll be right here when you awake."

I did not know what tomorrow would bring—either death, defeat, or victory. But knowing Ash would be by my side turned even the bleakest prospect into a blessing.

"Suddenly, I don't feel like sleeping anymore," I murmured.

Sensual laughter rumbled in his throat. "Don't you?" he whispered, his silken lips brushing my nape. "I can help with that."

I felt him smile.

CHAPTER THIRTY-FIVE

We arrived at Whitehaven an hour before dusk. Overcast skies announced an impending winter storm, painfully reminiscent of my late father's fateful wedding day.

As we advanced through the citadel, I stumbled time and time again upon royal decree scrolls pinned to the walls, commanding all people in the kingdom to attend King Raathiel's coronation.

Although the merry melody of drums and tambourines resounded in the citadel, the town folk huddled in the keep in frail restraint. Wonder gleamed in the people's eyes as they contemplated the grandeur of Whitehaven Castle. However, a thin layer of desolation veiled my kingdom's grounds.

The Evil Queen's Red Army guarded the gates zealously, alert and ready to act upon the slightest spark of turmoil. As we jostled through the crowd, I couldn't help glaring at the undead soldiers. Narrowing my eyes, I tried to catch a glimpse of the lifeless faces concealed in their fearsome spiked red helms. However, black masks shrouded the soldiers' dreary features underneath. And good thing that they did... Suddenly, I halted. A ripple of horror skittered down my spine when a guard's glazed eyes met mine for an instant.

"Don't stop," a hurried voice said in my ear.

I looked to my side to find Ash standing next to me. His fingers pinched the trim of his hood. He tugged it lower, shadowing his eyes. In a flash, Ash seized my hand and led me through the mob.

We scurried into the keep like ghosts, moving past the gates, into the great hall where a large dinner assortment waited, spread on several long tables. The queen's banquet surpassed the Seven's most lavish feast, with endless trays of mutton and lamb, boiling pots filled to the brim with steaming broths, and barrels of wine continuously wheeled into the warmed chambers.

Nobles and peasants gathered in the rooms. Puzzling that the queen would allow such an ensemble, when upon her wedding day she'd insisted on the contrary, casting off the townsfolk to the citadel.

That was not all. In the crowd, I recognized

many of the faces I'd seen in the Marble Hall, high fae lords and ladies garbed in their best outfits. Creatures of both realms mingled beneath the same roof for the first time in centuries... But no winged fairies stood amidst them. Surely, they'd not been invited.

I swept the room with a glance. Squads of trolls kept careful watch from the higher rooms. Scattered in the crowd, I recognized the others. Brindel and Thuriad lingered by their post at the western doors, casually sipping on wine. The fairy captain had taken the precaution of concealing her wings under a baggy green cloak.

Romni and Millindrel were standing by the dinner table, picking at a tray of sliced ham and cheese while glaring at their surroundings. Akron and Essgard stood guard at the main entrance, where Arthion's men were already rounding up.

The plan was simple. The outcome, unpredictable.

"I must speak to Brindel," Ash whispered in my ear. "I'll be back soon." Having said that, he dipped into the crowd and lurched towards the pair.

Standing in the middle sóf the great hall of what I'd once called my home, I strangely perceived myself as an outsider. I'd spent the longest hours dancing and laughing in these rooms... The place itself looked exactly as I'd left it. And yet, it felt so different. I was different.

A sigh escaped my lips. I glided away from the hordes and sought a moment's peace by the grand fireplace. My mouth went dry with restless anticipation. When a footman moved past me carrying a tray served with brimming wine glasses, I seized the chance and grabbed a drink. I took the glass to my mouth and eased the tasty wine down my throat in a single swig. One drink alone might not have been enough for an evening such as this, I thought.

"And then I told the monster, *'Of course you're doomed. Don't you know who I am?'*" someone in the crowd said, smooth yet loud enough to catch all ears. Laughter followed the boisterous remark.

I recognized his voice immediately. Looking back, it came to me as no surprise to see Phillip, surrounded by a welcoming committee. As usual, his bedazzled sycophants hooked their attention to his every word. Only this time, the group surrounding him comprised not only women young and old, but high fae ladies as well. The fae's violet eyes glimmered with magic as they praised Phillip's captivating stories. Stories in which he was always the hero.

A flash of awareness flickered through my being. *I must warn him. Phillip must be ready when the fight begins.* No swordsman was more skilled, no fighter more willing at the call of war than the heir of Steel-born Castle. With haste, I set aside the empty glass and started towards Phillip, keeping a safe distance from his party.

"Look at me," I whispered, dodging high fae lords and ladies as my stare locked on him. "See me now..."

Phillip failed to notice me. I'd have to find another way to steal his attention. Only one thought came to mind. Casually, as I drifted through the mob, I snatched a glass of wine from a drunken lord. When I stood mere inches away from Phillip, I purposely stumbled against his shoulder, spilling red wine on his lavish blue royal coat.

The prince started, an instant frown creasing his brow.

Gasps of fabricated consternation rose from the group of suitresses enveloping him. Their scrutinizing eyes glared at me as if I were the most loathsome and undesirable creature ever to have set a foot in this kingdom.

"Prince Phillip," a high fae lady said, smoothing a pale, delicate hand on his arm. "Are you all right?"

Phillip all but snarled. He jerked a silk napkin off the table and briefly attempted to dry his coat's sleeve. "Ugh. I honestly do not know," he mumbled, crossed. "Blasted peasants! I certainly do not appreciate being forced to mingle with them." He paused, setting a softened stare on the fae lady. "But, as those are my queen's wishes…"

I lowered my chin, careful not to reveal myself to unwanted eyes. "I'm sorry, my lord," I told him in a low voice.

Phillip whirled on the ball of his feet, a scowl marring his handsome countenance. "Yes, well. That's not good enough. Now, is it?" he spat. "Go away, filthy peasant! You reek of forest dew." The prince waved his hand dismissively.

His insufferable demeanor infuriated me. I pursed my lips tight and sucked in a sharp breath. "Your Highness," I said through gritting teeth, lifting my gaze as I stood before him, careful to shield myself from the others using Phillip's body.

He looked down at me with the same odious insouciance. "What do you want now?" he sneered, taking a hand to his waist as he squared his shoulders.

Foolish man. "Phillip," I muttered, eyes widened with exasperation. "It's me!"

As he finally focused his gaze on mine, Phillip's eyes flew open, swept in sheer shock. "Maleath!" he hissed. The prince then addressed his retinue and said, "Excuse me, I must see this servant girl is sternly punished." The sycophants nodded in agreement and clapped, celebrating his cruelty.

At once, Phillip snatched my hand and dragged me to the staircase. The same place where we used to hide to make love... It felt like ages had passed since those times. How different things were now.

The minute we were alone, Phillip slipped down my hood with tender care. His firm hands framed my face, his blue eyes inspecting me with desperate eagerness. "Fires of the Netherworld, it really *is* you!" He stepped back, raking me with a glance from head to toe. "Gods, what has happened to you, Maleath?" He scowled, gliding his fingers through my braids. "Your hair… And, your clothes…" His disconcerted stare traveled lower. Horrified, he seized my wrist and pulled it to eye level. "Is that a tattoo?"

"Will you please be quiet?" I all but hissed, grabbing his arms. "I must speak to you!"

Oh, but he was incapable of holding his tongue. "What on earth are you doing here?" he demanded, a glint of concern in his voice. "Don't you know they want your head for murdering King Edward?"

"Phillip, *please* listen to me!" I begged him. We had precious little time left. "Keep your sword close. Battle and blood are coming." The words sailed through my lips with unshakable conviction.

Phillip's body stiffened. Through the muffled din, he breathed the words, "Battle and blood?" He started.

A mirthless laugh escaped his mouth. "Maleath, have you lost your senses?" His tone became harsher. "This is a ball. Everyone knows there's no bloodshed in a ball—ever! Otherwise, it wouldn't be so fun. Now, would it?" He gave me half a smile.

"Be that as it may," I mumbled, increasingly annoyed, "I'm taking back my crown this evening."

His expression softened. "Oh... I see," he said. "That's nice, darling." Phillip caressed my cheek, a patronizing gesture, to say the least.

The blood rushed through my veins like wildfire. At once, I smacked his hand away with mine. "Phillip, I'm being perfectly serious!" I insisted, my voice's pitch heightened with frustration. "I will launch a coup at any moment!" When my hands dropped to my sides, I felt them slowly clenching into tight fists.

Phillip blinked, the words finally sinking in. "A coup?" he echoed in a wary tone. A muscle twitched along his strong jawline.

"Look around the hall," I told him gravely, pointing at the room. "Do you see the fae gathering near the musician's platform?" I waited as his gaze angled towards them. "They will fight for me." I paused. "See the men in the black hoods? They're powerful mages known as the Seven."

Phillip gasped. "Mercenaries of magic!" He scowled in disapproval. "They're real?"

"They are." I gave him a subtle nod. "And they're all with me."

Visibly shaken, Phillip raked his fingers through his wheat blonde hair. "Dear gods," he uttered, peering into the great hall once more. He faced me once more. "You're not teasing me. This is really happening."

"It is," I assured him, watching as concern grew on his countenance while he listened. "When the time comes, you must be ready to fight."

Phillip's features hardened. "No," he said with steely resolve. "No. I'm not staying for this." He took a step back.

Ice skittered down my nape when he turned away. My mouth slackened in disbelief. "Phillip!" I called, stopping him as he reached the threshold.

He looked back. "Maleath, I came here tonight seeking enjoyment," he began. "I'd hoped to find some reprieve from my burdens, if only for a moment." Undiluted grievance seeped through his words. "I did not come here to start a war. I will certainly not break our frail alliance with the fae." The bleakest silence drifted between us. "Now, if you'll excuse me. I've got my own kingdom to look after.

The gods know how your brashness might injure us all."

And thus, Prince Phillip Steelborn stormed into the great hall, disappearing into the crowd in an instant.

I stood there, stunned. I don't know for how long.

My gaze fixed on the hall, hoping he might realize his mistake and come back. "I can't believe he's gone," I stammered.

"Who? That pretty boy who just left?" Brindel asked, strolling into the stairway's tunnel. "Do you know him?"

A stuttered breath escaped me. "I thought I did," I told her, transfixed by Phillip's reaction. Never in a thousand years would I have expected such a vehement refusal coming from him.

Brindel eased a hand over my shoulder. "It's almost time," she said. "We should get going."

CHAPTER THIRTY-SIX

The festive melody dwindled as we joined Ash in the middle of the great hall. When the music finally died, throngs of guests huddled near the rostrum set at the end of the chamber before a grand, bifurcated white marble staircase.

A pair of lavish red velvet armchairs lay empty on the wooden dais. Behind them, I glimpsed the display of a dozen golden knight effigies presenting the sharpest spears. These masked guardians hinted at the fearsome force of years past, long before my father's reign. Seeing them now, dusted off and brought up from the dungeon, robbed the people of any reassurance.

"Let's move," Ash murmured.

At once, Brindel hurried to meet Thuriad by the

west doors while Ash and I drifted in the crowd, moving closer to the dais.

We halted a few feet away from the rostrum when the air suddenly shifted, becoming lighter, thinner... Instant lightheadedness assaulted me. The dizzying effect was all too familiar. I'd fallen prey to it once, in Valathüre Palace.

My wary eyes angled upwards. A slow breath escaped me when, standing on the left staircase near the marble balustrade, I spotted Lord Raathiel Ivasaar, the fae King of Deceit. He was impossibly dashing— clad in burnished black armor, dignified while holding his pristine helm under his arm. His long mane of silvery hair glistened in the candlelight, as did his stormy eyes as they looked down at the restless mob. A malicious grin curled his lips, smug as he flashed his pointy fangs.

Gasps of wonder rose from the gathering at the first glimpse of Queen Roslyn. She descended from the right staircase, each step slow and calculated. Her gown was black velvet, its cloak embroidered in exquisite golden flakes arranged in a manner evocative of scales. She'd pinned her hair into a low bun, topped with a black crown, glistening and adorned with merciless spikes like those of her Red Army. A long, dark veil concealed her countenance. Even now, she'd play the role of the widowed queen.

Queen Roslyn and the King of Deceit met at the stairs landing. The fae usurper escorted her to the front of the dais, then took a step aside and waited.

"He's so beautiful…" a woman whispered nearby, astonishment hanging from each word.

I stared at her sidelong, crushed by her bedazzlement. "If only you knew," I barely spoke, then turned my attention to the rostrum again.

"My dear friends and allies. People of Whitehaven…" the Evil Queen began. Her voice was terse and measured. "Welcome to Whitehaven Castle." Slowly, she pulled away the veil, and when it came off, a subtle smile thinned her crimson lips. Her softened stare swept the awestruck faces in the crowd. "Alas, with the cruel loss of our king, it now rests on me to continue his legacy." She paused. "And it's in that spirit that I've summoned you here tonight to celebrate an alliance without precedent."

The blood boiled in my veins to hear insult upon insult cast on my father's memory. I ground my jaw. My breathing quickened. Unconsciously, I took the heel of my hand to my sword's hilt.

"Easy, Snow…" Ash breathed in my ear, smoothing a hand on mine. "Not yet."

My gaze cut to Arthion Thamaris, standing on the left staircase, watching from above. "*A discrete signal,* he said," I told Ash. "How will we know when it's time?"

Ashton's impassive hazel eyes locked on my own. "We'll know," he assured me.

"Look around you," Queen Roslyn continued, extending her open hands as she addressed the gathering. "You will see trolls and fae standing by your sides. Do not fear them. Not only are they our guests this evening; but from now on, they become our friends." She clasped her hands over her gown, the bearing of a formidable monarch. The role suited her so well... A dark voice whispered in my grieving heart: *does this crown fit her head better than mine?*

I shut my eyes and dismissed the notion quickly.

"Tonight, we celebrate the rise of a new era for the realms of man and fae," the queen added. She gently whirled towards a footman who offered her a crystal box ornamented with a golden dragon. Queen Roslyn pulled back the lid and dipped her delicate hands into the container. "And what better way to commence our friendship than to honor the coronation of our brother, Raathiel Ivasaar, high fae lord and rightful sovereign of the Marble Court?" A black crown came out between her hands, shaped with crooked branches and twinkling diamonds sprinkled on its base.

The solemn beat of a drum rolled.

Raathiel Ivasaar stepped forward. At once, a retinue of fae lords and stewards descended from the staircase. Amid them was Arthion, garbed in servant clothes—a position purposely demeaning for someone who'd formerly enjoyed royal status.

Arthion bore his punishment well. Not a trace of fury marred his pale features. However, as he drew closer to the dais, his cobalt eye spotted me in the crowd. It burned with the fire of unrelenting bloodthirst.

Lord Raathiel shoved his black helm against Arthion's arm, eager to receive the royal investiture from Queen Roslyn's hands. He strutted closer and stopped inches away until the wicked pair faced each other on the rostrum's edge.

Unable to be still, my gaze wandered about the great hall. One by one I met eyes with each of the Seven, getting an approving nod of readiness every time. All but one stood dispersed inside the hall. The missing mage was their leader.

"Leander..." I mused with a frown.

Always brooding. Always keeping to himself and disappearing... Could he be trusted at all? His ties to the Evil Queen were much too strong. Would he not ultimately betray us?

A quick and disturbing thought.

"May this historic evening mark the start of our

alliance and bring forth centuries of peaceful ruling," Queen Roslyn said, easing the crown on the usurper's head.

Raathiel bowed. A crooked smirk twisted his lips. "Or not..." He mouthed the words, but no sound came through. Rounds of applause resounded in the high-vaulted room as undiluted dread washed over me. The prospect of Lord Raathiel's reign was absolutely horrifying.

Oblivious to the fae's vicious intent, Queen Roslyn took a pair of wineglasses from an approaching steward. Gracefully, she offered one to the King of Deceit, and with the same poised demeanor, the Evil Queen held up her drink. "Long live King Raathiel Ivasaar, first of his name," she proclaimed.

"Long live the king!" the crowd chanted back in unison.

The newly pronounced monarch lifted his glass, and after giving a quick nod of proud appreciation, he drew the drink to his lips. It took but one swig for him to grimace in immediate disgust. With a sneer, King Raathiel's head swung towards his shoulder. "Servant!" He growled, calling Arthion near with a pair of curled fingers. "Take this foulness away. Make yourself useful and fetch me some ale!" he commanded.

Arthion Thamaris bristled at the king's demand. His nostrils flared in contained fury, a sharp exhalation sailing through his lips. In a flash, he yanked the glass off Raathiel's hand, smashed it against the chair's arm, and plunged the lethal stem deep into the fae king's throat.

A drizzle of blue blood splashed on Arthion's face as shrieks of horror lifted from the multitude. The crowd jostled, spurred into panic, grappling to reach the nearest exit.

Wild fierceness contorted Arthion's face as he leaned closer to the falling king. "This crown wears heavy on your head, cousin," he all but spat, removing the royal treasure. "You can burn in the Netherworld. Your ruling days are over." Mercilessly, he thrust the splintered glass even further. When he drew it back, the wound became a pulsing fountain.

With a ruthless swing of his wrist, Arthion slashed open the fae king's throat, severing muscle and tendons and bone. In one quick move, he seized the king's jaw and jerked it back, snapping the spine. And just as swiftly, Arthion gripped the bodyless head by its blue smeared tendrils of hair, and held it high for all the present to behold.

I covered my mouth as a shot of bile hit my palate. Appalled, I faced Ash, hoping he might make some sense out of this horror.

His cold eyes fixed on the gruesome scene. "So much for a discrete signal," he mumbled with no inclination.

Raathiel's lifeless body dropped to his knees, then slammed on the ground. Dark blue vital liquid escaped through his neck and gently pooled around him. The dark ripple soon extended on the dais, inches away from reaching the black velvet hem of Queen Roslyn's gown.

The queen swept away her skirt and backed off fast, disgust and dismay tangling on her pale countenance.

I started. A rumble of clangs, one upon another, reverberated in the hall like the thunderous march of a behemoth. The powerful blasts instantly swallowed the people's desperate howls as heavy wood beams dropped on all doors, sealing the keep within seconds, holding the Red Army outside.

"It begins," Ash said, his voice cool and determined. With a flick of his fingers, he unlatched the pin of his cloak. The garment dropped behind him, heavy as a tapestry. It was then that through his rumpled shirt, I saw the Seven's brand inked on Ashton's neck. An owl's head with fierce, wide eyes.

No sooner had his blade swung free from its scabbard than the trolls' swords whispered from their sheaths.

CHAPTER THIRTY-SEVEN

A fearsome squad of mighty trolls lined up below the dais, protecting the Evil Queen. She stood there, frozen. Her widened eyes filled with horror, watching her headless ally lying stiff on the ground. I could tell her mind was fluttering away with keen anxiety. On a dark whim, I relished in her despair. If Queen Roslyn's suffering amounted to at least half the pain she'd caused me, then I would be satisfied.

The queen's pale lips parted. "Kill them," she managed, shuddering as she searched for the faces of rebellion in the crowd. Her wistful expression soon gave way to the harshest firmness. "Kill them all!" The order came harsh and unwavering.

"All?" I breathed, my heart sinking in my chest. My stare stumbled across the room. I watched trolls and fae crossing blades, reigniting the fires of their timeworn enmity. But beyond this tumult lay the men and women of my kingdom, cornered and help-less. What harm had they done to deserve this?

Time slowed down as reality crushed me, stark and vivid. Arthion's men were slaying indiscrimi-nately. He cared nothing for the fate of Man's chil-dren, as long as the crown was his to bear. And then a thought assaulted me, more haunting that the last: perhaps I'd been mistaken striking an alliance with the one-eyed fae. Perhaps Raathiel Ivasaar would have made a better king...

"Snow!" Ash called in the distance.

I blinked, snapping out of the daze. A loud snarl resounded behind me. I whirled and found a seething troll charging at me. In a flash, the soldier's throwing dagger skimmed my shoulder, ice cold alloy slicing through my clothes, biting at the tender flesh. Mean-while, the sword in the troll's grip swung high, then came thrashing down, ready to split my head open.

My mouth slackened in sheer dread. I couldn't move.

"Get down," Ash howled. "Now!"

I crouched, quickly picking up the mighty clang of steel against steel. With my heart pulsing hard in my throat and ears, I looked back and found Ash blocking the troll's attack with ruthless tenacity, forcing him away from me. And as soon as he'd gained a safe distance, his sword skewered the enemy in a flash of silver. Promptly, he shook the gore off his weapon.

Shivering, I took a hand to my throbbing shoulder. I rose to my knees, paralyzed in the middle of a whirlwind of steel, blood, and wails of despair. This was my first glimpse of war. True war. It was not the substance of song weaved by the bards, but the cruelest carnage... and I could not bear another minute of it.

Countless lives would be spared if only I reached Queen Roslyn and demanded her surrender. "I must finish this," I stammered with quivering lips and a vacant stare.

When Ashton's stare lodged on me, he darted to my side. His fingers were gentle but swift as they unfastened my cloak. "Fires of the Netherworld," he managed between hurried breaths, eagerly inspecting my shoulder. "Did he hurt you?"

My mouth opened, but not a sound came through. With haste, Ash peeled back my sliced shirt. "Oh, thank the gods..." he uttered. "It's just a graze." His voice was rushed, although laden with reassurance.

His hand cupped the side of my face with fondness as his hazel eyes leveled with mine. "Can you fight?" he asked.

I sucked in one deep breath and garnered my resolve. "I can," I said, giving him a quick nod. At once, my blade tore free from its scabbard.

"Good..." Ash said, relieved. "Because they're coming—behind you!"

I turned and glimpsed the frightful trolls emerging from the mob, flashing blades smeared in crimson and blue, thirsty for our blood.

"That's the princess! She's the one we want!" a troll soldier advised the others, pointing at me with his sword. "Kill her!"

Ice skittered down my nape at those words. I swallowed hard and steadied my grip. Back to back, Ash and I braced ourselves for an imminent attack.

At the first clang of steel as my sword met the troll's blade, rage rushed through my veins like wildfire. I parried the blow and counterattacked. My sword's song was death, dusted with the venom Ash had once given me. In a practiced arc, I sliced a crimson swath through the snarling troll, sealing his doom. The wound itself was deadly, but the venom acted faster, sending his body convulsing to the ground.

By the time his friend came after me, I was ready. And in a flash of silver, my blade skewered the fiend.

Together, Ash and I formed a wall of death, slaying the entire troll squad that attacked us until he faced the last one, fighting valiantly. I swept clean my sword on my enemy's clothes when my gaze wandered a few feet ahead to a small adjacent chamber. My people were flocking there, seeking refuge, unknowingly becoming the perfect prey, trapped in a sealed room—although it wasn't.

Without giving it another thought, I rushed to the room, dodging the dead, stabbing and slicing the queen's forces of death. I stopped at the threshold to catch my breath, my face flushing from the effort.

"It's the princess," someone blurted in a jittery voice.

Disheartening as it was, my people feared me. I was a traitor, for all they knew. Even so, I strolled inside. "Please, do not be frightened," I hurried to say, an appeasing hand raised in the air. "I know a way out." Slowly, I moved closer, heading to the wall where a grand tapestry hung, depicting one of my father's victories.

"You came back," an old woman said. Her piercing blue eyes brimmed with tears as they tracked my movements.

As I reached the wall, I stared at her, bemused.

"We thought you'd abandoned us," the man

continued with a firmer voice, anything but scared of me.

Strange and disquieting thoughts raced through my mind. My brow creased into a frown. "I did not kill..." I breathed, and the words got caught in my clenched throat.

"We know." A younger woman stepped forward. Her green eyes glinted with conviction as they met mine.

"We've always known," a young man followed, standing beside her. "We saw everything."

The warmth of forthcoming tears rose to my eyes. Unable to speak a word, I pursed my lips and nodded. And in a flash, I grabbed the tapestry and dragged it aside.

When the precious drape shifted, it revealed a secret door embedded in the oak paneled wall. I rushed to push the panel until it clicked, then opened the door. "Hurry now," I told them. "Don't stop until you reach the forest."

The gathering quickly scurried down the darkened passageway, fleeing to safety. But the old woman halted on the threshold and turned. "You make sure you get your throne back," she said, steadfast.

My expression hardened. "I will," I assured her, and the woman trudged into the tunnel. Immediately after that, I closed the door and covered it with the tapestry.

When I reached the great hall, the rage and violence had not waned. My shoulders jittered at a powerful blow that shook the castle to its foundation. A breath's time passed, and another strike came, pounding hard against the keep's doors.

"A battering ram..." I stammered in dismay. Outside, the Red Army grew impatient.

Fearful of my friends' fates, I swept the hall with a glance. To my left, I found Akron, taking on a pair of trolls. The mage caught one's head locked in his muscular arm, while the other faced the wrath of his sword. Not far from him, Romni and Millindrel paired an attack against a full troll squad. Their combat showed the harmony of a dance, ripping through the fiends with finely honed blades.

Essgard and Thuriad led the battle at the great hall's entrance. They commanded a troop of Arthion's soldiers, rounding up a battered horde of fae and trolls into submission.

But Leander. Where was he? I raked the castle with another glance, but to no avail... Leander had abandoned us.

"Snow!" Ash called in the distance. He was standing in the middle of the left staircase, waving a hand.

I darted to his side, at once noticing the trail of bodies—some clustered against the dais, others leading to the stairway where Ash stood. Ashton's sword had slain them all... He really was paving the way. Just as he'd promised.

With no time to lose, I mounted on the rostrum. As I stepped near the curdling pool of dark blue blood, something was amiss. Raathiel's body... it was... gone. And so was his head.

I winced, astounded. Who would steal the King of Deceit's corpse and why?

"Snow, she's getting away!" Ash uttered in a desperate roar.

Shock and anger tangled in my being. "Oh, no. She's not," I said. My voice, though quiet, sailed with an undertone of icy contempt. Prompted by that feeling, I climbed the stairs and met Ash.

"She went that way," he hurried to tell me. In one quick move, Ash grabbed my arm and pulled me behind him. In a flash of silver, his sword stabbed a troll who'd dropped from the upper landing.

"Go!" Ash turned to say, facing yet another soldier. This time, one of Raathiel's loyal guards.

I nodded. The stairs I'd climbed hundreds of times before now seemed taller, wider, and infinite. As soon as I reached the landing, I stopped by the balustrade and looked back. Ash was following, when a troll dropped from the upper floor and landed between us. He snarled at Ash, facing him viciously, armed with a fearsome axe and sword. Completely unaware of my presence.

The battleaxe's crescent head swung clean, death riding in its wake, boldly blocked and countered by Ashton's sword. But he was no match against the massive troll's strength, and he stepped back as the beast lunged forward. Brazenly, Ash slid out a knife cinched to his thigh, crouched, and slit the troll's heel tendon. The soldier collapsed to one knee. Infuriated, his axe swung one mighty blow against the sword, shooting both weapons down the stairway, out of reach.

With no weapon left save the dagger, Ash was at full disadvantage. And the troll warrior, though wounded, rose to his feet, pushing through his injury's pain as though it were nonexistent. This time, he unsheathed his sword.

In a flash, a memory came to me—Ashton's owl, almost crushed by the vicious barghest. I'd picked up a rock to save him back then... But this time, the earth would not crumble underneath our feet.

I ground my jaw, tightening my hands on the sword's grip. And as a dozen lessons of Sir Trevan played in my mind, I marched forward.

"Hey," I called, shifting my feet into a fight stance. "You, there."

The formidable troll slowly whirled back. My gaze angled skywards to meet violet eyes wild with fury. Upon noticing the broad difference in our heights, the creature grinned. "I'll watch you die, human." His grating voice made me shudder.

"Not if I kill you first," I told him, taking the step that would unleash the fight between us.

When our swords clashed, they rang like the chime of a silver bell. A mournful one. Realizing my weakness, I disengaged fast and dodged the forthcoming swing. The troll, no matter how imposing, had one fatal disadvantage. He was wounded, and that hindered his speed.

I crouched when the next slash came. It swung dangerously close to my head and bit into the wall. The blow had been so powerful that the blade had sunk into the stone. A growl rumbled in the troll's throat as he fought to free his weapon. For a moment, everything was a blur. Then I realized the troll's legs stood before me. The corner of my lips curled, and with one swift jab, I sliced through the soldier's unscathed heel.

The creature came tumbling down, heavy like a falling tree. He snarled and scrambled his limbs, slamming back against the balustrade. Before I lost heart, I kicked the troll's chest and pushed him off the stairway several feet down. When I rushed to the handrail, I saw his body meet the spear of a knight effigy below.

"You saved my life," Ash spoke, breathless as he stood beside me, also looking down.

My head swung to face him, the thrill of uncertainty shooting ripples through my being. "I know," I managed, wide-eyed.

Ash cracked a smile, but his amusement was short-lived. "She headed that way." He pointed at the corridor.

I swallowed hard. "To the North Tower."

CHAPTER THIRTY-EIGHT

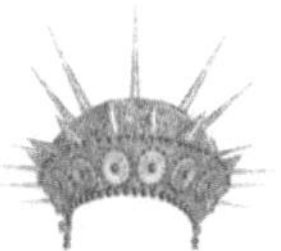

I reached the room first and halted at the doorway, crushed by the dark memories the throne room evoked in me. Even as flickering chandeliers spilled amber radiance in the chamber, the grim backdrop of the crumbling wall behind the dais turned everything bleak.

The harshest winter storm lashed outside as dusk smoothly settled. Myriad lacy snowflakes drifted in the room, immaculate crystal petals piling on the rostrum.

"By all the gods!" Queen Roslyn growled, desperately pacing in the central aisle. As her marching footsteps geared towards the cursed throne, the queen snapped her fingers in a rush, instantly unveiling every piece of furniture concealed beneath frail linens, tattered and tarnished with dust and old ashes.

"Where the devil is it?" she all but hissed, her knuckles whitening as she clenched her gown tight.

Ash joined me in the doorway. He leaned against the door's jamb, watching the queen with a derisive stare. "Looking for your morals, Your Majesty?" he taunted, grinding his jaw. The sword hung loose in his grip as he strolled into the throne room. I moved along with him.

When the Evil Queen locked stares with Ash, her piercing blue eyes shot ablaze with spirited contempt. "What do you think you're doing, Ashton?" she demanded in defiance. "Do you think coming here flashing the Seven's brand makes you a hero?" She paused. "Do not fool yourself, boy. You're the same coward who deserted his kingdom. You'll be running away from here too before you know it."

We stopped in the middle of the central nave.

"I am done with running," Ash told her in a dispassionate tone. Slowly, he swung the blade and braced it before him, locking his limbs into a guarding stance.

The queen's expression hardened, spite marring her features. "I cursed you once. I'll do it again!" Roslyn sneered. "This time, if you're lucky, I might turn you into a barghest."

A stuttered gasp escaped him. The blade slightly quivered as Ash tightened its grip. "I'd rather *die* than live a shifter's life!" His voice broke, laden with undiluted pain.

Feigned sympathy twisted Queen Roslyn's crimson lips. "Oh no, dear boy. We can't have that," she said, the beginning of a frown creasing her brow. "You're too pretty to die."

A mirthless laugh burst from her mouth as she turned to the White Throne, her lavish skirt twirling like a black rose. The seat looked barely recognizable, coated in red ink. Stifling her amusement, she dropped onto the chair, resting her temple against a pair of fingers. "And you," she added, spearing me with a daunting glare. "Do you realize the harm you've caused my kingdom?"

Instant rage swept through my being. "It's *my* kingdom!" I spat.

Queen Roslyn pursed her lips, failing to suppress a disparaging smirk. "Maleath, you're just a child," she said with a dismissive hand wave. "You know nothing about ruling. And there's your proof!" She pointed to the break in the wall behind her, signaling the devastation unleashed at my expense.

Her gaze lingered on the wintry sky as the last evening sunbeams vanished, when the queen's countenance slipped into a frown. She faced Ash immediately. "Why haven't you shifted?" she demanded from him in a hurried voice.

"Arthion helped... *and* a griffin," he spat, matching Queen Roslyn's hushed ire with his. "I guess your magic isn't that powerful after all."

Her jaw slackened at a sudden realization. "Arthion—that treacherous fae," she muttered. Her hands, like claws, clutched the seat's armrests as she leaned forward. "He stole my griffin tears!" Acute panic flickered across her face. "He stole them from me and gave them to *you*!"

Ash turned to me, thrown by the queen's revelation. Inextricable dread loomed in his stare.

At once, the Evil Queen shot off the seat. She rushed down the nave at unnatural speed, reaching Ash so unexpectedly that she quickly disarmed him. "Where is it?" she pressed, yanking on his shirt's collar. "Give it to me!"

"Let him go!" I roared, lunging at her, my sword thirsting for her blood. But quick as lightning, with a single flash of her palm, the Evil Queen unleashed a wind with the force of a powerful hurricane. The blow hit me full force. It swept my body off the ground and sent it flying. I crashed several feet away.

"Ashton," she continued, lodging her focus on him, "give me that vial right now or you will pay dearly." The queen spoke through clenched teeth.

Frozen by Queen Roslyn's spell, Ash parted his lips when, abruptly, the queen winced, deeply affected. She took a hand to her chest and stepped back.

I got on my feet and cautiously ambled towards Ash. Now I was the victim of the queen's glare. Again, she scowled in pain, the blow so harsh it made her stumble. And as I reached Ash, to our sheer astonishment, Queen Roslyn dropped to her knees.

Summoning all her strength against the forthcoming waves of ache assaulting her, the queen crawled back to the dais. As soon as her delicate hands reached the ancestral seat, she dragged her body farther, and promptly found refuge behind the cursed throne.

Doleful sobs echoed in the dilapidated throne room. A shiver rippled through my being as the torturous sound gained volume and intensity, quickly shifting into unsettling laughter.

My brow creased with uncertainty. "What's happening?" I breathed, moving closer to the dais with wary steps, trying to catch a glimpse of Queen Roslyn.

When I stood before the rostrum, an icy draft lashed into the room, smothering all candlelight in an instant. Anxiety spurted through me. My breathing quickened, white mist fleeing through my quivering lips.

The hazy clouds drifted with the breeze, bleeding

slanted beams of silver moonlight through the crumbling wall. Against the mournful rays, the throne's shadow stretched and spilled over me. Meanwhile, the queen's mysterious stillness prevailed. Not a sound slipped from her throat. And as the howling wind died, a chill, black silence surrounded us.

"Snow…" Ash whispered, but I paid no mind to his warning.

In the chamber's twilight, the throne's shadow thickened. It expanded more and more until it touched the ceiling and reached beyond the dais. And inside this impenetrable shroud of darkness appeared a pair of flaming blue eyes. Large and feral.

A great muzzle emerged above the throne. The growl that lingered in its throat echoed in my chest and shot shivers through my limbs. Outlined in the gleaming moonlight, exquisite black scales scintillated, etching wide, magnificent wings.

The beast rushed a sudden huff through its flaring nostrils, and with it, a bank of fog scurried down the central nave, quickly enveloping Ash and me. Gradually, the creature's neck elongated out of the dark, its purpose hindered by the ceiling. My gaze shot skywards, humbled by the beast's enormity. Every inch of my body went taut.

Another growl resounded in the room. A warning of death and destruction to come.

I cringed. "Ash?" I managed without moving an inch. "She's a..." The words flitted into silence.

"A dragon," he added, standing next to me.

My head whipped towards him with an instant scowl. "You knew?!" I all but screeched while I threw him a glare. "You should have told me!"

Ash started, confused. "I *did* tell you. At the Seven's lair," he hurried to explain. "I thought you understood."

"I thought you were being poetic!" I snapped back, my expression slackening as I faced the fuming firebreather.

"I'm sorry about that," Ash uttered in the gravest tone. "I'll be clearer in the future."

"If we have one," I replied, then swallowed hard.

The mighty beast raised its hand a few feet high, only to slam it against the floor seconds later. At once, the entire tower shook to its foundation, rattling rubble and a cloud of dust from the frail, broken wall. Ash and I braced ourselves, struggling to hold our bearings, when the firebreather's head slowly stretched towards me, stopping perilous inches away.

My breathing hitched. Fathomless dread clenched like a tight fist around my chest.

The dragon tilted its head. Black spikes sprung along its jaw and snout, and a pair of silver horns crowned its head, glinting like spotless mirrors in the dark. The creature's slanted pupils suddenly narrowed, sweeping me with an appraising stare. And sparked by its nearness, memories of years back flashed before my mind.

Sheer black dread washed over me. "Gods of the Netherworld," I breathed, eyes widened at a sudden understanding. "I know you..." Unmitigated fury displaced all fear in my heart as I faced the fire-breathing monster. I ground my teeth. "You killed my mother!"

At once, the dragon's throat blazed alight like burning coals. The firebreather's jaws lazily unhinged, exposing fearsome ivory fangs sharp as spears and a thick grazing tongue, ready to ignite the warm air that streamed through its flaring neck... And then, I understood. The rumble in the dragon's throat was not a growl at all, but a roaring fire ball brewing in the beast's core.

"Snow!" Ash called. His voice was muffled in the distance, followed by a metal clang that echoed in the room.

As long as the beast's ensnaring stare was locked on mine, I could not move, tethered to its hunting gaze by the means of the darkest magic. Tears brimmed my eyes as the realization stabbed me like the fiercest blade. *She killed my mother.* The words whirled in my mind. *Galhöe killed my mother.*

The dragon's growl grew louder, menacing, and vicious. And yet, my fear subsided into numbness. For as the violent flames clambered up the beast's throat and filled its snout, the gleaming light felt welcoming and warm—an open doorway to the Netherworld. A summons to meet my parents again. A promise, so beautiful...

"Snow, move!"

In a flash, Ashton's body rose in front of me, a fae shield braced on his arm. With one quick swing, he blocked the firestorm that clashed against the worn-out metal. A scorching gust of wind rushed past us as unforgiving flames filled the throne room with vivid amber light. Sparks and embers spattered off the shield's gleaming rim. I couldn't resist the blinding blaze. I shut my eyes and turned my face away, praying to all the gods the firestorm might end quickly. It seemed to last forever.

When the dragon fire finally died, a freezing wave swept through the chamber. The silence was unbearable. With my pulse pounding hard in my throat, I opened my eyes. Ash and snow tangled in the air, a frightful rain gently pouring in the smoldering room.

Lacy flakes dusted my lashes. I blinked. Before me, I saw Ash. He was lying on the ground, his shield discarded feet away, melting. Instant horror froze the blood in my veins.

A sharp gasp escaped me. I darted to his side, careless of all else. Panic rioted inside me as I swept him in my arms, unconscious. "Ash!" I managed between scant breaths, my soul spiraling into fathomless darkness. "Ash, please!" My hand glided along his strong jawline, desperate to see his eyes suddenly open.

Seconds drifted in raw agony until my tears finally burst, confronted with the harsh truth. "*Please!*" I cried in a roar of grief. "*Please,* don't leave me!" I buried my face in his chest and sobbed bitterly, knowing my heart forever ruined beyond repair.

But my misery was short-lived as the grounds shook with the force of a powerful earthquake. At once, I lifted my gaze, lodging it on the frightful fire-breather barely fitting in the room. The creature's focus shifted from me to the crumbling wall when the clamor of war sailed in the wind. The quake came not from the dragon, but from the battling ram below, successfully breaching the Red Army into the castle... And thus, my hope subsided.

I had no kingdom. No army. Only the will of a few, and our numbers were dwindling by the minute. My greatest loss in this rebellion lay between my arms and my crown's future steadily dimmed.

"She's a dragon," I breathed. "How can I ever slay a dragon?"

The firebreather's newborn growl rumbled in its chest. In a flash, its head whipped towards me, all fury and viciousness rekindled.

I met the dragon's fearsome eyes and watched its neck growing aflame, admonishing my doom.

CHAPTER THIRTY-NINE

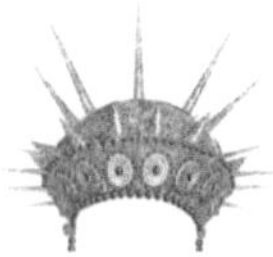

"If all is lost, I've nothing left to lose..." I mused, easing my hands around my sword's grip. Slowly, I got to my feet.

As I ambled towards the dais, I tightened my hold on the blade, permeating it with all the anger and grief that filled my being.

The dragon cocked its head, its glare following me, curious to unveil my intention as I stood my ground before it. Quick as lightning, the creature snapped its massive jaws, threatening to eat me whole in a single bite. But I was faster and dodged the attack, slashing its snout in a single swing. The sword sliced through the surface of the beast's nostril, barely causing any damage, but forcing the dragon to recoil from me.

Foolish thoughts concerning Queen Roslyn arose

in my mind. As the deadline of her curse drew near, did she keep any awareness while trapped in her shifter form? Was I fighting her or the firebreather which had conquered her soul? What did it matter when the thundering march of countless undead soldiers resounded in the tower's spiral staircase?

"I'm not leaving this world without putting up a fight," I muttered, finding courage where there was none before.

The rumble in the stairway came to a stop. Out of the corner of my eye, I watched as incoming rows of the Red Army lined against the throne room's walls. "Roslyn or not," I managed, stepping closer to the firebreather, "you *will* remember me."

A shriek broke the silence as the beast launched another attack. This time, I was ready, and when the monster opened its ferocious maw, I swung my sword in a practiced arc. My slim blade successfully slashed through the creature's crimson tongue, splitting the tip in half. At once, a raucous screech poured from the dragon's throat. Its head violently swayed, shattering a massive chandelier that toppled to the ground.

I shielded my eyes with my forearm at the forthcoming cloud of dirt and ash scurrying my way. And as soon as the dust began to settle, I shook the gore off my blade between coughs and shallow breaths burning my lungs with each inhalation. Merciless shocks of pain rippled through my being, beating down at my worn-out limbs.

The beast came back, charging at me with reignited fierceness. And as its vicious jaws unhinged, and the fireball built up inside its throat, the sword slipped from my quivering hands, chiming like a silver bell as it kissed the sooted ground. A stuttered breath escaped me. This was the moment. There was no happy ending in this tale. Even so, I carried no regrets. This path had led me to the cruelest defeat, but the journey had outshone any victory. I had loved and known the love of friends, and that was what I chose to take with me.

I closed my eyes, preparing to receive the final blow.

As the dragon's warm breath lashed at my face, my thoughts turned to Ashton, to my father, and to my mother. I was praying to see them again when a hand folded in mine.

Startled, I opened my eyes to meet an ice-blue stare locked on me with infinite kindness. A secretive smile curled the corner of his lips. "Leander..." I gave him a faint smile, relieved to see him with me. He was no traitor, but the truest friend.

All mirth faded from the mage's countenance. His head swung towards the dragon. "It's time to make things right," he said in a quiet voice. "I've hurt you long enough." Leander nodded gravely. "Galhöe, please forgive me."

A flood of light spilled on our faces as incandescent flames poured into the dragon's widened mouth. My expression slipped into a frown. "Leander?" I breathed, bemused.

He stared at me sidelong with cool, unwavering eyes. "GO!" he roared, shoving me out of the way with one quick push.

At the mage's mighty blow, I tumbled to the floor and rolled, stopping several feet away from them. When my gaze angled towards Leander, a firestorm blasted out of the dragon's mouth and descended on the mage. The creature's unforgiving flames swiftly engulfed him in one lethal embrace.

My soul splintered into a thousand shards. "NOOOOOOOOOOOOOOOOO!" I broke down, clenching my fists tight against the shuddering ground. I pushed myself to stand, unable to do so as long as the tower was shaking.

When the fire died, a shrill cry echoed in the throne room. The ghastly sound came from the black dragon as it recoiled into a corner, whimpering in despair.

Tears streamed down my cheeks while I managed to rise on my knees, watching as thick swirls of dark vapors lifted from the beast, now crawling closer to the mage. The black smoke continued to rise, becoming denser until it swathed the dragon fully.

As frail morning rays strayed into the tower, the dragon slowly vanished, leaving the mortal mage Galhöe behind. A broken woman, overwhelmed with fathomless grief, stumbling over the seemingly unscathed body of her lifeless brother.

"Why, Leander?" Galhöe sobbed miserably. "I longed to be free. But not like this!" she whimpered. "Not like this!"

A loud clang resounded in the chamber. At once, I swept the room with a glance, witnessing as row after row of undead soldiers collapsed to the ground until none remained standing. It became painfully clear to me then. Leander's death had saved us all.

With a heavy heart, I picked myself up off the ground, swept in the cool draft as the drifting ash gently settled. Slowly, I turned and looked down the chamber's central nave. Legions of faeries stepped inside the room across the hall's ancient mirrors, surrounding us within seconds. Amid those many faces, I recognized Queen Inoue and her royal guard, and Brindel moving down the hall beside her.

My blurred gaze shifted towards the dais. Galhöe's curse had been lifted. The Red Army's dark spell had been broken. Red no longer stained the White

Throne. My family's ancestral seat shone pristinely, as it always had. I turned my hand over, catching the last flakes of snow that floated in the room and watched them thaw in my palm into precious cherry blossom petals. When I looked past the crumbling wall, for the first time in five centuries, the sun glared through my kingdom.

But what about Ash? Crushed, I found my way back to him. *What about my handsome love?* I sat by his side on the ground, silently weeping.

Brindel strolled past me, followed by the royal guard. With a solemn expression, she took a knee next to Leander's body, and bowed her head in hushed recognition. After a moment, she raised her gaze, stern green eyes fixed on Galhöe. "It's time you come with us," she told her in a low, mournful tone. The faery captain then got to her feet and waited.

Galhöe sniffed, clearing the tears from her blotching face. Struggling to garner the will to rise, she straightened, agreed to the captain's command with a swift nod and sauntered behind her. In silence, they strolled down the central aisle, heading towards the mirror.

"No." A voice rang through the chamber. I recognized it instantly as Thuriad's. "Leander—Ash!" Hurried steps darted down the hall. In a flash, the mage stopped before the dais. "My brother... and my dear boy!" He took a hand to cover his mouth and stepped towards me, where his knees finally buckled and pinned him to the ground.

My throat clenched tight with revived grief when Thuriad's free hand pulled me to him, his arm wrapping me in a warm embrace. "I'm sorry, m'darling..." Tears rolled down his blushing cheeks. "So sorry."

"You have magic..." I sniffed. "Can't you save them?"

Thuriad shook his head.

"What about Leander?" I managed in a broken whisper. "The dragon fire should have consumed him to ashes, but—"

"He's a mage," Essgard said in a doleful tone, standing beside me. "When death comes for us, it shows us kindness."

Soon, the others joined us, desolated as one by one they knelt before our fallen.

"Maleath," Galhöe said, subdued.

Lazily, I turned to face her. Magic radiated from her as she stood in the middle of the aisle. It was compelling as the moonlight and shared the same pulsing gleam as her brother's. "Tears are the most powerful spell in the world," she added, "*if* you know how to use them."

Galhöe lowered her chin. She gathered her hands over her gown and stepped into the mirror.

CHAPTER FORTY

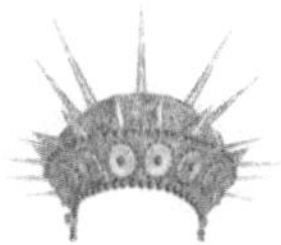

The sky was darkening through the gaping hole of the throne room's broken wall when guards—*my* guards—discarded the Evil Queen's crimson banners over the edge. They fell, lazily swaying in the wind with a raucous flap. Columns of smoke rose on the horizon from great pyres roaring ablaze. People were already burning the dead, as bursts of victorious clamors from the crowded streets reached my ears. They tangled with the wail of countless grieving widows and children. I joined them in silence, mourning not only for their losses but also for my own.

My lips thinned into a frail, bitter smile as I looked down at Ash, still lying in my lap on the marble floor. "We did it, Ash..." I told him in a broken whisper, gently pushing away a stray lock of hair from his brow. "We did it." I knew then his death had scarred my heart forever. I could not foresee happiness touching my life ever again.

Victory was ours, at last—spoiled with the stalest aftertaste. Exhausted in body and soul, I loosened a sigh and rubbed my eyes, burning from so much weeping. As I opened them, I noticed the most peculiar glint. Bewildered by the mysterious shimmering, my gaze drifted towards Leander. The light emanated from his body. Sparks burst from the mage, subtly colliding over him, small as fireflies.

"What's happening to him?" I managed.

The Seven gave no reply, but stared at their fallen brother in stern silence.

Soon, a magnificent radiance enveloped him, obliterating any vestige of Leander's mortal vessel. The pulsing gleam gave one powerful burst and shattered into myriad stars that swirled about the room, shooting out of the broken wall in an instant.

My chest tightened with sudden apprehension. "He's gone!" I blurted.

Thuriad knelt beside me. His green eyes remained serene as they found mine. "Not really," he assured me, faintly curling the corner of his lips. But the smile faded just as quickly. "Now, about Ash..."

"I will not bury him!" I snapped, my lips quivering after uttering such bleak words.

"Snow," Akron said, easing a hand on my shoulder. "Our boy is gone."

"Gone..." I echoed, my mind helplessly numbed while I stared at Ashton's chiseled profile, glistening against the golden sunlight. His beautiful features were still flushing with the gleam of life—a cruel deception of the dragon's toxic fumes. I'd noticed the same bloom in my mother's countenance after the black beast attacked her all those years ago.

"He was a mighty warrior," Romni spoke, standing beside me.

Essgard crouched next to me, wrapping an arm around my shoulders. "Took down an entire troll squad by himself," he said.

"We will always remember him," Millindrel added as he joined his brothers.

I blinked, and my withheld tears streamed down my burning cheeks. "Oh, Ash..." I whispered, holding his hand. "Life's already grim without you." An invisible fist gripped my throat. "I am dead, and you thrive beyond my reach." I tilted towards him, close enough to capture every inch of his face. In this nearness, I lingered upon his blonde eyelashes, his sculpted nose, the set of his mouth, the sun-kissed skin pulled taut over the ridge of his cheekbones... If I was to never see him again, then I would learn every detail and lock it in my heart.

Pursing my lips to stifle my quiet sobs, I smoothed a hand over his firm chest. When it glided over his doublet's pocket, I halted. My fingers stumbled on something. I dipped them into the opening and extracted the vial, its precious elixir all but gone.

I heaved a sigh. "Galhöe's griffin tears." I winced, shaking my head. "You should have given her the tears..." The words sailed into silence before a sob shattered my resilience and overcame me completely. I couldn't breathe, tears were flooding my sight and this mere idea hurt my core as a blade stabbing me countless times would. I wailed and cried until I stopped. Another thought had slithered into my brain with fearful clarity.

"Snow?" Thuriad frowned, inching closer.

"Galhöe said tears were the most powerful magic in the world..." I stammered, pulling the vial's cap open.

"Snow, don't!" Essgard urged, suspicious of my intentions. "It's dangerous!"

My narrowing gaze cut to his, defiant. "He's already dead," I wryly answered, and tilted the vial over Ashton's mouth. The last silvery bead in the container scurried to the brim and dripped on his lips, then smoothly rolled inside.

I waited, my sanity pending from a thread, hoping for a sign that he'd come back to us. My gaze raked him desperately, watching his motionless chest intently... And still, nothing happened.

"It was worth trying," Romni uttered in a low voice. He sighed, disheartened, and paced away.

"Say goodbye to him, lass," Thuriad bid me, warmly easing a cupped hand to the back of my head. "We'll take care of him."

My heart stuttered, caught in a falling sensation, as silent tears spilled down my cheeks. No words would drift through the tightness in my throat, so I forced myself to nod.

Torn in agony, I leaned close to Ash and gave one last kiss to his lips. His mouth's temperate warmth expanded through my being, nuzzling awake every nerve. And it was as if his gentle fingers trailed along the slope of my neck, climbing it tenderly, gliding to my jawline... I only wished that would be true, but I knew better than to trust a mourning mind's deception.

As I barely parted from him, I tumbled to his chest and began to snivel.

"Snow?" a voice said, calm and laden with tenderness.

My eyes opened, shuddering, fearful. Every inch of me went taut when Ashton's chest rose beneath me. Soothing fingers dipped between the black locks of my hair.

"What happened?" he asked.

"Ash?" I managed in a tremulous whisper, lifting my stare to meet his. I found his hazel eyes, no longer gleaming with the spark of his curse but watching me with profound sweetness.

I startled. "Ash, you're alive!" I gasped, taking my quivering fingers to his firm jaw.

A subtle frown creased his brow. "Of course I am," he replied with unwavering confidence. His hand trailed the way to cover mine. "What happened?" He glanced about the dilapidated throne room, stopping to notice each of the mages as they gathered around him, speechless. "Why is everyone here? Did we win?"

My vision blurred with renewed, joyful tears. "We won, my love," I told him, my pulse fluttering with emotion as I held the side of his face. "We won." A dry smile curled my lips.

Behind me, murmurs of relief burst from the Seven. With Ashton back, a ray of sunshine had beamed into the darkest day, healing our wounded hearts with revived hope and limitless gratitude.

"I'm parched," Ash uttered while I aided him to sit on the ground.

Thuriad stooped before him, holding his shoulder in reassurance. "I know exactly what you need, lad," the mage said. And turning his green eyes towards me, he added, "What we *all* need."

CHAPTER FORTY-ONE

*A*mber rays pierced the hallway's stained-glass windows as the sun kissed the horizon. Ash and I moved down the corridor in silence. We'd barely spoken a word since I'd told him of Leander's passing..

Steps away from reaching the room where the mages gathered, Ash halted in the middle of the desolated hallway. A stuttered breath sailed through his lips. "I can't believe we lost him," he whispered hurriedly, with teary eyes, jaded with exhaustion. As he ran his fingers through his hair, desperate to make sense of the dire news, I wished with all my being I could have spared him from this pain.

"We owe him our victory," I managed, smoothing a hand over his chest. At once, my touch picked up the pace of Ashton's racing heartbeat.

Bowing my head, I pursed my lips, struggling to fight back the tears that brimmed in my eyes.

Ashton's fingers glided along my jawline and stopped under my chin, gently lifting it until our stares leveled. "And you saved my life… for the *second* time," he said, his voice laden with the sweetness of honey. "I promise you one thing, my beautiful love…" His eyes blazed with determination. "I will *not* waste the gift you've given me."

I bit my lower lip, unable to stop the tears now streaming down my face.

In one quick move, Ash seized my waist and pulled me to him. He wrapped me in his strong arms in a heartfelt embrace, long and meaningful. Words were needless.

I buried my face in his chest, yielding to his hold. Many were the trying moments we'd shared. I longed for brighter days by Ashton's side, and closing my eyes for an instant, I escaped my grief, contemplating the prospect of us building joyful memories.

Minutes passed until he slowly parted from me. "Come," Ash said, regaining his aplomb while his fingers laced with my own. "Let's go meet the Seven."

I nodded and walked with him down the remaining steps in silence.

When we reached the chamber's threshold, I couldn't help but flinch. "I don't recall this room being so..." My gaze drifted through the mages, picking up each of the interior's details—from the lavish silk embroidered drapes hanging from the walls to the portraits that depicted gorgeous landscapes taken out of a fairytale. "Splendid," I mumbled, taken aback.

In the middle of the vast room, where the old strategy map had once stood, now lay a large oak table topped with a feast worthy of the gods. "That even looks like the Seven's dinner table," I pointed out to Ash, noticing dozens of ale jugs and fragrant delicacies as we strolled in.

"That's because it *is* our table," Romni said, smug as he crossed his arms over his chest, standing conveniently close to a tray crammed with aromatic roasted lamb chops.

My brow slipped into a frown. "How did you—?" I uttered.

Essgard, who was passing by, stopped short in front of me. He threw me a knowing look, a dark eyebrow shooting skywards.

"Oh... That's right," I added. "Magic."

The mage inclined his head in approval. He then whirled on the ball of his feet, swinging his zither over his shoulder. A pleasant melody hummed in his mouth as Essgard grabbed the back of a chair and strolled to the hearth, dragging it with him. And when he eased into the seat and hugged the instrument on his lap, the mage streamed his soothing song into the zither's strings.

"We thought you could use a bit of our *decor* in your palace," Millindrel said, offering us a pair of ale mugs. A twinkle of mischief glinted in his blue eyes.

"It's a castle!" Akron promptly corrected from the other side of the room. The towering mage grinned, satisfied, as he poured himself a drink. Judging by his ruddy cheeks, it wasn't his first one.

Vexed, Millindrel shrugged. "What does he know?" he mumbled to himself, and on second thought, he glared at Akron. "What would you know?" He scowled. "You're drunk!"

Akron's eyes widened in steely amusement. "Aye, I'm drunk," he retorted, unable to clear the smirk that twisted his lips. "But not daft!" And staring at his drink, the mage laughed infectiously.

"Yeah, whatever..." Millindrel scoffed. Then shedding from all anger, he turned to us to say, "Tonight lads, we dine and we drink, and thus we honor our fallen brother." Stretching his lips into a bitter smile, the mage slipped the large wooden mugs into our hands.

Ash and I nodded in agreement.

"To the most formidable mage in all the realms,"

Akron cheered, lifting his drink as he addressed the room.

The bustling group came to a stop. "To Leander!" all replied in unison, holding up their mugs.

Ashton's gaze cut to mine. "To Leander," he told me in a dour tone, then took a long swig of ale.

I held my mug between both hands, staring at the brew with empty eyes, when a hand slipped on my shoulder. "Soon, you will be crowned," someone said. "He would have been proud."

My head swung towards the voice. "Brindel," I said, acknowledging her presence. A sigh sailed through my lips. "I dearly hope so."

The fairy captain flinched, puzzled by my answer. "Don't you know Leander never doubted you?" she added, knitting her smooth brow. "Had he not persuaded Queen Inoue to cross her troops through the mirrors in the throne room, our cause might not have prevailed." She paused. "You might not know this, but it was the Diamond Army that quickly disbanded the Usurper's following after the Red Army's fall."

"Leander persuaded Queen Inoue?" I stammered in disbelief.

"Oh, yes," Brindel added, unwavering. "It was the way he spoke of your character, how he presented you as the fierce leader who would smooth the ridge between our realms, that convinced Queen Inoue and every faery in the Diamond Court that this was a battle worth fighting."

My expression hopelessly slackened at Brindel's revelation. "Leander truly was formidable." I paused. "I will not disappoint him," I assured her. "*Or* your people."

The captain's green eyes regarded me with quiet contentment. "I know that," she said, and drawing her mug to her lips, she took a swig of ale.

"Brindel," Thuriad intervened in the gravest of voices. A stern expression etched his face as he inched forward. "May I speak with you?"

Brindel started, her usual collected bearing shattered as never before. "You may," she replied. Her graceful hand faintly quivered as she set aside her drink.

My inquisitive gaze followed the pair as they sauntered to the chamber's arched tall windows. There, Thuriad and Brindel stood face to face, and behind them, the sky tinged in dark blue and fading purple, flickering with countless stars.

With utmost care, the mage's fingers trailed down the faery's temple, pushing away a stray lock of fawn hair. Thuriad's green eyes found hers, full of life, pain, and insatiable warmth. He leaned lightly toward her and spoke into the fairy's ear. His furtive words broke

Brindel's lips into a bashful smile, her gossamer wings lightly fluttering. Instant relief washed through the mage's features, and finally, his hand folded on hers.

"Is this *really* happening?" Ash spoke in awe, standing behind me.

"I think it is," I replied, stunned and unable to part eyes from them.

Dipping her head slightly, Brindel said *yes*. And delighted beyond any measure, Thuriad's thumb gently caressed the back of Brindel's hand, then pulled it near and pressed it against his lips.

At once, teasing *oohs* resounded in the room.

This did not sit well with Thuriad. "Shut it, Romni!" he barked back.

"Come on, Thuriad. Let the mage be!" Akron pleaded in an appeasing tone. "We've waited half a century to see this moment." He took a hand to his waist, the other holding up his mug.

"Now listen, brother..." With a scowl creasing his countenance, the redhead mage turned toward Akron, ready to snap when Brindel's hand eased on his jawline, and tugging him to her, the faery captain pressed her lips to his, ending all quarrels.

Thuriad's might waned as he melted into Brindel's hold, returning her kiss with sweet intensity.

"More drinks, please!" Essgard called, waving an

empty mug in the air. "And this time, open up the good ale!"

I took a hand to my mouth, stifling a giggle. "Fifty years… Thuriad certainly took his time, didn't he?" I uttered. But when I looked over my shoulder, Ash was gone.

CHAPTER FORTY-TWO

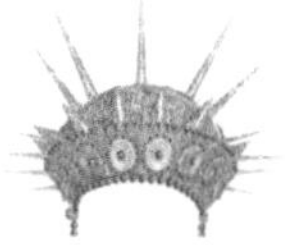

I found Ash standing in the darkened courtyard. The air was cool. The evening, embellished with the soothing croon of crickets. Moving further in the hallway, as I reached the threshold, I picked up his voice, tangled with another in a heated discussion. I narrowed my eyes and peeped through the door's crevice, trying to discern the stranger's features, but failed to in the feeble light.

"Not now," Ash said to the man, adamant. "This isn't a good time."

A gust of wind blew, scattering the clouds and spilling glistening rays of silver moonlight. It didn't surprise me then to see the Marble Court's one-eyed king—his army had set camp nearby before undertaking the journey back to Valathüre Palace. What raised my awareness was the fact that he'd come unescorted. A dangerous venture for someone of his stature. These were treacherous times. Why would he take such a risk?

"It's as good as any," Arthion replied in a vigorous, yet strained, tone. "This cannot wait." The fae monarch clasped his hands over his lavish dark blue robes. The rich fabric swayed in the breeze, flapping and ruffling against the fae's taut body as loose tendrils of his silvery hair stroked his cheeks.

With a quick sweep of his fingers, Ash raked back the golden locks of hair that had strayed to his brow. A harsh gasp of frustration escaped him. "Your people and ours... we're *all* in mourning," Ashton argued, hardening his expression. "Can we not grieve in peace for a single evening?"

Arthion inched closer. "Ash, you know I hold you in a high esteem," he told him coolly. "But if you force my hand, I will *not* be as gentle." His voice dropped into a sinister whisper as his hand eased to his sword's hilt. "I am here as the king of the Marble Court and *I will* see Whitehaven's sovereign."

"Is that a threat, Arthion," Ash purred in a velvety voice, raising his chin, "or a challenge?" Spurred by pain and the ale streaming in his blood, he reached for his sword. "You see, I *too* can be less than charming."

"I'm here," I said, standing in the middle of the

doorway.

The fae king started. "Princess Maleath," he said with a swift bow, lowering his arms.

Ash winced at the sound of my voice. He lowered his head, and pursing his lips, he stepped aside, clearing the path between Arthion and me. His hand, however, remained locked in the sword's grip.

"What is this urgent business?" I asked, sauntering to meet the fae ruler. My interest escalated with each passing second.

"I appreciate your candor, Your Highness," Arthion said, giving me an approving nod. "Allow me to extend you the same courtesy." He paused. "The matter at hand is your coronation."

"My coronation," I echoed in a flat tone. The thought far from thrilled me. The last coronation to have taken place in the castle hadn't gone all that well —fortunately for us. Despite that, I could not shake from my mind the gruesome images of the headless fae king lying on the dais.

"Yes," Arthion said. "We must proceed with the ceremony at once."

"Why the rush?" I asked, leery of the one-eyed fae's intentions. *Be wary of these high fae lords,* Leander had once warned me. His advice rung true now more than ever.

"Because, Your Highness," he continued, self-assured, "nothing is as tempting as an empty throne." Arthion inclined his head in a feigned display of humility. "Surely you realize that regardless of our victory, your position at present is most vulnerable."

I stared at him, expressionless.

"As vulnerable as yours," Ash uttered knowingly. His mouth took on an unpleasant twist. With fiery eyes locked on the fae king, he strolled towards me, and did not stop until he stood by my side. "Lest we forget that, given our circumstances, Whitehaven's crown legitimizes your own." His voice came low, determined.

Arthion's face slackened the slightest bit, rattled as his purpose now lay in the open. His shuddering cobalt eye cut to Ash.

"There will be a coronation shortly," I told the fae king, wearied by the conversation. "And your court will be summoned..." The words faded into silence as the thought dawned on me. I had the upper hand. "*Provided* you agree to the terms of our alliance, which I will relay to you at my earliest convenience."

A flash of discomfort crossed Arthion's face. "I understand." He took a hand to his chest. "Your Highness." The fae king bowed his head. "Ashton," he added as he straightened. He then turned away, strolling into the night.

"I don't trust him," Ash sneered, his face flushing

with fury while his narrowing gaze tracked the fae ruler. "Not after what he did... ordering his army to slay so recklessly."

"Neither do I," I confessed, watching Arthion's figure dissolve into the shadows. "But as my father used to say, '*This is the game, and one must play or forfeit*.'"

I heaved a heavy sigh.

"Snow," Ash breathed, standing before me. "I know that from now on, life will be different." His eyes bored into mine, and my heart turned over, as it did unfailingly each time our stares met. "But do you think we can have this night for us—just the two of us? One night, my love, free from the forthcoming troubles of politics?" His voice was a soft caress. "The gods know I've got my own to solve." At this, Ash lowered his head, creasing his brow with unease.

His last words shook me into the harshest realization. Ash was the crown prince of Thornwood. A battle of his own lay ahead of him, if he would claim back his throne... But would he? And would such plans not force him away from me? The sole notion shot a flicker of apprehension through my being. I had to know, but I daren't ask. Not now, when I was about to make this promise.

"We can," I assured him, and wrapping a hand around his arm, I led him inside.

CHAPTER FORTY-THREE

I stared down at my dress—pristine white Lathiriua silk embroidered in gold. My hands glided over the tight bodice, sewn with pearls and twinkling rubies. As I faced forward, I sucked in one long breath and released it slowly, hoping to appease my restless heart.

The throne room's doors creaked opened.

The chamber gleamed alive with the fire of torch-light and countless candles. Clad in white steel armor, members of the Diamond Court's army lined both sides of the central nave. High fae lords and ladies of the Marble Court stood up front, headed by Arthion Thamaris, the one-eyed king. And behind them, throngs of townspeople filled the chamber, stirring restlessly, eager to catch a glimpse of their fated sovereign.

When I took the first step across the threshold, no wariness stirred inside me. This no longer was a room foreclosed, never to be mentioned. Misery and devastation touched it no more. Not only had the furnishing been restored from the ashes, but hope and the promise of a new era lay before us, a time of peace and abundance.

Upon my command, the crumbling wall remained untouched, with the addition of a vast platform beyond it that overlooked the entire kingdom. A memorial plaque minted on stone hung in loving remembrance of the king and queen. Scripted into the slab of marble were the words: *Here death swept our beloved Queen Laeessa, and King Edward, her adoring husband, joined her in the Netherworld.*

As I strolled further down the crimson carpeting, white and gold banners dropped from the ceiling, flashing the red rose that branded my family name. Every mirror remained burnished spotless. Every tapestry repaired and mounted on the walls. The White Throne waited ahead, pristine as before.

Ash stood at the bottom of the dais, watching me with calm sternness. Next to him, the Seven lined up, garbed in formal leather jerkins and trousers, with trimmed beards and clean hairstyles that suited their former positions as heads of their magedoms. I couldn't imagine them ever straying from their leisurely lifestyles, however.

"Your Highness," Brindel called.

"Captain," I said, stopping to admire her glistening plated armor. I particularly appreciated the single red rose chiseled on its breastplate. The corner of my mouth curled. "Are you pleased with your new position?"

"It is my honor to serve you," Brindel said, inclining her head. "I'll escort you to the throne."

I silently agreed, and as we reached the dais, Captain Brindel stood beside me. No one was worthier or more competent than her to lead my Royal Guard. Parting from Brindel's service had raised some resistance from the fairy queen—I'd hardly expected otherwise. But the gesture showed unity between our reigns, and so she'd conceded.

My hands glided on the ancestral seat's arms as I slid into the throne, and it was as if my parents' fondness seeped through the carved stone, lacing my heart in perpetual warmth.

Brindel stepped forward, carrying a golden crown. I'd seen my mother's precious spiked headdress many times when I was a child, and more recently, inside the black mirror's reflection. As I took it in my hands, glinting with myriad precious gems, I received it as the last gift from my parents. A most demanding one.

It was in their name that I eased the golden crown on my head. Instant cheers resounded in the room, followed by the chant of *Long live the Queen.*

When the last clamors died, my lips parted to speak.

"Beloved people of Whitehaven. Brothers and sisters of the Realm of Fae," I began, noticing each of their faces. "Our lands have endured through the darkest times." I paused, as a ripple of memories flashed in my mind's eye. Memories of the bleak road that had led me away from my kingdom and into the mages' lives. Into my sweetest Ashton's life. And how that journey now came to an end as we prepared to forge a new one.

"At long last, the time to heal our kingdoms has arrived." A faint smile thinned my lips. "Love," I added, locking eyes with Ash. "Fraternity." My stare drifted to the Seven, and from them to the crowd. "Unity... There lies our answer."

Slowly, I rose from the throne. "We walk out of these trying times, not as bystanders of our destinies, but as the bards that sing their stories," I said. "None of this would have taken place without the loyalty of our friends. To the Diamond Court and the Marble Court, we are beholden. But there are also those who deserve a special recognition."

"Prince Ashton of Thornwood," I called,

delighted, as I watched him climb the dais. When Ash knelt before me, he bowed his head, a hand resting on one knee. "You are my champion. I commend you for your valor." I slowly opened my hand and waited until Brindel eased the weapon in my grip. "To you, I gift this sword. It belonged to the most formidable mage of all the realms." I offered him the glinting blade. "May it guide you in wisdom and passion as it did to our dear friend Leander."

When Ashton's hand closed on the sword's grip, his eyes shimmered, brimming with tears. "Your Majesty," he said, lowering his head. He slipped the sword into his scabbard, then straightened and returned to the bottom of the dais.

The next time Brindel approached me, she carried a wooden chest. My captain opened the lid swiftly, revealing an interior covered with a red velvet sheet. I peeled back the layer, exposing several golden livery collars embedded with precious gems. "To the brotherhood of the mighty Seven," I continued. "I'm pleased to announce that King Arthion Thamaris has reinstated your magedoms to you in their entirety."

The mages stirred, swept in sheer shock.

"A new council has been born from our alliance with the Diamond and Marble Courts. The Council of Three Crowns," I added. "Your foresight and experience will be crucial for its undertaking. Please look after this endeavor with the same care you once showed me."

The Seven bowed in gracious acceptance. One by one, I called upon the mages to receive their chains of office. Rubies for Thuriad, sapphires for Essgard, pearls for Romni and Millindrel, and onyx for Akron.

"The long winter is over!" a man in the crowd yelped.

At once, renewed cheers rose in the throne room. The music of legendary minstrels gently drifted in the warm air, and glasses brimming with spirits passed hands.

At last, it was over. Instant relief swept over me, though my pulse throbbed hard in my chest.

"Your Highness," a small group of high fae ladies said, lingering near the rostrum.

A tumult of human and fae aristocracy surrounded me before I even realized it. I acknowledged their curtsies, wondering all the while what my father would have made of such an alliance. I could imagine him being pleasantly surprised. Although I became the cynosure of their buzzing conversation, after those initial seconds of contact, none of them addressed me personally.

"Princess Maleath," someone called in a grave tone.

I whirled towards the voice, and discovered

Queen Inoue standing before me, watching me with patient blue eyes. "I remember my coronation day," she said, easing her lips into a warm smile. "Allow me to be the first to congratulate you." The fairy queen startled as her gaze on me drifted downward. "My, that's a beautiful gown."

I spread my hands over the tight bodice, painfully aware of myself. As I faced the queen again, I glimpsed Ash behind her. He was standing on the balcony, his stare drifting to the horizon.

"I appreciate your kind gesture, Your Majesty," I told her, my gaze drifting towards Ash. "I look forward to visiting you at the Diamond Court." My lips thinned into a warm smile.

"That would be lovely," she said, genuinely delighted.

I smoothed my hands over hers, delicate and cold. "I'm afraid I must go on," I said. "Please excuse me."

CHAPTER FORTY-FOUR

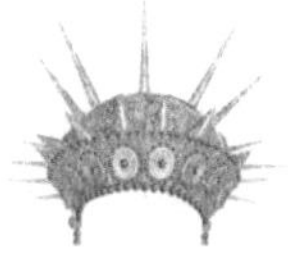

*I*mmediate relief washed over me as I strolled outside onto the platform, leaving behind the stifling throne room. The stillness and beauty of my kingdom eased my worries. A blanket of feverish stars spread across the clear night sky. And for the first time in the season, the fire serpents gleamed in the heavens, with magic swirls of green and vivid blue.

Ash was standing by the balustrade, marveling at the play of lights. I watched him without making a sound, relishing his delight. When I was but a few inches from his ear, I whispered, "Enjoying the view?"

His tall, black-clad figure stiffened. As his head swung my way, Ash broke into an irresistibly devastating grin. "I am now," he replied with quiet emphasis.

We stood face to face. My senses spun at his nearness. I smoothed a hand over his firm chest and lifted my stare to meet his, delighted, as his fresh cologne permeated my lungs.

"You look radiant." His voice broke with huskiness.

"Honestly?" I began, slightly raising my eyebrows. "After weeks of wearing comfortably snug trousers, easing into this heavy gown has been quite a challenge."

Ash tilted forward, narrowing the distance between us. "I'd gladly rid you of it," he purred, roving my face with sultry hazel eyes. His firm hands locked on the small of my back, tugging me near. "I've missed you."

I blushed like a fool. "And yet," I stammered, "you chose to be alone." I weighed him with a calculating squint. The crown rested on my head, and I now ruled the most influential kingdom in the realm, but that power had its limits. Picking apart Ashton's concerns was one of them.

"I was thinking," he said, and breaking away from me, he smoothed his hands on the balustrade.

"Mm..." I uttered, patiently waiting.

A troubled expression marred his countenance. "I'm wondering why I've not shifted since the night of the dragon," he finally said. "Galhöe lives. I've got no griffin tears left. It makes no sense." He shrugged. "Leander said a curse could only be broken by destroying the sorcerer who'd cast it."

"Unless..." I mumbled pensively, looking back on that long conversation, "said sorcerer lifts it."

Ash stared at me, dead in the eye. "Galhöe lifted my curse," he said in a flat tone. "The Evil Queen chose to spare me. Is that what you're saying?" His eyes narrowed in outright disbelief.

I silently nodded.

A soft gasp escaped him. Knitting his brow, he mouthed soundless words, disturbed and astonished. "Well then," he managed, recovering his aplomb. "It's the least she could have done after all the harm she's caused."

"And now that the Evil Queen's curse no longer touches you," I said, gliding my hand over his, "what will you do?" Swept with apprehension, my heart jolted into a wild gallop.

His stare drifted skyward and locked on the dancing green lights. "I will return to my kingdom," Ash said offhandedly. "I can only hope to serve Thornwood the way I've served the house of Whitehaven."

My breathing hitched, crushed by the dire news. I gathered my bearing as fast as I could and forced my lips into a brief smile. "I know you will," I whispered, unable to stop myself from admiring his selflessness, his genuine valiant character.

I could never deter him from his destiny, even if that meant our painful estrangement. I vowed right then to offer him my unconditional support and encouragement, as he'd given me. And biting hard on my lower lip, I mustered the courage to ask, "Will I ever see you again?" A shiver spread through my being, more vulnerable than ever before.

Ashton's face slowly swung towards me. His gentle eyes froze on mine. "That depends," he said, and his voice laced with fathomless longing. "Would you like to have dinner with me?"

"Tonight?" I blurted. "That sounds lovely."

Ash took hold of my hand and gently stroked his thumb over it. His mouth curved with tenderness. "Then perhaps you might join me the evening after that," he added with quiet resolve.

I looked at him, charmed and confused.

His expression stilled and grew serious as he pulled a stray lock of hair behind my ear. He then said, "And *every* evening that follows."

My heart fluttered with unmitigated bliss. "Perhaps I will," I breathed.

Ash laced his fingers with mine and pressed my hand against his chest, pulling me in. I held my breath, trying to throttle the dizzying current racing through my being. Each day after we'd met, my love for him had only deepened and intensified. He had unlocked me, heart and soul.

His firm hand eased along my jawline, and inching forward, his mouth brushed mine like a whisper, then became warm and sweet as our lips sealed in one dreamy kiss.

ACKNOWLEDGMENTS

It's because of my dear friend Jaclyn Roche, that Maleath Snow breathes. That one day you messaged me with, *"Hey, I think we should write twisted fairy tales!"* got us our first letters and marked the beginning of this series. I'm forever grateful to you for nudging me to explore the wonders of dark fantasy.

My dearest Julie Cocaigne, your marvelous insight gave this story its heart and soul. Once again, I am in awe of your wonderful editing skills, and I recognize myself lost in the grammar world without you. You're simply brilliant.

To Gina Kincade and to our wonderful Brat Pack, thank you for your invaluable encouragement. I'm so lucky and honored to be part of such a talented group of authors.

My boys, Iker (†) and David. You're the magic in my life. I love you. And to you, Eric. Your unending support made Ash and Snow a reality. You're always around to remind me who I am and that I've got this, rooting for me since day one. (D1).

And last but not least, I want to thank my readers. You mean the world to me. Thanks for putting up with my shenanigans, and thank you for sticking around, because I promise you… it'll be worth it!

ABOUT THE AUTHOR

USA TODAY bestselling author, Silvana G. Sánchez loves to write monsters with a heart of gold, villains who are heroes and get their happy endings, and more recently, she writes twisted fairytales.

She lives in Mexico with her husband Eric, twins Iker (†) and David, and two Shih-Tzu puppies she lovingly calls her *dragons*—Wookie and Padme.

When not writing dark fantasy novels in her writing den, she's known to poke eyes in her practice as an Ophthalmologist.

You'll often find her in her reader's group the Reader's Den and on TikTok.

Stop by to say hello. She doesn't bite—not always, anyway.

For more information:
silvanagsanchez.com
sgs.author@gmail.com

9 781736 804223